Totally Bound Publishing books by Mimi B. Rose

The Laurentian Mountain Clan
Love's Anchor
Heart's Ease
Mind's Peace

I0611422

The Laurentian Mountain Clan

MIND'S PEACE

MIMI B. ROSE

Mind's Peace
ISBN # 978-1-80250-538-2
©Copyright Mimi B. Rose 2023
Cover Art by Kelly Martin ©Copyright May 2023
Interior text design by Claire Siemaszkiewicz
Totally Bound Publishing

MIND'S PEACE

Dedication

To Jennifer M., Nancy M., Nancy P., Cindy S. and
Kerri W. for getting me through hard times.

Note about Québécois French

This novel uses some Québécois expressions the reader may not be familiar with. Most are profanities or exclamations that do not translate easily into English, but their use can be understood in the context. Others are explained when they occur in the story.

Chapter One

Thomas Ducharme cursed. He looked out of the helicopter windows at the snowy village below and his heart sank.

He should have taken the all-terrain vehicle.

Using the helicopter was the fastest way to get through the forested peaks from their clan's compound in northern Québec. Still, he hadn't anticipated what seeing the tiny town from the air would do to him.

Five hundred souls had called the little town home.

Five hundred bodies littered the streets and yards.

It made him sick to his stomach. It made his wolf thirsty for vengeance. Their neighbour and rival Roland Reynard—Alpha of the Trois-Rivières Clan—had struck back against Thomas' family and the Laurentian Mountains Clan.

Six months ago, Roland and his son René had targeted Thomas' pack. Thomas' brother and Alpha of the clan, Charles, had stopped them with the help of his mate, Chantelle. When they had turned René over to the local authorities and he had gone to prison for kidnapping and assault, René's father had vowed to make Charles and Chantelle — and their clan — pay.

Thomas closed his eyes. He was not going to let the Trois-Rivières Clan win. After seeing this violence, he would redouble his efforts to protect their clan and support Charles.

When the helicopter landed in a clearing, he disembarked and ran out of range while the pilot took off again. He put a grey blazer over his white button-up and jeans, then marched towards the perimeter team waiting on the edge of the town. Pushing back his shoulders, he smoothed down his short, dark hair and combed his fingers through his beard. He had to appear strong and confident for his people. He was their Lieutenant, after all.

He looked at the team, catching each person's eye in turn. "Report," he said, feeling another headache coming on.

Anne, the team leader, took a step forward, her long braid swinging down her back. "Last week there was news of rogue shifters in the area. This week we were checking on the smaller communities. We tried calling the village elders here to tell them we were stopping by, but there was no answer."

Thomas nodded. "So you drove out."

"There was nobody alive."

"Nobody?" Thomas choked out.

"Nobody." Anne exhaled a shaky breath. "We estimate it happened in the night, several hours before we arrived."

"Let me see it. Everything." If they all had to die, then he would honour their lives. And he would avenge every single one of them.

As they walked through the streets and houses, the team leader asked, "Is it true the son of the Trois-

Rivières Alpha tried to assault our Alpha's mate when she was a teenager?"

"He's a sick man," Thomas replied.

"It's not right. We need to stop their clan from taking it out on the territory."

Thomas should have protected his people better. Now that he was Lieutenant, and Charles was trying to find a work-life balance between clan business and his mate, Thomas felt every attack as if it were an assault on his own person.

Another member of the perimeter team approached. "We've taken a census. A few people are missing. Women and children."

"*Calisse!*" Thomas swore again. His wolf growled inside. It was pack instinct to protect the young. His clan treated everyone equally, regardless of gender, sexuality and race — although he knew Roland's clan was different.

He stepped away and called his brother. "Charles, you'd better come down here."

While he waited for his Alpha to arrive, Thomas continued the walk-through. He tried to keep his calm while he surveyed the scene. He couldn't believe the whole village had been wiped out. All those innocent souls. He pulled out his phone and keyed in the number for their Head of Security, Juana Aguirre, to discuss increasing the patrols on the border to Trois-Rivière territory.

"We need someone from the family to have a presence in the area as well. Is Henri ready?" Thomas asked. His younger brother Henri had been shaken by their father's and older brother's deaths three years ago, though he was getting back on track.

Juana paused. "It would be a test for him."

"This could be a chance for him to step up," Thomas said. They could use Henri's help, but they couldn't push him.

Juana agreed to think about it.

Thomas hung up just as Charles' helicopter arrived. He rushed over in the swirl of wind and noise.

Charles looked like Thomas felt...angry, unsettled and ready for a fight.

"Lieutenant," Charles said, his eyes sparking. "You're right, it's bad."

Thomas spent the next half-hour retracing his steps with Charles. They ended up at the small parish hall, where the perimeter team had set up coffee and snacks for the security and clean-up crews.

"What's your plan?" Charles asked, sipping his coffee.

"Increase security on the border between territories." It would be a challenge, since the communities were spread out along the large boundary. There were hundreds of kilometres of forest and mountainous terrain. "We'll send Henri out as your representative to meet with village leaders and discuss other options."

"What else?" Charles asked, brow wrinkled.

Thomas inspected his brother. "You won't sanction retaliation."

"This attack might change my mind. Until now, we've been dealing with small forays, minor thefts and violence," Charles said. "This is a new level."

Thomas started a mental checklist. "I'll get started then. We'll want to beef up patrols, increase monitoring stations and begin planning our offensive strategy."

"I'm sending you to Montréal. Juana and Henri will deal with this."

Thomas huffed in frustration. "You're not sidelining me, are you?"

Charles shook his head. "I want you to find out all you can about the Frères Gris Consortium."

"I know they are connected to the Trois-Rivières Clan," Thomas said, "even if we can't prove it yet."

"Chantelle thinks they are supernaturals. They may have been in Canada for centuries."

"Your wife has been right about a lot of things. But what is their goal then?"

"That's what I want you to discover. Are they using Roland's clan for their own ends? Is there something else going on that we should know about?" Thomas asked.

His head throbbed. "I still think I should be here."

"Roland is the knowable factor. We can give him to someone else."

"I know I've been off my game." Thomas wondered if his brother was losing confidence in him. He couldn't stand it if it were true.

"Thomas, it isn't about that. You're going to Montréal because I need your brains and your ability to solve puzzles." Charles sighed. "What's bothering you, bro?"

Thomas took in a big breath. "I've been doubting myself since Aimée dumped me. I can't stop it."

"You need to find your confidence again. She did a number on you." Charles patted his shoulder.

Thomas sighed. When she'd cheated on him and they broke up, he'd thought he'd lost his chance at happiness. "I worked so hard to figure out what she wanted. But then she changed the rules. I didn't know which side was up."

"You're still strong. You have to learn to rely on yourself again. When you trust yourself, you can do anything."

Thomas knew his brother was right. Still, it hurt that he was doubting his abilities. Maybe he needed to get angry and fight against this side of himself. Or maybe he just needed a little time away to think.

* * * *

Tatienne Laflamme checked her watch. Her boss at the Montréal Diocese Records Office was away on holiday and she was expecting a call from Archbishop Lacroix. The archbishop's assistant had said he had a favour to ask.

While she waited, she gathered up the archival documents a patron had used in the Reading Room and returned them to the storage rooms at the back. She straightened her pencil skirt and returned to her desk. It was quiet in the basement archives, but it would likely pick up in the afternoon. The Montréal Diocese Records Office saw its share of researchers, students and family genealogists, but it was never noisy or overwhelming. She liked the peacefulness of the space.

She had worked as an archivist's assistant since she had finished community college, what they called CEGEP in Québec. She'd always intended to go back to school and get her library and information science degree, but she had been too busy looking after her sister, Céline, and making sure they had food on the table. Now that Céline was older, it might be time to pursue that dream.

Making sure her sister was cared for had been her responsibility since their parents had died ten years ago. The foster system had wanted to separate them, but Tatienne had fought them and won. Céline had been a special-needs nine-year-old, and Tatienne didn't think her sister would have made it without her. And vice versa — it had been a dark time, for many reasons, and Tatienne had relied on her sister for stability and comfort. They were a team.

The landline at the desk rang. It was the archbishop.

"Tatienne, so nice to talk with you," he said in his kind, deep voice. "How is your sister?"

"Well, thank you. She's loving the community programme you got her into."

"Oh, that's wonderful. Your parish priest, Father Andre, was the one who did the heavy lifting."

"Still, I appreciate your help." Father Andre had always been in her corner. He had known the archbishop in Rome before they had both moved here, and had asked him to pull some strings to help with Céline's community support. It was one of many things Father Andre had done to assist Tatienne and her sister.

"I'm hoping you can return the favour, please?" the archbishop asked.

"Certainly, Monseigneur." She waited on the phone.

"Do you know the Ducharme family?" he asked.

"No," Tatienne said.

"They're an old family. Live in the mountains, but they have a place in the city. They are big supporters of the diocese's Soup Kitchen programme."

So, they're entitled rich people. They were often demanding and insensitive when they came to the records office. She wasn't their servant — she was an employee of the records office.

"They sound important," Tatienne said, keeping her voice neutral.

"Yes, we want to make a good impression. They're sending someone to look through the diocese records. I'd like you to take good care of them."

She could certainly handle a major donor. It might be irritating and disruptive, but she could manage it. "What do they need?"

"They are looking for references to a group of friars who settled in New France in the eighteenth century. Can you direct the family to any relevant records? Help them look through the resources?" he asked.

"I'll do everything I can to help." She enjoyed solving mysteries and putting together the pieces of the puzzles folks brought to the archives. This request was unusual compared to many others, but she would do her best to find the information they wanted.

"Thank you," Archbishop Lacroix said. "Thing is, they can only come on the weekend. Could you take the next couple days off and work Saturday and Sunday instead?"

Tatienne thought. Father Andre could probably help with Céline on Saturday, then for Sunday she could ask their neighbour. "Yes, I think I can swing it."

"Bless you, Tatienne," said the Monseigneur. "I'm sorry it will cut into your family time. And—" He paused.

"Yes, I know. This family is important. I'll take care of them."

"I know you will." He signed off.

Tatienne sighed. The Ducharmes were probably like the mean girls at high school, but she couldn't let her feelings get in the way of her job. She would try to keep an open mind.

When she checked her messages, the archbishop's assistant had already emailed her the details on the search. She decided to get a head-start while it was still quiet.

The Ducharme family was looking into a group called the Frères Gris — the Grey Brothers. She'd heard of the Grey Nuns. The small group of religious women had set up an abbey, a school and a hospital in eighteenth-century Montréal. Maybe the Brothers had been affiliated with that community?

She went through the Reading Room to access the storage rooms. She stared at their eighteenth-century collections. Notebooks, ledgers and documents from several local churches formed the bulk of the resources. There were family albums, posters and newspapers as well.

Where should I start? First things first, my sister.

She went back to the landline and called Father Andre.

"Hello, my dear. How are you?" he asked.

"Good, thanks. I won't be at church on Sunday. I have work. And could you help me with Céline on Saturday?"

"Sure. We've got youth group that afternoon. She could come in the morning and help me set up. Then we could have lunch and join the youth group. Will that work?"

"That would be fantastic. Will Yousuf be there, or any of Céline's other friends?" If Céline's routine had to be disrupted, she hoped her sister would have some friendly faces around her.

"Yousuf is planning to be there," he said.

"Thanks." Tatienne breathed a sigh of relief.

"What do you have to do?" the priest asked.

"Help some rich guy with his family tree, I think. Have you heard of the Frères Gris? They were a group of friars during the New France era. I'm supposed to research them for the family."

Andre paused on the end of the line. "I might have a book that mentions them in my library. Do you have time to come by?"

"Yes. I have some pepper sauce for you, too."

"My grandmother's recipe?" he asked. Father Andre still followed many of his Guyanese family's traditions, even in the "cold and frozen city" — as he called Montréal.

"Of course. Extra hot." Tatienne was still surprised he had entrusted her with the recipe. Céline could eat it by the jarful, and Father Andre did too.

"Oh, lovely! I'll look through my library," he said.

"Thank you."

Tatienne hung up, a little more hopeful about her weekend. She should be able to find a few leads for the Ducharmes, send them on their way and get back to her life.

Chapter Two

Thomas hated being late.

The fridge at the family's condo had been unplugged. He had forgotten to pack his favourite button-up shirt. And to top it off, there had been a snowstorm last night and traffic was slow as the snow-removal vehicles worked to clear streets and sidewalks.

He'd only had coffee this morning. His brothers laughed at him for insisting breakfast was the most important meal, but the morning routine set him on the right path each day. The lack of breakfast was an inauspicious start to what was likely to be a wild goose chase in the basement of a records office, while his brothers took care of the real problems back home.

His driver, Isabelle, pulled the town car up in front of an unassuming five-story brick building in the college district. He pulled out his briefcase and straightened his tie. He must look like a mess. *Oh well, there's nothing to be done about it. Just get this over with and get home.*

He stomped through the snow and up the five stairs to the front doors. The snow had been shovelled in front of the building, but the lights were off. He banged on the door.

A light turned on inside. A woman's silhouette appeared a second later. She was curvy, medium height, with a topknot of kinky hair. She moved like a dancer. It was a deliberate, sensuous glide towards the door. When she reached the door, she gave him a withering look.

He suppressed a growl. Her stare reminded him of the nuns at his Catholic high school. The ones with the rulers and pursed lips who didn't like it when he and his friends messed around in class. *This is going to be a long day.*

When she opened the door, he took a step forward and stumbled. He looked into her black eyes and his heart slammed into his chest. Her light-brown face was stunning. He couldn't stop staring at her.

His wolf sat up and looked too. *Mate?* his wolf asked.

He tried to tamp down the desire rising inside him. Nuns weren't supposed to be this young and sexy. He was going to have to control himself.

She put her hand on her hip and blocked the doorway. He was half-aroused and half-ashamed until he caught a hint of her scent. Thomas struggled to push his wolf down but couldn't stop his beast from breathing deeply.

He put on his best penitential schoolboy look. "I'm sorry, Sister. I thought there was nobody here."

She pursed her lips. "You were late, so I went to set up."

"My apologies. Sister—?" Today was going to be torture. He was painfully alert to her eyes, her curves, her intoxicating fragrance. *Hibiscus? Musky, sweet and tart.*

She fixed him with another withering look. As she stood up straighter, his body tingled with awareness. She said, "I'm not a nun. My name is Tatienne Laflamme. My boss is away, and he asked me to assist you this weekend."

As he apologised again, he re-evaluated the situation. She was not a nun. She was sexy and smart, and for the first time in months, his body was reacting sexually. He could almost feel the ice melting in his chest.

"You are the Ducharmes' lawyer?" she — Tatienne — asked.

He chuckled. They both had expected something different. *This might be fun.* "Why would you think that?"

"Accountant, then? Who works out a lot?" She ran her gaze over his shoulders, and he found himself sticking out his chest, like a teenager.

Smiling, he shook his head. He should explain, but he was enjoying the guessing game.

She paused. "Security guard for Mrs Ducharme?"

He laughed, the action coursing through his whole body. He hadn't done that for a long time. She was a delectable morsel with a fine mind. This would not be so bad, after all.

Reaching out his hand, he said, "Thomas Ducharme at your service. My older brother Charles is the head of the family and his wife, Ms Mizuki-Ducharme, does *not* need me to look after her. I am very pleased to make your acquaintance."

She stammered and shook his hand, her cheeks turning an adorable shade of red. "I'm so sorry. I thought Mr Ducharme would be much older and less..." She waved her hands around. "Ummm, less Adonis-like."

His wolf chuffed at this remark and sat down to lick his paws. "No apology needed. I thought I was going to be spending the weekend with an old nun."

Her face got redder, then he saw a little spark in her eye. "We were both wrong. But we're here for business, that's all."

He schooled his face. He hardly knew her, he should maintain his distance, but there was something about her that made him want to get close to her. To make her laugh or blush or even get mad at him. "I only meant it would be nice to make a friend. I don't get a chance to do that often." He hadn't intended to be serious, but there it was. The truth.

Her dark eyes softened a little. She sighed, a hint of a smile at the corners of her mouth. "It would make a more pleasant experience if we could be friendly." She opened her mouth, then closed it. Then she ushered him out of the snow and cold.

He followed her inside, trying not to ogle her tantalising ass as she walked down the stairs into the basement. He fought the urge to run his hands down her backside, tracing the line of her dangerous curves. She was splendid.

At the bottom of the stairs, she stopped and turned to look at him. "So, Monsieur Ducharme—"

He held up a hand. "Please, call me Thomas." He suddenly had a picture of her whispering his name as he kissed her throat and shoulders. He tried to keep his face blank. But when she smiled and said his name, he almost lost control.

"Thomas, Monseigneur Lacroix wishes you to know how much he appreciates your family's generosity in the parish. I'm to help you with anything you require—"

She blushed. His cock got hard as he thought about what he wanted from her. But he had to act like the Lieutenant he was and be professional.

He cleared his throat and pretended she hadn't said something that had given him dirty thoughts. "Thank you very much, Mademoiselle — or Madame?"

"Mademoiselle." The blush was back again. "Just Tatienne."

"You are anything but 'just Tatienne.'" He stopped himself from saying more. "But Tatienne it is."

She walked down the hall and opened the door to the archives. It was a well-lit and cosy space. The furniture was good quality, outdated but well-cared for. Several walnut tables stood in a neat formation in the large room, presided over by a reception desk and computer by the entrance. At the back of the room was a door — to back rooms he supposed — and he spotted some book stacks and shelves through a bank of windows on the left.

She gestured to the right. "Please leave your belongings in this area." There was a small closet for coats and boots. He saw a well-made and well-used wool coat with a colourful scarf and hat in the closet.

"We can forgo the usual checking-in process, since you are a special guest."

He protested, "I don't want special treatment."

She fixed him with another fierce glare. His wolf rumbled, enjoying her fire.

"I'm sorry," he said. "You're here on the weekend because my family gets special treatment." He should have thought before he spoke. "I'm grateful to you for doing this."

She inclined her head. "You're welcome."

He had a thought he couldn't keep to himself. "Do you have a boyfriend or anyone who you couldn't be with this weekend?"

When she shook her head, relief coursed through his body.

"It's me and my sister. She's being looked after by friends."

It was odd. He had only just met her, but he felt comfortable sharing things with her. "I'm a family person. I have two brothers, and my cousins work with us, too. We're very close."

"My sister and I have our found family. Just a few of us, but they are the 'ride or die' types."

He shared a smile with her. Thomas was strangely glad she had found her people.

After a pause, her gaze flicked away, and she turned to the tables. "I've pulled out some documents and reference texts for you to look at first. Once you've examined those, we'll make a plan for the rest of your time."

He sat at a table beside some large encyclopaedia-type volumes and a file box. The large books had several pieces of coloured paper marking what he assumed were the relevant sections for his inquiry. He opened the plastic file box.

She took the lid from him, her fingers brushing against his. "Some of these are quite old. I'll get you some cotton gloves. We use them to protect the sources."

He nodded as she bustled away. He opened one of the large books, a volume from *The Canadian Centennial Series*. There were short entries describing the brothers' emigration to New France and their charity work in Montréal. The additional volumes came from the *Omnibus Canadiana* series, written in Québec in the nineteenth century. They included articles describing both the history and the myths about the Frères Gris.

By the Victorian period, French-Canadian villagers were telling stories about these grey-robed missionaries as boogeymen to frighten children during the long winter nights. There wasn't a lot of evidence to support the claims that they stole children and young women in their sleep, but it was an effective way to keep young folk from straying into the mountains.

Thomas became so engrossed in the descriptions that he almost forgot about the enchanting woman until she came back with another stack of books. As she approached him, her scent wafted to his nostrils. *Delicious. Panty-rippingly delectable, luscious, mouthwatering.* He looked up and met her beautiful black eyes. This was going to be an interesting weekend.

Tatienne took a deep breath and placed the old volumes on the table beside Thomas Ducharme. This man was…irresistible. He had an animal magnetism that pulled her into his orbit. She couldn't stay away.

When she had seen him first thing this morning, standing outside the door, she had almost turned and left him there. *Dangerous*, her body and mind had said. But that was ridiculous. He was just here for the weekend to do some family research. There was nothing dangerous about that.

So she had opened the door and fixed him with her best librarian stare. That kept most men in their place.

It hadn't worked on him.

It had made him smile and tell her it was going to be he wanted to be "friends." Friends they would never be, but at least she could relax for the next two days. This time, she wouldn't have to worry about some rich old man getting handsy or reporting her to Monseigneur for being uppity.

Thomas had quickly skimmed through the first set of documents she had pulled out for him. He was smart and capable. She didn't need to babysit him.

He was rocking the geek chic look, with his suit jacket off and his sleeves rolled up to show off his sexy, muscled arms. And his reading glasses were adorable. She tried to pry her gaze away from his body, reminding herself it was easy to look effortlessly sexy with unlimited resources at one's disposal.

He thanked her and opened up the new file box she had delivered.

She was glad she had put on her best sweater and blouse for today. Her thrift-store skirt was well worn but clean. Her neighbour had given her the sweater, which she had bought from a good store ten years ago. Tatienne liked classic clothes. She loved the forties era and if she could, she would wear vintage clothes from the period all the time. They were power clothes — shoulder pads, menswear silhouettes, but with a dash of femininity and a bucket of elegance.

She moved the papers and books he'd already read to another table. Since there were no other patrons for the weekend, she would leave it out and put it all away tomorrow when the visit concluded. That would save her having to retrieve materials again if Mr Ducharme — Thomas — wanted to see something again.

She moved closer to him, trying not to touch him as she rearranged the books.

When they had first touched, electricity had pulsed through her. There was an immediate connection, something she had never felt before. It was full of flames and passion — overwhelming and familiar all at once.

She had connected with people like this before. Her sister said she had been a mystic in another lifetime. Usually, she felt a twinge of an emotion or a ghost of thought. Sometimes she had tiny premonitions. But this time was different. His connection brought her peace.

She shook her head and asked him if he had found anything useful yet.

"There are some newspaper articles with illustrations of the priests," he said. "Their faces are mostly covered by hoods, but the caption includes the names of three of them and mentions some acolytes who were apprenticing with them."

"Names?"

"Bellaine, Agravaine and Sagramor." He wrinkled his brow. "They don't sound like priests, do they?"

"I thought missionaries were named John and Luke. Biblical names." She wondered where they came from.

"They're old country," Thomas said. "My family emigrated from Brittany. We're steeped in Celtic spirituality and language."

"Do you think the priests came from the same area?" she asked.

Thomas nodded. "I need to get this to my family."

"Coming right up," Tatienne said. She took the documents, made paper copies then uploaded digital versions to the cloud.

When she returned the papers to him, her fingers grazed his hand. He started and looked in her eyes. Grabbing her hand, he brought it close to his chest and massaged it with his fingers. His coolness pulsed through her, mingling with her heat as it spread through her torso.

Fire and ice.

She had an urge to run her hands along his chest and do naughty things to him. Undo the buttons on his shirt, feel his taut skin under her fingers, straddle him in the chair…

The phone rang. Tatienne jumped back and her face grew hot. His gaze followed her, intense and hungry. She walked to the landline at the reception desk. After taking a deep breath, she answered the phone.

It was the food Thomas had ordered for lunch. Tatienne asked his driver, Isabelle, to bring it in and showed Thomas upstairs to the lunchroom. Isabelle arrived, her brown curly hair in a messy bun and snowflakes on her thick wool sweater. She brought in several bags from a local Jewish deli.

"Do you want to eat with us?" Tatienne asked Isabelle.

"No, thanks. You two enjoy a quiet break."

After Isabelle left, Thomas opened the bags. "I don't know if you have any dietary restrictions. I got an assortment of smoked meat sandwiches, egg sandwiches and bagels and lox."

Tatienne looked at a tower of salads in takeout containers. "I love all of it. I'll start with pastrami and egg and take some salads. It's too bad my sister isn't here. She loves bagels and lox."

"Please take the smoked salmon and bagels back to her. She can have it for breakfast tomorrow."

"And for several days after. Although she would eat a dozen bagels in one sitting if she could."

Thomas looked at her. Her heart sped up when she saw the twinkle in his eye. He was even more handsome when he opened up to her like that. "She's a girl after my own heart. When I was a teen, I could demolish half a dozen bagels and go back for more."

Tatienne laughed. "Céline has her favourite foods. Others she just won't touch."

"That's her name, Céline? Are your parents fans of the singer?"

Tatienne had made a mistake by telling him her sister's name. That was private information she rarely shared with others. Certainly not at work or with a date.

Not that this was a date. Still, she didn't tell near-strangers about her family. That was a rule.

She wasn't upset, though, to break it. Maybe it was because he was easy to talk to and very accepting. She felt comfortable around him.

"My parents died years ago. But yes, my mother loved our homegrown celebrity. And our Céline knows all the singer's pieces by heart. We're very loyal."

"I'm sorry to hear about your parents. My mother died when I was young. And then we lost my father and oldest brother a few years ago. It's been hard on everyone."

Tatienne nodded. "I wish they could see how well we are doing now."

"We have to move on, don't we? Things change, we change and we have to make peace with the past."

She chewed on her sandwich. "All of it shapes us. I know it made me stronger. It brought me and my sister closer together. But I wish it were different."

Thomas reached over and placed a hand on her shoulder. His calmness flowed through her. He understood her, and she him.

Chapter Three

After they'd finished their lunch, Thomas offered to clean up the space. "You go downstairs. I'll tidy up and take the compostables and extra food to the town car."

"There's so much going to waste," Tatienne said.

Thomas grinned. "Don't worry. We'll pack some up for you and your sister, then Isabelle will take the rest to her friends who live under the bypass."

"How does she know them?" she asked.

"She experienced homelessness for a while as a youth. She's kept up her connections in the community. We do what we can to support some of the folks."

Tatienne looked away from him.

"Did I upset you?" he asked. *What did I say?*

"No, I'm fine."

"Tell me, please. I don't always pick up on social cues. I can say the wrong thing." He had screwed things up somehow.

She gave him a small smile. "You're not what I expected. And you're surprisingly easy to talk to. I like how well you listen."

A warm glow went through him. "Thank you," he said. "Now, scoot! *Vas-y!* I'll see you in a few minutes."

As soon as she'd left the room, he picked up the bags and trash then texted Isabelle to bring the town car around. He checked his watch. Four more hours with this lovely flower. She was not frail or timid, but a vibrant hibiscus blossom—tough and strong. He wanted to do whatever it took to watch her bloom and grow.

But in the meantime he would spend his time wisely and hope she would agree to see him again.

He walked down the stairs and entered the Reading Room. It was dark and quiet. No Tatienne. The door to the back storage rooms was open. He poked his head through the door and called her name.

"I'm at the back!" she said.

He followed her voice, peering down the aisles. At the last row, he found her facing the wall, her back to him. There were boxes and a trunk on the floor beside her.

He did a double take and almost whistled. Inappropriate, he knew, but she was a gorgeous sight.

She was on all fours looking in the bottom shelf of a cabinet. Her shapely ass wiggled in the air as she tried to reach something inside the cabinet. Her curves did not quit.

He leaned on a shelf, taking in the luscious sight. A low rumble of appreciation emanated from his chest and his wolf slammed in the front of his mind.

Mate? his wolf asked.

Thomas tried to shake it off. "*Belle,*" he said. "What are you doing?"

Sitting back on her haunches, she cast a glance at him. "What are *you* doing?" She shot him a glare, just like the one he'd received that morning.

He grinned, running his eyes over her form. "You're going to have to work harder than that if you want to scare me off."

She raised her eyebrows in surprise. "That's enough to intimidate most men."

He sauntered halfway down the aisle, his wolf still at the surface. He paused and put a hand on his hip. "I'm not most men."

She snorted. "I noticed."

"I guess many guys would be afraid of such a striking, intelligent and accomplished woman." He closed the remaining distance between them and crouched to the same level as her. "But they're wrong. I find your strength and independence very attractive."

He reached towards her with a hand, intending to brush or skim along her shoulder, but paused. "I don't usually come on this strong."

She shrugged, her eyes glittering. "I'm not afraid of physical contact."

The hair on his arms and neck stood up.

He leaned over and caressed her chin, using his fingers to tip her mouth up to his. He pressed his lips to hers—a sweet kiss, but a taste of the hunger in his belly. She was tart and sweet, a luscious combination that filled him with desire. He broke off and looked in her eyes.

Immediately, she leaned forward and kissed him back. Something inside him shifted as they let their hands and mouths explore each other.

A minute later, she pulled away. "I shouldn't mess around at work," she said breathlessly, putting her fingers to her kiss-swollen lips. "This isn't a hospital drama."

"The archbishop would not approve," he said. Still, he kept his hands on her, caressing her back.

She smiled wistfully. "And we're on a timeline."

He knew she was right, but logic be damned. He just wanted to spend the afternoon in this chilly old room touching and pleasing her. "I hope this doesn't make things awkward."

"No. That was…nice." She looked at the ground.

"Nice?" He sat back and crossed his arms. That was a blow to his ego.

Turning her eyes up to him, she said, "It was more than nice. But we have to behave professionally."

"Got it." He took in a big breath. "Okay, back to work. What were you looking at anyway?"

She handed him some books and stood up. He watched her curves undulate as she led him back to the Reading Room.

When they had deposited the volumes on the table, she spoke. "I remembered we kept the old parish records and family albums in the cabinet at the back of the storage rooms. They reminded me of some books in the basement of my local church."

"Do you think there's something in them?" he asked, brushing his fingers against hers.

"I found the set belonging to the parish where the Frères Gris had their mission church when they first settled in New France."

She selected a volume and passed it to him. He opened it. "There's a city block in the parish that's owned today by a company called Frères Gris. We're hoping to establish a connection between that company and the historical group."

"Do you think you'll find some dirt on them? Corporate espionage?"

He shook his head. "They're engaged in some questionable business practices and we're trying to uncover their motivations."

"Like a secret society or something?" Her eyes lit up. "That's a lot more exciting than most information requests we deal with."

"It might turn out to be nothing. But if we can understand why the company is blocking some of our business deals and working with our rivals, then maybe we can figure out how to stop them."

"It seems like a long shot." She pursed her full lips, and he resisted the urge to run his finger along them. "I'm game to keep looking, though."

He smiled. She was a treasure, that was certain.

* * * *

At the end of the day, Tatienne took a moment by the coat closet to compose herself. This morning, she hadn't expected to be getting hot and heavy with a sexy businessman in the archives. She shook her head. He was good looking and very kind, but way out of her league. It couldn't be anything serious.

Not that she was looking for anything serious. Casual was always better. Besides, she couldn't suddenly fall for a stranger. She hadn't dated in a few weeks—obviously she was just starved for sex.

Maybe she could indulge herself this weekend. Have some fun. If he wanted to pursue it. No, she should put him out of her mind. He probably had lovers falling over him all the time. She didn't need a boyfriend.

She picked up his overcoat, stroking the soft wool and catching the scent of pine and wood smoke. It was like he had stepped out of the forest. She chuckled at her overactive imagination.

She returned to Thomas, and he smiled as she passed him his coat. If only he wasn't so hot, she could keep her distance. It was going to be a struggle to stay professional tomorrow.

After she had locked up the basement, he paused at the bottom of the stairs. "I'd like to get to know you better," he said. "Would you go out with me tonight?"

She looked at him and melted. She wanted to say yes.

"I have plans," she said. "Tonight is my dance class."

"You take dancing lessons?"

She shook her head. "I'm the dance teacher's demonstration partner."

"Are you dating this teacher?" He frowned.

"He's my dance partner. Nothing else." If she didn't know better, she'd think he looked jealous. That was funny, that he could be jealous of her friend.

"Does your partner know this?" His eyes were dark and smoky.

"Yeah." She rolled her eyes. "He's my best friend."

"That doesn't mean he's not interested. How could he not be?" When he ran his eyes over her body, heat rushed to her centre.

"You don't know him," she said. "Besides, it's none of your business."

He sighed. "You're right. Can I drive you home?" He put his hand on the small of her back as they walked up the stairs to the main floor.

She liked having him close to her. He was tall and broad-shouldered, but not intimidating. He made her feel safe.

After she'd closed up the building, Thomas steered her over to the waiting limo. Isabelle greeted them both and opened the car door.

She had forgotten how rich he was when they were working in the records office, but now she couldn't ignore it. A driver who was being paid to take him around the city, a fancy limo and an expensive suit that probably cost more than she made in a month. It was too much for her. She had grown up in hand-me-downs, always trying to go unnoticed at school—to avoid being a target of the mean girls.

She could live it up for the weekend, though. Only one more day. Then he'd be gone, and she'd go back to her regular life. She would miss him a little, but everything would be fine.

When Thomas got in the car from the other side, he leaned back and turned his knee towards her. As he unbuttoned his coat, his eyes met hers.

Her heart pounded. Warmth pooled in her belly. His already familiar scent wrapped around her like a cosy blanket. She unbuttoned her coat and matched his stance.

"So, what is your family like?" he asked, resting his hand beside her leg on the seat.

"My sister is a handful—stubborn and opinionated. Don't get me wrong, she's also kind and compassionate. We have lots of fun together."

"She sounds like you," Thomas said, chuckling. He brushed his fingers along her thigh and her whole side tingled.

She cleared her throat. "My neighbour, Lynne, helps out a lot. And my best friend does too."

He nodded. "You have good friends."

"They are my family. I trust them completely."

"My family means the world to me, too. Growing up, my brothers and I were really close with our cousins. When my mother died and my father was busy running the family business, we had to look after ourselves more. I was the third of four sons— important, but not the main focus for my dad's

36

mentorship activities. But since my oldest brother died in the same accident as my father, things have changed. Charles became head of the family and we've grown closer again." Thomas reached up and cupped her cheek. Her heart ached for his tragedy. It was such a blow to lose family like that.

"Father Andre has been there for me and Céline since the beginning. He pushed really hard for the two of us to stay together in foster care — that was tricky, but he pulled it off. Since then, he's always looked out for us, making time to visit and help out when he can." She rubbed her face on his hand, savouring his touch.

"I'm glad you have a champion like him."

She looked into his eyes. There were little yellow glints in the grey irises that she hadn't noticed before.

The car stopped and Isabelle announced through the speaker that they were at Tatienne's address. Tatienne looked at the three-story walk-up building with different eyes. It had good bones, but it was almost a century old and showing its age. Thomas was probably used to the best of everything.

"I love the old apartments in this neighbourhood. One of my college friends used to live around here," Thomas said.

I shouldn't invite him in.

"Would you like to see the inside?"

I can't believe I'm doing this. It's against my rules. She prided herself on keeping her romantic life separate from her home life.

"Hell, yes," he said.

What could it hurt? When he met her family, he would probably run away. And it was better to know that now than later.

Wait, is there going to be a later?

She pushed her shoulders back and walked with Thomas into the building and up to her second-floor apartment. She turned the key and opened the door.

Céline was sitting with Diego at the small kitchen counter. Diego had a plate of sugar cookies in front of him. Céline held a small tube of icing in one hand and a cookie in the other.

"Hello!" Céline said, through a mouthful of cookie.

"Hey, *mon chou*." Tatienne came over and kissed her cheek.

Diego waved and blew an air-kiss. "It looks like you brought dessert, too, Tati." Her best friend ran his eyes over Thomas' large form and grinned.

Tatienne's face grew hot. She turned and saw Thomas smiling, that adorable twinkle in his eyes. "This is Monsieur Ducharme. I'm helping him with a research project this weekend. Thomas, this is Céline, and the annoying one is Diego." She stuck her tongue out at her best friend.

"Your dance partner?" Thomas asked.

"My dance partner," Tati agreed.

"Would you like a cookie?" Céline held out a cookie festooned with three colours of icing and two kinds of sprinkles.

"Yes, please," said Thomas. He took the treat and bit into it with gusto. "This is delicious. Céline, you are an excellent baker."

Céline giggled. "Diego helped a bit."

Thomas finished the cookie with exaggerated relish.

"How is the project going?" Diego asked.

"We found some references to a secret society or something in the standard early histories. And some news articles with mysterious accounts of people disappearing. Very spooky!"

"This is the kind of stuff Tatienne loves," Diego said. "When she was in college, she could spend hours talking about her history courses."

"She's been very helpful," Thomas said. "I don't know what I would have done without her."

After a moment, Tatienne broke the silence. "Thomas wanted to see the apartment before he leaves."

"Let me show him," Céline said.

Tatienne nodded and Céline led Thomas around the small place. He asked questions and examined the tchotchkes and knick-knacks she handed him. Tatienne relaxed. Even though she hadn't thought he would be judgemental—after all, he'd been kind and thoughtful all day—she hadn't known if he'd been around someone with Down syndrome before or how he'd react. Of course, he was everything she could have hoped for.

When Céline brought Thomas back to the kitchen, Tatienne smiled at them both. "What do you think?" she asked.

"I like him," Céline pronounced, grabbing another cookie.

"I was talking to Thomas," Tatienne said.

Thomas smiled. "I like her, too." When Tatienne opened her mouth, he added, "I like the apartment. Thanks for letting me see it."

Tatienne stood there awkwardly for a moment, twisting her hands together. "I should get ready for dance class."

"Right," Thomas said. "See you in the morning. I won't be late this time."

"It's all right." Tatienne smiled. "It's different now that we've met."

He looked down and reached for her arm. She went to shake his hand, but he grasped her fingers and brought them to his mouth. When he brushed his lips against the back of her hand, she squeezed his fingers as a rush of calm passed through her.

In a flash, he was out of the door, and she was shutting it behind him. She sighed. Tomorrow was going to be interesting.

Chapter Four

Thomas arrived at nine sharp. He found the door unlocked and made his way down the stairs to the archives. He paused a moment when he saw Tatienne was wearing glasses and had swept her hair into a bun—his sexy librarian fantasies were sitting right in front of him. She, however, was busy sorting through the file boxes. There was a new stack of albums and ledgers on the table.

"Have you discovered something?" he asked, trying to focus on business and failing miserably.

Her eyes lit up and she pushed a stray curl from her face. "I had an idea last night. We should focus on the property and the educational records."

"Wait, I'm pretty sure I read yesterday that the brothers started a school," Thomas said. He resisted the urge to fold her up in his arms. Instead, he walked to the nearest chair and sat down to look at what she handed him.

"Yes," Tatienne replied. "There was a school for local boys from well-off families. Then they started a mission school outside of town. I found a news article detailing rumours about some of the Indigenous children and youth who attended and went missing."

"You're kidding," Thomas said. This information shut down his lusty thoughts. "That sounds like the residential schools, when the Catholic and Anglican churches took Indigenous children from their families to force them to learn how to be white."

"The residential schools were instituted in the nineteenth century, though." Tatienne said. "My college friend Grace's mom and grandmother went through the schools, and it sounded horrible. They lost their culture and community. Many Indigenous children were abused and mistreated."

Thomas thought for a moment. "Why were the Frères Gris doing this in the eighteenth century?"

"If they were like the Jesuit missionaries, then they were going to use whatever tactics they could to bring God into the lives of the non-Christians," Tatienne said. "Father Andre studied this period in seminary. I can ask him if he knows more."

"Good. This might be useful information." Thomas debated whether to reveal his family's early history to Tatienne. She was still a relative stranger. His family had to be careful about whom they entrusted with the knowledge of their shifter status. He had a feeling in his gut that he could place his faith in her. Yet the information could be a burden for those who knew. It was safer to wait.

He looked through the file box for more educational records. When he didn't find any, he went to the pile of books on the table, selected one then moved to a chair beside Tatienne. She was frowning at some blueprints, her cute nose crinkling up as she focused. She put down the papers and picked up one of the family albums. It held a collection of calling cards, notes and programmes from local performances a society mother had gathered into the scrapbook.

She murmured to herself. Thomas turned and faced her, putting an arm on the back of her chair. "Did you find something?" he asked.

"Another illustration of the brothers. This one is an original drawing."

"Who made it?" Thomas asked, standing up to get a better look.

Tatienne placed the album flat on the table and looked up at him. He was close enough to catch her scent, but he tried to focus on the book. "There's a set of initials in the corner – M. E. D. D'Aoust – in English, Doe – is the name of the family who kept the album. Geneviève D'Aoust is the mother, and she had three daughters – Agnes, Marie Elisabeth and Nicolette."

"M. E. D. So it could be Marie Elisabeth D'Aoust who made it?"

Tatienne nodded. Thomas placed his hands on the back of her chair, resting his fingers against her shoulders. "Let's see if the family wrote about them. There has to be a clue here," she said.

Thomas leaned over as she flipped through the pages. "Not much," he said. "What about the wedding announcement?" He showed her a page decorated with flowers.

"It's for Marie Elisabeth. She was marrying a seigneur and they were travelling up north to take possession of their land. And look, one of the Frères Gris officiated. Here's his name, Bellaine."

"I'm not sure what it means, but it feels like a victory," Thomas said.

"This kind of research can be time-intensive and sometimes uncovers very small clues, but every little piece brings us nearer to understanding who these priests were."

"And hopefully what their descendants or followers might be doing today." Thomas knew Tatienne could help him discover the truth. They just needed to keep digging.

They both jumped when someone knocked on the archives door. Tatienne opened it and Isabelle, Thomas' driver, was standing there.

"I'm sorry to interrupt," Isabelle said. "I couldn't get a call through."

Thomas checked his phone. No reception. "Sorry. What is it?"

"Your brother Charles is trying to reach you."

Thomas wondered what was wrong. It wasn't like Charles to track him down, unless there was an emergency. Not another attack? He looked at Tati. "Sorry, I'd better check."

"You'll have better cell reception upstairs," she said.

He stepped out of the Reading Room and walked up the stairs to the main floor. He asked Isabelle to wait as he dialled his brother's number.

"Thomas," Charles answered.

"What's up?" Thomas' stomach tensed up.

"We need you back right away."

Thomas sighed. "It must be bad if we can't do it over the phone." He wished he could stay with Tatienne for the rest of the day.

"Yes," his brother said. "Pea said something is coming. They're not certain what it is, so Chantelle wants the family to sit down and come up with some plans."

Thomas' stomach sank. "Do you think it's another border attack?"

"Possibly. But we have to be prepared for an attack on the compound, too. We need all hands on deck."

"Yes," Thomas said. "I'll need to come back this week to continue the research. We've found a couple of interesting things."

"Mid-week? That should give us time to set up our strategies."

"Yes. That will be fine. And Charles…" What did he want to say? That he'd found someone who put the fire back in him after his heart had been frozen for months? It sounded ridiculous when he thought about saying it out loud.

"Everything okay, Thomas?" Charles paused on the other end of the phone.

"Yeah, it's all good. I need a couple hours to wrap things up and head home."

"The helo will pick you up at the condo in two hours. We'll meet tonight."

"Later," Thomas said. There was little time to tell Tatienne how he felt. Could he put his feelings out in the open? What if he was wrong and she was just a pretty distraction? What if he was thinking with his cock, not his head? He'd spent months second-guessing himself. He didn't know if he could trust his heart.

"Fuck it," he said. At the least, he wanted to make a physical connection with her and see if it led to anything. He wasn't proposing marriage or anything. Just a date or two. Maybe they would click.

* * * *

Tatienne tidied up some of the papers while Thomas was on a call. He must have to go back to work, so she'd finish up the research on her own. This was better in the long run. She knew it couldn't last. They'd had a hot kiss and now he would return to his glamorous life.

The door opened and Thomas' gaze locked in on her. He stalked towards her, yellow glints in his eyes.

"You need to go home?" she asked, her heart sinking.

"I had planned to seduce you after dinner," he said, reaching for her hands.

"I had planned to undress you in the limo," she replied.

He licked his lips, and a rumble went through his chest. Her body stood at attention, nipples hardening to stiff peaks while the apex at her thighs grew damp. He pulled her tight against his body, then tangled his hands in her hair and brought her lips to his. There was a hint of citrus as he explored all the nooks and crannies of her mouth.

She moaned.

"Are you all right with this?" he asked, dragging in a deep breath before kissing her again.

"I want you, too," she whispered.

He groaned and lifted her onto the table, running his hands over her backside before perching her close to the edge and pressing his entire body against hers. He was tight and hard, his bulging cock pushing against her centre while she wrapped her legs around his waist. She couldn't stop herself from grinding against him, the sensations rippling through her.

He pulled up her skirt. She skimmed her hands along his back. She was like a fire, and he was the match. They couldn't stop now.

She loosened his tie and struggled with his shirt buttons, while he pulled her white blouse down and cupped her breast with one hand. He devoured first one nipple then the other, kneading and pulling until she gasped in delight.

Returning his mouth to her lips, he kissed her and pushed her pencil skirt up to her hips. He gripped her skin with his bare hands, as warmth spread through her torso. She pushed against him, moaning.

He skimmed his fingers along the outline of her bikini panties and her centre started to ache. He rumbled and nipped at her neck as she kissed his ear and tugged at his short hair. Then he grabbed the strings on the sides of her panties. Growling, he ripped the strings, pulling off her panties and grabbing her ass.

She pulled back and gasped. "Did you just…"

"Yes," he said, his voice low and guttural. "I have a thing with gorgeous lingerie on my lovers. It drives me wild and once we start fucking, I have to remove it immediately. With my hands or mouth — whatever's closest."

She almost climaxed at his words, her pussy gushing in response to his admission. She didn't have any kinks, but she enjoyed wearing lace and silk underthings. She liked the contrast of soft and feminine undergarments under her menswear styles and classic separates.

He pulled her close, then reached down her thighs towards her slick, wet folds. She gasped as he ran a finger lightly around her outer lips, stopping at her cluster of sensitive nerves. She trembled against his touch. He manipulated her clit, flicking and making little circles as she moaned. She thought she might explode when he inserted a finger inside her pussy. She gasped and wriggled as he added another finger, taking them deep within her.

She thought it couldn't get any better. But then he started thrusting a little faster, rubbing her clit in the same rhythm. He undid the last buttons on her blouse and brought his mouth to her chest. He licked a trail between her breasts to the front fastening of her bra. Her breath hitched as he bit through the fastener, releasing her plentiful breasts. Moaning, he grazed her nipple with his teeth, and she arched her back.

He thrust his fingers in her pussy faster, and she wiggled her hips. She was floating on clouds of pleasure. He whispered, "Fuck, yes." When her breathing sped up, she pulled her hands through his hair, panting. She was close to the edge.

He shifted a little, then curved his fingers into the sensitive spot on her walls. Breathing in her ear, he murmured "Tatienne," and her pussy clenched around him. She gasped as her cream flowed over his fingers, then held him tight until the pulses subsided.

He kissed her face and hair, drowning her in light, feathery kisses while she came down from the high. When the aftershocks subsided, he pulled out his fingers and held them up. With a wicked grin, he licked her come off his fingers. "You are a tasty morsel."

"And you are too much." She reached for his belt and unfastened the zipper of his trousers.

"I am more than enough," he replied, a smug look on his face.

When she pulled out his stiff cock, she looked in his eyes and smiled. "You're right." She pumped her hand along its exquisite length, feeling the softness over top of the hard shaft. When she ran a finger around the tip, he moaned.

She knelt down to have a closer look. "So big and hard," she said. "I want to suck it, swallow it down until you come deep in my mouth and throat."

"Tatienne, yes," he moaned, his hips gyrating while she squeezed his cock. Then his smoky eyes searched her face. He looked hungry, and she wanted to give him what he had given her.

She tasted his swollen member, swirling her tongue around its width and finding a droplet at the slit. As he groaned, she grabbed his length at the base and licked down the shaft, enjoying the taste and feel of his salty maleness. Her nipples hardened and her pussy ached for more.

She bobbed up and down, taking time to play with the head, then pulling him in her mouth with long draws. He held her hair, losing himself in the sensations. "Your beautiful mouth is perfect. I don't want anything else," he whispered.

She sucked harder and faster as he thrust in and out of her mouth, loving how she made him hard and hot.

She cupped his ball sac with her other hand, making it draw up nice and tight. He was getting close. "Oh, Tatienne," he breathed. She hummed her satisfaction and squeezed with both hands while taking him in deep. She sucked as he started thrusting faster, making little rumbling noises in the back of his throat.

Then he stopped for a second and drew back, moaning and closing his eyes. "Here it comes, *ma belle*. Everything just for you." He thrust deep once more, spurting hot come in her mouth. She swallowed it down, loving the taste and feel of him.

After he slowed down, he gently removed his cock and sank down to kneel in front of her, kissing her face and holding her close to his body.

"*Belle*, you are magnificent. Thank you for that gift."

She smiled. "That was fun."

He hugged her, tucking her head on his shoulder as he leaned back on his haunches. "I'm sorry about your panties and bra."

"You're an animal," she said. "But I don't mind."

"You have no idea." He grinned. "I want to replace your underthings. I'm not a pervert, I don't collect panties. I just want to make sure I get the right size."

"I'm too thick," she said, blushing. "I can't let you."

"Nonsense."

"My breasts are too big." She looked at the ground.

"You're kidding, right? I've had a raging hard-on since I first saw you. You are goddamn perfect."

He did seem to like her body. And guys usually said her breasts and ass were a turn-on. Maybe they were right. She pulled her bra off and handed it to him.

He scooped up her panties from the floor. "I wish we had more time. I'll be back on Wednesday, though." He kissed her, short and sweet.

"You should get going." She ran a hand through his hair. "I'll see you then."

After he left, she shook her head. She didn't know what had possessed her to get freaky with the gorgeous man in the killer suit. But she didn't regret it. Not one single moment.

She pulled herself together and started sorting boxes and making notes. No more time for daydreams.

Chapter Five

It was Monday morning. Tatienne was back at work, putting away the last of the books and boxes from the weekend. Her boss was still away, and there were no other researchers booked for Monday and Tuesday. While she sorted, she made digital copies of the important passages and papers, saving them to the cloud for Thomas. She wished it was Wednesday already. She knew she shouldn't get her hopes up, since a million things could stop him from visiting.

When she had almost finished, she got a phone call from Father Andre on the landline.

"I found a trunk in the corner of the church basement you should see," he said.

"What is it?"

"Musty old church records on top. Underneath, there are some books that you might find interesting."

"Oh?" Tatienne sat up.

"Among the volumes, there's a diary from a Bernadette Lavalle. She lived in the parish in the early 1820s, then travelled with her husband into the bush."

"This could be a significant find for the record office," Tatienne said.

"There's more. In the opening pages, she talks about meeting the Frères Gris," he replied.

Tatienne gasped. "Really?" She didn't believe in miracles, but she had her faith. Sometimes things happened for a reason.

"I made a video of the finds. Hang on, I'm sending it to you now."

When her phone pinged, Tatienne downloaded the video. "Can I pick them up tomorrow?"

"I've been called out of town for a few days. I might be able to drop the diary by before I leave. If not, I'll take copies of the first section and text them to you. Then we can meet when I get back, okay?"

"Sure. Thomas — Mr Ducharme — returns to the city on Wednesday. I'll let him know there will be more information later in the week."

"Thomas? You're on a first-name basis?"

Tatienne squirmed in her chair. "He wasn't what I was expecting. I shouldn't have been so quick to judge."

The priest chuckled. "I admire your strength and confidence. It's nice to see a little humility, when it is warranted."

"I know I shouldn't stereotype people — God knows it happens enough to me and Céline."

"It's not easy to trust strangers. Did he find what he was looking for?"

"We've got some leads. But we haven't determined where they relocated in the Laurentians. Maybe your books will help solve that mystery."

"I hope they help."

After they said goodbye, Tatienne watched the short video.

The trunk was in the dark and dusty basement, surrounded by seasonal decorations, old candles and the fancy lanterns — censers — clergymen used for burning incense. Father Andre was holding the trunk lid open. He brought his phone camera forward to pan over the contents of the trunk — all Tatienne could see was a jumble of papers and corners of old books. The priest took out the documents and placed them on the floor beside the trunk.

Then he reached in and pulled out a small volume with a dark brown leather cover. He set it on the table and opened the brass clasp. He leafed through the first pages. There was no title page. Instead, on the flyleaf was the inscription "Bernadette Lavalle, Lac Saint-Patrice." The handwritten entries began on the first page. Scrawled in the upper right-hand corner was the date, "le 8 septembre, 1822." *September 8, 1822.*

Her heart raced. She loved looking through the family albums and young lady's diaries in the archives. They provided glimpses into family dynamics and the social world of the French settlers. At the very least, this book would contribute to their knowledge of the colonial era. In addition, it might provide some information for Thomas' search. He would be thrilled.

Was it too soon to call him? Thinking about it caused butterflies in her stomach. She didn't want to seem needy. Maybe she should email him instead.

The phone rang again. It was the archivist, asking how the visit with the Ducharmes had gone.

"Very well. We made good progress and I'm going to keep looking this week."

"Great. The archbishop wants us to keep the Ducharmes happy."

"I know, he told me several times already. I might have another lead, from Father Andre, too. I'll talk to him later in the week."

"Good," said her boss. "The archbishop will be very pleased with your work."

After Tatienne said goodbye, she returned to making notes and sorting file boxes. She smiled. Everything was going well. She should have it all in order by Wednesday, when Thomas arrived.

* * * *

Tuesday, Thomas sat in a board meeting and tried to focus on the crisis. It was the third meeting he and his brother had held since his return. Although he was worried about the clan, his thoughts kept wandering to Tatienne.

Had she received his package yet? He'd ordered several items online from his cousin Clem's favourite lingerie store. Tatienne would like the place, a local shop in Montréal with inclusive sizing that paid their staff a living wage. Her bra and panties from Victoria's Secret were gorgeous—especially on her—but he'd wanted to give Tatienne something extra special.

He'd gone a little overboard at the pricey shop, buying a half-dozen lingerie sets in various tones of taupe, chocolate and burgundy. It was just money. He'd also selected a royal blue garter and matching bustier he thought would look glorious on her light-brown skin. Thinking about it made his cock stiffen. He shifted in his chair, trying to adjust himself under the boardroom table.

Charles cleared his throat. Thomas realised everyone was looking at him.

"What was the question?"

His brother raised an eyebrow. "Do you agree with the plan to tighten patrols along the Trois-Rivières Clan border?"

Their rivals were getting bolder, and their sprite Pea thought there was another attack coming. Pea was not psychic. They had a different view of time and sometimes spoke in riddles. But they protected the clan and looked out for its safety in ways humans and shifters couldn't.

"I don't want more innocent people getting hurt," Thomas said. "If we can put in additional safety measures, then we should."

"Roland has always been a bully," added one of the elders, Soleil, whose long grey hair was in a single braid down her back. "We can't stand by while he hurts more people. There's a lot of ground for the patrols to cover, though. Can we do anything else to support the communities that are in danger?"

Chantelle, Charles' mate, spoke up. "In addition to the security teams, we could send out groups of volunteers to help the villages prepare for emergencies."

"Some of the volunteers could train community members to set up and monitor surveillance equipment," Soleil suggested.

"And many of the villagers know how to shoot hunting rifles. We could do some target practice sessions and teach those who want to learn," Thomas said. They were reaching a consensus. Still, he wished he could be more active here at the compound and in the border towns. He wanted to show his clan that their Lieutenant was present and willing to protect them.

At the same time, he was counting down the hours until he saw Tatienne. Twenty-two hours, to be exact. He was falling for her already, but was she looking for anything serious? She'd allowed him to meet her family. She was a private person, and he respected that. So, it must be a good sign that she had let him into her personal life. Even if she wasn't looking for a relationship, she had gotten closer to him on the weekend. He knew in his heart that it was meant to be more. Now he had to convince her, too.

Thomas interjected a few more times in the conversation until all the decisions had been made. The clan would start implementing the enhanced measures this week. Then next week he would go out and review the progress along the border. He was comfortable with that compromise. The clan was too large to run as a mom-and-pop organisation. They were better from having strong members throughout the clan. Encouraging leaders and providing opportunities for others was an important part of his role as well.

Perhaps he needed to have a similar attitude with Tatienne. She wouldn't respond well to being pushed into anything and he wouldn't like her if she did. He needed to trust her, to encourage her to grow into a relationship with him. Take his time, show her his respect. Shower her with attention. And orgasms — lots of orgasms.

Chapter Six

Wednesday morning, Tatienne was shelving books from a genealogy project when her phone rang. It was Thomas.

"What's up?" she asked.

"I can't make lunch." He growled. "I wanted to spend some time with you today."

"Me too." Her heart sank. "What about dinner?"

"What about Céline? Wait, bring her with you and I'll get an adjoining suite. She can watch movies with my PA."

"Your assistant is not a babysitter," she said reluctantly.

"Frédérique volunteers with our community centre programme for youth with special needs. And I'll pay her double time for it."

"I'm sure that's more than a babysitter makes and Céline would enjoy the adventure." She sighed. "Okay."

"Great. I'll send the car for you."

"What time?" Tatienne couldn't stop herself from grinning.

"I'll push through the meetings and finish by five," Thomas said, his tone brighter.

"I'll bring my research and we'll go over it. I haven't been able to see Father Andre, though. He was called away for a few days."

"We could talk on Friday about his books. Do you think you'll see him by then?"

"I hope so," she said. "I'll call you when I know more."

After they'd hung up, Tati sat at her desk for a few minutes. He wasn't blowing her off. He was making time for her and thinking about her priorities at the same time. The butterflies in her stomach fluttered rapidly. Was it just a week's fling? She was starting to hope it was more, even though that was ridiculous. They were so different.

While she waited for the workday to be over, she finished her shelving tasks and gathered her research for Thomas. She called Céline and asked her to be ready for a movie night.

Underneath her work clothes, she had worn one of the new lingerie sets Thomas had sent her. It gave her a chance to think about him during the day—his scent, his hands fingering and ripping her panties, his mouth hot on her breasts. Her panties had been damp all day. Although she had thought she'd be showing him the bra and panties in his limo, it looked like it was a hotel rendezvous instead. She had never been to a fancy hotel for a booty call. Thomas probably had the penthouse suite or something equally impressive.

At four-thirty p.m., Tatienne locked up, put on her coat and slogged through the snow to the waiting town car.

Isabelle was waiting, dressed in a puffy down coat and knit hat. She smiled and opened the car door. "Thomas is sorry he couldn't be here to pick you up."

Tatienne nodded and got into the vehicle. "He's a busy man."

Isabelle peered in, still holding the door open. "Thomas doesn't date much. Not anymore."

"I don't know if I'd call this dating," Tatienne said.

"Trust me, he is courting you. When he chooses a course of action, he pursues it single-mindedly. There's a lot going on in the company right now, but you are on his mind."

"I really like him," Tati confessed. "But it won't work out. How could it?"

"Thomas doesn't care about privilege and money. Look at me. I was living on the street before he found me and hired me."

"He has a big heart," Tati said.

"And I'm glad he's found someone who is the same." Isabelle closed the door and went around to the driver's seat. They started moving.

Tatienne was thankful she hadn't been expected to reply. It made her happy to know Thomas liked her. Was she ready for him to court her? As Isabelle said, it was already happening. Tati had said yes to meeting him at the hotel and bringing Céline as well. And she didn't regret those decisions.

The car stopped at her apartment building, and she went to get Céline. Tatienne kept on her work clothes since they were probably more suitable for the hotel, but she packed jeans and a T-shirt in case she wanted to change. When the two of them returned to the car, Isabelle had drawn down the partition. Céline chatted amiably with Isabelle for the drive downtown.

Isabelle stopped at the front of the hotel and a striking middle-aged woman in a trim black pantsuit ran out to meet them.

"I'm Frédérique. You must be Tatienne and Céline. Nice to meet you!" She escorted them past the uniformed footman and concierge towards the back of the hotel. They turned left at the lifts down a long hallway.

"Mr Ducharme is in Boardroom A. I'll show you where it is." The three of them walked down to the end of the hall. Frédérique showed them a couple of chairs outside the door and asked if they wanted water. When they shook their heads, the woman said, "Céline, would you like to look in the gift shop with me and pick out some snacks? Then I can take you up to your room and we'll make our movie choices."

Céline nodded and looked at Tati. "Will you be okay without me?" Céline asked.

Tatienne sat down. "Yes, *mon chou*. I'm sure Thomas will be done soon, and we can meet you upstairs."

Céline waved and skipped away, Thomas' assistant trailing a step behind her. Céline was growing up so fast and Tatienne wasn't sure she could keep up either. But it made her heart happy to see Céline smile like that. Maybe the sad times were in the past and new opportunities were opening up.

The boardroom door opened and several people spilled out of the room talking animatedly to each other. She heard Thomas' voice. He was holding the door and saying goodbye to each person. As the last one left, he looked out and made eye contact with Tatienne, a smile spreading across his face.

He marched up to Tatienne and took her hand, pulling her up from the chair and leading her into the conference room. After closing the door, he kissed her, hot and wet. Then he scooped her up, spun her around and sat her on the edge of the table, just as he had done in the records office. Tatienne hooked her legs around his waist. He snaked his arms around her shoulders. They kissed again, Thomas leaning in and holding her closer.

"Let's get the business out of the way so we can do more of that," he said with a wicked grin.

Tatienne showed him the hard copies she had made and gave him a thumb drive with digital images of all the research materials. "I couldn't find any other drawings in family albums, apart from the one you saw on Sunday. But there were some letters from Marie Elisabeth at the back of the scrapbook. I included copies of them for you. And I found a few more references to the Frères Gris in newspapers and periodicals. They were linked to a series of disappearances which they tried to blame on Indigenous communities. They used some local legends about Wendigo and werewolves to try and cover up their involvement."

Thomas narrowed his grey eyes. "Local legends, eh? Were they punished?"

"No. They left before they could be apprehended. It was like they just disappeared. There were some sightings in the Laurentian Mountains. People talked about a red castle in the sky inhabited by grey-robed ghosts who ate humans."

Thomas harrumphed. "Do you think there's more to find out?"

"I still want to look at Father Andre's books. I should be done by the end of the week." She looked at him, waiting. Would he ask to see her again? Would she ask him?

"I'll try to come back Friday. I could take you out on a proper date. What do you think?"

The butterflies came back. "Yes, I would love that." She smiled and kissed him.

"Good. Now, I want to bring you to my suite."

He took her hand and led her to the lift. When he touched her, her muscles relaxed, warmth spreading across her skin. Her whole body tingled with desire, and she couldn't wait to get upstairs.

Thomas hoped the lift would be empty when it opened. He couldn't wait to kiss Tatienne again.

It was.

Still holding her hand, he walked with her into the lift and used the key card for the penthouse. When the doors closed, he leaned over and planted his mouth on hers. Sweet and tart she was, a delectable combination. When his tongue sought entry, she opened her lips with a moan and ran her hands down his back. Everything she did lit a fire in him, melting the ice he'd packed around his heart.

She moaned again and he walked her backwards to the lift wall. Taking her hands and holding them above her head, he rubbed his torso against her soft form. The friction just made his cock throb more. He skimmed a hand down her arm, lingering a moment on her waist, before he squeezed her ample bottom. Those cheeks — they would be his undoing. He could spend the rest of his days worshipping them.

He released her other arm and brought his hand down to the hem of her grey pencil skirt. Sighing into her mouth, he lifted her skirt and ran his palm along her bare thigh. Her head fell backward, and she groaned when he used his fingers to trace the outline of her cheeky panties. She was wearing the taupe lingerie he had sent, with a criss-cross pattern at the back. His fantasies were coming true. He couldn't wait to see her in this set.

The bell dinged, and the lift came to a stop. "We're here." He helped smooth their clothes in place as the doors swooshed open to an elegant square space with three doors — one on each wall, apart from the lift side. "There are only three suites on this floor, so I booked them all. I'm in the one at the end," — he pointed to the door across from the lift — "and you and Céline are in the one on the left. Frédérique is on the right."

Tatienne squeezed his hand. "Can I check on Céline for a minute?"

"Of course," he said. He wouldn't want her if she wasn't loyal and loving to her family. The Ducharmes believed family was everything, too.

While he unlocked the penthouse, she went to the other suite. After looking over the rooms, he nodded in approval. Everything was ready.

There was a knock on the door. He let Tatienne in and handed her a glass of champagne. "I thought we'd eat in."

She walked to a nearby table, where there was a charcuterie board made up of local meats and cheeses, a large bowl of fruit salad and French bread on an artisanal board. Finally, there was a box of pastries beside the champagne bottle. "This looks delicious," she said.

"So do you," he said.

She turned and granted him one of her brilliant smiles. She picked up a piece of pineapple from the fruit salad and held it out to him. He opened his mouth, and she plopped the fruit on his tongue, withdrawing before he could lick her fingers. He took a slice of buttered French bread and fed it to her, bite by bite, allowing his fingers to linger near her lips. She obliged him by licking and sucking his digits as she ate. After a few more exchanges, she pulled him to a nearby leather couch and sat him down. Kneeling in front of him, she started unbuttoning his shirt, leaving a trail of kisses to mark her progress. He held her head in his hands for a brief moment, feeling content. When she reached his navel, he shuddered with pleasure. Then he whispered, "Stop. Let me take you to the bedroom."

She looked up at him with eyes so willing and trusting that his wolf jumped up and rumbled, *Mate*.

Calisse, he could take her now and claim her. Spend the rest of his days bathing in her gaze, sating himself with her gorgeous body and loving her generosity and kindness.

It was too soon. This he knew. But his wolf was impatient now that he had found the one.

Give me time, he said to his wolf. *We'll make it happen, just not today*.

His wolf whined but sat back down, resigned to wait for now.

Thomas stood. He picked up Tatienne and carried her through to the primary bedroom, a sleek and modern space filled with chrome and black. He licked his lips as he lay her down on the giant bed and pushed away several pillows and cushions of various shades of grey. As she pulled his open shirt out of his trousers, he undid the buttons of her blouse. The silky lavender fabric floated through his fingers as he pulled back the shirt and massaged her breasts. Unhooking her bra, he admired her generous bounty and leaned over to suck one nipple, rolling the other one between his fingers. Tatienne squirmed beneath him as she unzipped his trousers. He moaned when she reached in to caress his aching member. Then he pulled her hips up and tugged down her skirt.

"Let me get a better look at you," he growled, kneeling above her. He raked his gaze over her body, running his hands along her hips and thighs. The lingerie was perfect. Form-fitting, soft and comfortable, it showed off her assets beautifully.

He leaned down and licked her belly button. She shivered and grabbed his head.

"You don't know what it does to me to see you like this," he murmured.

"Do it, it's okay," she moaned.

"Are you sure?" he asked, grazing his teeth on the edge of the panties.

"Yes, I liked it last time."

A rumble came from his chest as he grabbed the fabric in his mouth and bit into it. She gasped as he brought his hands forward to finish ripping the panties. When he threw them on the floor, he made a trail with his tongue down the landing strip of clipped hair hugging her sex.

He gripped her thighs and bent to kiss her folds. After lightly teasing her with his lips and tongue, he spread her legs open and planted her feet on his shoulders. He took his time sucking her clit, enjoying the taste of her. She moaned and writhed as he made long strokes of his tongue along her lips. When he flicked his tongue on her clit, she bucked and squeezed her thighs around his head. He plunged his fingers into her pussy and revelled in the sensations of her rippling walls.

When she had stopped gyrating, he sighed in contentment. "I love to hear you come. Those little moans and panting sounds when you get close to climax make me hot."

Breathless, she pulled his head up and tasted his lips, wrapping her legs around his waist. "I was thinking about you all day."

He lay down so they were side by side on the bed. She planted her hands on his naked chest and he shivered.

"Let me take off the rest of your clothes," she whispered, pulling down his trousers and boxers. When his cock sprang out, hard and thick, she murmured, "You're beautiful." She stroked his length reverently, then looked in his eyes.

Fuck. I'm in over my head.

"I want you to fill me."

I'll do anything you ask.

He reached down, took a condom from his trouser pocket and placed it on his aching cock.

He supported himself on a forearm and kissed her before gently pushing her onto her back. He climbed on top of her, rubbing his cock against her thighs and spreading her legs to receive him.

When he brought his aching member to her entrance, she moaned. He pressed in slowly but insistently, her juices surrounding his cock. He pushed in to the hilt, filling up her tight, wet pussy. Loving every second, he pulled out and thrust back in, kissing her face and neck.

They settled into a rhythm, but then he slowed down to make long, luxurious strokes in and out of her channel. Taking her nipple between his teeth, he teased her until she groaned. When her panting accelerated, he arched his back and cried out. She surrendered, shuddering around him as he spurted hot and deep inside her.

He was caught up in the moment of their joining, wishing they could stay there forever. When they came down from their highs, he collapsed on top of her, panting heavily. Catching his breath, he held her tight and rolled them to their sides.

As he lay beside her, he kissed her like she was the only thing in the world. If only they had time to explore each other fully, to pleasure one another and learn each other's secrets.

Sighing, he excused himself for a moment and removed the used condom, disposing of it in the bathroom trash. Then he brought some plates of food to the bed and went back to fetch their champagne glasses.

"Céline picked out two movies. We've still got some time until they're finished," Tatienne said.

"What do you want to do?" He lay back down beside her and pulled her into his arms.

"I want to stay just like this," she said. Her hair tickled his chest as she snuggled her face against him. And he couldn't ask for anything more.

"That's fine with me," he murmured and closed his eyes.

Chapter Seven

Tatienne couldn't believe Thomas had talked her and Céline into staying the night at the hotel. He had to leave at dawn, so after they had finished their cuddling session and Céline's movie had ended, he said goodbye and left the women to themselves in the junior penthouse suite.

There was nothing junior about the suite. Even though it wasn't as gigantic as Thomas' rooms, it was still twice as large as their entire apartment. The TV screen where Céline had her movie night was as large as her bed at home. And they had separate bedrooms with queen beds encased in the whitest linens she had ever seen.

She called her best friend Diego while Céline brushed her teeth and put on her pyjamas.

"How was your date?" Diego asked.

"Good. We're staying over at the hotel."

"Wait, what?" he said. "You're sleeping over with him?"

"Not exactly. He got rooms for Céline and me, so we're staying there." Tatienne's face grew hot. She didn't know why that bothered her. She'd slept with other guys before.

"Is it serious?"

"No!" Tatienne replied. "Maybe. I'm not looking for a relationship, though." She checked on Céline, then sat down on a tufted armchair in her bedroom.

Diego sighed. "That's what you always say."

"It's always true," Tatienne said.

"Sweetie, you can't keep sacrificing your needs for everyone else's."

"I take care of my needs," she said, shifting in her chair.

"I mean your emotional needs, your needs for intimacy and support."

She scoffed, but she knew he was right. It was scary to contemplate, though. "It's been me and Céline for so long."

"I get that. But maybe it's time for you to open up and take a chance."

Tatienne fiddled with a silk throw pillow. "Thomas is way out of my league. I'm afraid he'll regret being with poor, ugly, old me."

"You have no idea how amazing you are. He'd be lucky to get you."

Tatienne laughed and threw the pillow onto her bed. "All right, I'll give it a try. But you'll be the one buying the ice cream when he doesn't call me back next week."

When Céline appeared to say she was ready for bed, Tatienne said goodnight to Diego and hung up the phone. Tatienne tucked her sister in. Then she brushed her own teeth and climbed into the softest, fluffiest bed she'd ever encountered in her whole life.

She closed her eyes. She knew she should give Thomas a chance. Well, she should give herself a chance. Céline was happy, and things were good. She could take a risk and see if there was something between her and Thomas. He was worth it. And damn it, so was she.

* * * *

Several hours later, she thrashed in her sleep, caught in a nightmare.

Flames. Just like when their parents had died.

She was a teenager standing outside their house, holding a nine-year-old Céline's head to her chest. They were both sobbing.

I could have stopped it. I could have stopped it. If only I'd listened...

The litany had run through her head for years. The inner voice had fed her guilt and shame since the accident. She knew it had been an accident, but she still took the blame.

Why am I so hard on myself?

Then the dream scene had changed. She was in the parish church with Father Andre. He was bleeding and there were more flames.

Is it the same fire or a new one?

She was confused and afraid, her stomach in knots. Yet someone—something—was there with her, comforting her, radiating calm. She held them tight while books and shelves fell all around them.

The scene shifted again, and she found herself in a dark space. A dungeon? A cavern?

This time, the flames were contained to a fire pit where a large iron cauldron sat. Three shadowy figures in robes stood around the vessel, chanting and stirring. The same someone or something was with her, but it was multiplied somehow. She felt more reassurance, more peace—like a family. But that couldn't be true. It was only her and Céline.

The dark figures in robes stopped casting their spell—*that's what they're doing!*—and looked towards her. She couldn't see their faces, just shining, white orbs where their eyes should have been. But human eyes didn't glow like that.

Who are they?

The eyes drew her towards them. She took a step forward. Cursing, she tried to shake off the compulsion. She closed her eyes and stepped back.

Suddenly, she was running down a tunnel towards a moonlight entrance.

Tatienne woke. Sat upright in the hotel bed. There was no fire, no crying, no creepy sorcerers.

She stumbled to the bathroom, then poured a glass of water and drank it down. Her heart raced and she took some deep breaths.

She hadn't had a nightmare like that in a long time. Maybe her brain was reacting to the new environment. Or she was having doubts about a relationship with Thomas.

Someone knocked on the bathroom door. Tatienne opened it to find her sister rubbing her eyes.

"Bad dream?" Céline asked.

"I'll be okay. I just need to clear my mind."

"Was it a regular dream? Or…"

"I don't know." Tatienne hugged Céline. "Our parents were in it and some new stuff I didn't understand."

"Did you see fire?"

"Yes." Tatienne swiped at her eyes. "I can't tell if it means something, since the premonitions are hard to decipher. It could just be a dream."

"You can't keep blaming yourself because you had a fire dream before our parents died. We don't know if the dream was a sign."

"What if something happens this time and I could have stopped it?" Tears fell down her cheeks.

"I'll make you some warm milk," Céline said. "Come to the kitchen." She grabbed Tati's hand and tugged her out of the bathroom and down the hall to the kitchen area. Tatienne sat at the kitchen island while Céline found the milk, poured it into a mug and put it in the microwave.

Tati tried to shake off the bad feeling and forced herself to smile. "What would I do without you, Céline?"

"Will you be able to sleep after this?" her sister asked.

She hoped to hell she would.

* * * *

Thursday afternoon, Thomas took an hour to go to the resort's pool. He needed to work out some stress. The meetings had been positive today, but there were so many angles to consider. Even with the volunteer training and enhanced security measures underway, it was a massive job. They couldn't secure the entire border between the two clans — it was simply too long. He thought a judicious use of cameras at key points that could be monitored from the villages would help a lot. Although that would take a lot of effort to coordinate, it could be worth it.

After changing into his swim trunks, he entered the Olympic-size community pool. There was a seniors' fitness class taking place in the shallow end. The deep end was divided into lanes for those who wanted to do laps.

He saw his sister-in-law Chantelle bobbing up and down near the dividing line in the middle of the pool. When she waved, he dove in and swam to her. "Hey, what's up?"

She smiled. "I was feeling a little peaked. Thought a swim would clear my mind and settle my stomach."

"Do you want to swim laps with me?" Maybe some company would help him sort out his thoughts.

She shook her head. "I'm the paddle type of swimmer. I couldn't keep up with the captain of the swim team."

"I was never captain." He ducked his head. "I just placed at nationals a couple times."

She chuckled. "Don't be embarrassed! I really admire how athletic you are."

"It's a struggle to keep fit these days. There's so much going on with the clan."

Chantelle swam to the edge of the pool and put a hand on the ledge. Thomas followed her. "I appreciate you stepping into the Lieutenant role," she said. "Charles and I are grateful for your work—I know it hasn't been easy."

Warmth spread through his chest. He was making a difference for his clan. And its leaders. "I wish we knew what the Trois-Rivières Clan wanted."

"Did you find out anything in the city?"

"Yes," he said. "I need to go back and pursue some leads..." He trailed off. Was he thinking about the rival clan or about Tatienne? Maybe both.

When he paused, Chantelle's eyes opened wide. "You met someone, didn't you?"

His face went hot and he gripped the ledge of the pool beside Chantelle. "She's gorgeous and smart and strong. But she doesn't want to have a relationship. I don't know if I do, either."

"Is this because of that spoiled brat Aimée?" Chantelle frowned.

Thomas looked down at the water. "I don't think I'm ready to date someone. I'm not a very good boyfriend."

"Nonsense. She's still in your head." Chantelle rested her hand on his shoulder.

Thomas sighed. "She was pretty critical when she dumped me. And very demanding when we were together." It hit him that he had internalised her criticisms and started thinking they were true.

"She used you and then discarded you when she wanted a new toy." Chantelle pursed her lips. "I know you were really devoted to her, but you can do so much better."

"I wish I could believe this. I want to believe it."

Chantelle put a hand on his chest and a soothing sensation radiated from her palm. She let him feel how much she and Charles loved him, how important he was to the clan. His confidence boosted, he considered his options.

"The woman I met is very private, closed off," he said. "It's going to take some effort to convince her to take a chance on me." Thomas didn't realise until he said it out loud how much he wanted to make it work with her.

"Be yourself. You are kind, compassionate, handsome — all the things anyone could want in a boyfriend." When she smiled at him, he thought again how lucky his brother Charles was to have found her.

"What if I do the wrong thing? What if she doesn't like me?"

"You worry too much!"

"Aimée had all these rules. It was so hard to keep track of everything. Then she would change the rules or demand something else when I thought I had it all figured out. It made me doubt myself." Her behaviour affected him still. He needed to get out from under her shadow.

Chantelle spoke up. "Is this new woman— "

"Tatienne."

"Is Tatienne like this at all? From what you've seen so far?" She tilted her head and waited for his answer.

"She's surprisingly easy to read. I can tell what she's thinking by the look on her face. And she doesn't hold back with her opinions."

"I like her already," said Chantelle. "Did she change her mind or act inconsistently with you?"

He thought for a moment. "No. We had trouble keeping our hands off each other, even when we agreed we should stick to business. We were both a little confused by our attraction, but we were honest about our feelings."

Chantelle crinkled her forehead. "Was it an immediate attraction?"

"When I first saw her, it was like I'd known her all my life. Or maybe in a previous life?" He laughed and shook his head. "I know, that sounds ridiculous. Forget I mentioned it."

"Love is a funny thing." Chantelle chuckled.

"Love?" He sputtered. "I just met her." His mind spun. "Wait, you don't mean…" *Is she talking about what I think she is?*

"There are stranger things in the world than Fated Mates. A year ago, I would have laughed if you had said this would happen to me." Chantelle practically lit up when she talked about her courtship with Charles.

"That's not possible." Thomas furrowed his brow. He wasn't special, he didn't deserve to find this kind of romance and love.

"What about your brother and me?" Chantelle raised an eyebrow.

Thomas considered his words carefully. "You two are different. Unique. I'll never find what you have."

"Don't be so sure." Chantelle squeezed his arm. "You are worthy of a great love. Just keep an open mind."

"All right," he grumbled. "If it were anyone else, I'd tell them to mind their own business."

"Then it's a good thing I'm not anyone else," she said, chuckling. "Now, go do your laps."

Thomas excused himself and swam away to the lane markers.

Maybe he wouldn't find his Fated Mate, but he needed to stop living in the past. Chantelle was right. He shouldn't think of himself as broken or incapable. He was better than Aimée had made him feel. It was time to move on.

He could use this opportunity to regain his confidence in the company of a fine woman. It might not lead anywhere. They weren't—they couldn't be—Fated Mates. Still, they had made a connection. She was smart, loyal, fun and attractive…and the sex was great.

They didn't have to get married. It was just a few dates. He just had to trust himself and be open with her. He could do it.

Chapter Eight

Friday evening, Tatienne tried to sit still on her bed while Céline gathered her curls into a side ponytail. Beside her, their neighbour, Lynne Bernal, unzipped a garment bag and pulled out a deep-gold gown. The shimmers in the tight bodice gave way to a flowy, diaphanous skirt with a top layer of sheer georgette.

"I remember wearing this to a benefit hosted by my law firm. It's a good thing we both have full figures, otherwise the dress wouldn't work," Lynne said.

Tatienne tried to turn and look, but her sister held her shoulders in place.

"Stop fidgeting!" Céline said.

"Remind me why I'm doing this?" Tatienne asked.

"Because a rich, handsome man invited you on a date."

"It's ridiculous."

Lynne handed her a pair of gold high heels. "You'll be gorgeous. Come on, you deserve to have a little fun."

Tatienne looked at the expensive shoes. Maybe that was the problem. She didn't think she deserved it. She always ended up putting herself at the bottom of the list.

"It's just a fun night, not the rest of your life! Enjoy yourself while you're young," Céline said.

Tatienne put her shoulders back. "Okay, my wise little sister. I'll give it a try."

"That's my girl," said Lynne. "I'll stay with Céline overnight if you decide to stay out late." She winked. "Then you can tell me *all* about your date in the morning."

Tatienne shooed the women out so she could get dressed in peace.

Ten minutes later, there was a knock on the apartment door. Her sister let Thomas in. She took a deep breath, left the room and found Céline in the living room laughing at something Thomas had said.

"What's so funny?" Tatienne asked.

"He likes to tell me jokes," Céline answered, as Thomas turned to face Tatienne.

"Our reservation is —" His jaw dropped. "Beautiful, you — you look beautiful," he breathed. "Well, you always look beautiful, but —" he stammered. "You are stunning, like a queen."

Tati fidgeted but did a spin so her skirt twirled up. "I'm glad you approve."

"That dress is perfect on you," he said.

She smiled. "I don't think I'll be able to walk in these heels, though."

"I'll have to carry you then." Thomas' eyes twinkled. "Come on, we have to get to the restaurant."

When they exited the small walk-up building, Thomas' driver, Isabelle, pulled up in a vintage silver Aston Martin.

Tatienne gasped. "Is this what you usually drive in the city?"

"It's my fun car." The glint in Thomas' eye gave Tati a thrill.

Isabelle gave Thomas the keys while he helped Tatienne into the passenger seat. "I feel just like one of the Bond girls." She ran her hands over the soft leather. "Very glamourous."

"My brother Charles made us watch all the Bond films when we were teens. He loves old movies," said Thomas. "I like to drive fast, but I won't drive James Bond-fast, I promise."

As they pulled away, Tatienne waved at Isabelle, who waved back. Then she stared out through the window, watching the city lights go by. "I feel like the paparazzi are going to mob us when we get out."

Thomas laughed. "They don't usually bother with me these days. When I went out with an influencer, they tracked us. She enjoyed the attention." He glanced over at her before returning his attention to the road. "I just want a nice, quiet night with you."

"You've probably dated celebrities and supermodels," Tatienne said. She couldn't measure up to them.

"My younger brother Henri is into that scene. It's not for me."

"What's not to like about that scene?" she asked.

"A lot of them are obsessed with their appearance. And there are lots of parties, lots of drama. I had other priorities."

They pulled up to a building with a red carpet leading to an imposing oak double door. Two staff in uniform were waiting on the stairs.

Thomas got out of the car and gave the keys to the waiting valet. The other staff member opened Tatienne's door and offered a hand as she got out of the car. She looked up at the six-storey building. The windows were tall—new but designed to suit the historic property. The dark green marble foundation and brass accents were intimidating, but Tatienne remembered what Céline and her neighbour had said. *Have fun, enjoy myself.*

Thomas appeared at her side and presented his arm. She took a deep breath. Then she put her arm through his and they ventured up the stairs and through the open door.

It was quieter than she had expected. There were hushed conversations amid the low soundtrack of smooth jazz and the clinking of expensive china. Delicious smells wafted out to the foyer.

A handsome man approached, his medium-brown skin gleaming in the candlelight. The maître-d' greeted Thomas warmly. "The special chef's table is waiting for you and your companion, Monsieur Ducharme."

"*Merçi*, Jacques," Thomas inclined his head.

Her date was so at home in this chic atmosphere. Tatienne was sure she stuck out like a sore thumb. As the maître-d' seated her, Thomas spoke. "Jacques, this is Mademoiselle Laflamme."

"Welcome to Club St Patrice," he said with a flourish.

She smiled tentatively, feeling a little shy.

"If I may, Mademoiselle, you are an improvement over Monsieur Ducharme's previous girlfriend."

Tatienne looked at Thomas.

"My ex would start complaining as soon as we walked in the door to the club. She was never satisfied," he said.

"I'm sorry you had to go through that," she said to Jacques.

Jacques bowed. "I will send over your server right away. Wine is on the house tonight, in appreciation of the lovely lady." He slipped away.

Thomas regarded her, one side of his mouth quirking up. "This is already an enjoyable evening. I was so uptight when I came here with my ex, I couldn't wait to get away. Tonight, I can imagine lingering over drinks and dessert, talking into the wee hours with you."

Her face grew hot, and she took a sip of water. "I want you—us—to have a good time. And my neighbour is staying the night at my apartment with Céline, so we can talk all night, if you like."

Thomas stared at her hungrily, a low rumble sounding in his chest. She liked the noises he made.

"I might want to do more than talk, if you're interested."

She nodded and reached for his hand. Looking into his eyes made her whole body hum.

The sommelier brought a bottle of wine, and the server added a bread basket to the table.

"Do you want to taste the wine?" Thomas asked her.

"I don't know how. You go ahead."

She watched as Thomas swirled a small amount in his glass, sniffed it and took two small sips. He closed his eyes then nodded. "*Merçi*," he said to the sommelier, who poured the wine into their glasses.

The server asked if they wanted to know the special features.

"Please tell Chef Marc-François he has full rein of our meal selection."

Tatienne was impressed. He wasn't worried about looking sophisticated in front of her. He just wanted them to enjoy the evening and for the club to do what it did best. That was a thoughtful gesture.

After the server had left, Tatienne tried the wine. It was good, even if she didn't know much about it.

"This club is exclusive. I've always wanted to eat here," she said.

"You're going to love it. Marc-François' food is fantastic."

They continued to chat until the server arrived, announcing an *amuse-bouche* with local ingredients. When the maître d' came to check on them, Tatienne asked about the history of the building. "I worked on an exhibit for the Business Association in this area. I was helping research the freed slaves who came north and worked in Montréal hotels."

"One of my ancestors came up through the Underground Railroad," said Jacques. "My *grandpère* used to tell us stories about them. I'd love a chance to compare notes. Would you come back during the day sometime to chat with me?"

Tatienne blinked. *A nobody like me?* "Sure, I'd love to. If you mean it."

Jacques raised his eyebrows. "I never say something I don't mean."

Tatienne felt her face grow hot again. "Then yes."

"I'll be in touch," Jacques said, as he disappeared to greet more guests.

"How...?" Tatienne looked at Thomas.

"I'll give him your number," he said. "You are amazing! I bet you can make authentic connections with anyone."

"My grandmother always told us, 'You can talk to any folks. We're all the same.' There are differences, for sure, but we can always find something in common."

"My *grandmère* is a wise lady, too. She taught me a lot about respect and dignity."

Their next course arrived, with an elaborate explanation from the chef via their server. The meal was the best Tatienne had eaten. She was very full when they got to dessert, but Thomas insisted they sit and talk while they shared a few bites of the chocolate confections they received.

After Thomas paid the bill with his platinum credit card, Jacques came back to escort them to the foyer. "Mademoiselle Laflamme, I hope we will see you again soon. Monsieur Ducharme, if you bring her back, I will ask Chef to make his cassoulet for you."

Thomas' eyes lit up. "Really? It's a deal."

As they walked out of the club, Thomas explained that Chef Marc-François only made this signature dish for special occasions. "And Jacques knows it's my favourite."

Tatienne laughed. "I'm uncomfortable being part of this shady bribe."

"You will be glad once you taste it. Trust me."

Tatienne realised she did trust him. And that didn't frighten her.

The valet arrived with the sports car. After opening the door and seating her, Thomas got in himself.

"Are you an old-fashioned gentleman? I mean about opening doors for a lady kind of thing?" Tatienne asked.

"Not exactly." Thomas shrugged. "My father was unconventionally traditional. He was a hippie in his beliefs — especially about treating everyone with courtesy. I learned a lot about leadership from him."

"You admired him." She eased off her shoes and rubbed her toes.

Thomas nodded and stole a glance at her. "It was my mother who taught me the importance of being generous and observant in a relationship. She said it showed respect when you attended to your date's needs, and all relationships needed to be founded on mutual appreciation and kindness."

"She sounds like a wonderful woman."

"I treasure the talks we had before she was gone." His eyes shone as he turned down a side street.

Tatienne squeezed his knee. "My mother was traditional in some ways. She was proud of her Laurentian heritage. My father was proud of his heritage — his father had come from Jamaica. Both of them instilled in me a love of family and culture."

"Is that why you became an archivist?"

Tatienne thought about her family. "My father was such a good storyteller. I loved stories when I was a child. It was such a treat when Papa would spin a yarn after dinner."

"In my family it was music — fiddles and banjos and traditional Québécois songs. I learned how to play the accordion and sing at a young age." He laughed. "It didn't help me make friends."

"That sounds like a lovely tradition." She tried to imagine a bespectacled young Thomas playing while his family danced and sang.

Thomas nodded. "Family music time is some of my best memories of childhood. One day I want to bring that to my children."

"You want to raise a family?" she asked. She hadn't expected such a serious conversation. In fact, she usually avoided them. But the discussion flowed so easily with Thomas. And she wanted to know the answer.

"Yes. Things are too busy with work now, but someday I'd like to. How about you?"

"Céline is the centre of my life. I've practically raised her since our parents died." She fiddled with the hemline of her dress. "I haven't really been in a place where I could consider having a child of my own."

Thomas looked thoughtful as he passed another car. "Is it lonely? Just the two of you?"

"You have a big family, yes? It's different. But we are close, almost inseparable. We've got Diego and his partner and our neighbour. And Father Andre. It's a good family. We love each other."

He smiled at her. "That's how I feel about my brothers and cousins. That loyalty and love feeds me. It's the same for you, isn't it?"

"Yes." *He gets it.* "Do you look after your little brother?"

Thomas rolled his eyes. "He's a good man, but he's still young. At least in his heart. He took it hard when our father and oldest brother died — we all did, but he was in his teens, and it was difficult for him to lose that guidance."

"I can imagine. But you've been there for him." She could see how much Thomas cared for his brother.

Thomas nodded. "I've tried my best. He treats me like a father sometimes, though. Ignores me, thinks he knows better—"

"Just like Céline," Tatienne added. "Younger siblings can be a challenge."

"You know what I mean." His gaze met hers briefly before it returned to the road. "In contrast, my older brother Charles puts all the responsibility of the family on his shoulders."

"That's a big burden. I can sympathise with that." Father Andre and Lynne kept telling her she needed to take better care of herself, but it was hard when there was always so much to do.

"Now that he has a wife, he's less stressed and he takes more time off. There's a better work-life balance." He shifted gears and passed a car.

She wished she could find that balance for herself. And for Thomas, too. "Do you think that has put more responsibility on you?"

"In some ways, yes." Thomas nodded. "But I like helping out. I'm Charles' right-hand man. I support him and advise him."

"He's lucky to have you." She squeezed his knee again and he placed his hand over hers for a moment before changing gears.

"It can be challenging sometimes to live up to expectations."

"I know that feeling. You think you're letting everyone down."

He looked briefly at her before returning his gaze to the road. "You are doing an amazing job with your sister. She is loved and happy."

Tatienne smiled and tried to take it in. "It's easy to doubt yourself, but she's doing really well. We've got good routines, loving adults and caregivers in our lives. She is happy." She realised she was happy, too. Life was good.

Thomas drove through the city streets, sneaking glances at the beguiling woman beside him. She had won over Jacques at the club almost immediately. Most people had to put in months of effort to get a smile from him, let alone an invitation to talk. He had always wondered why Aimée couldn't get along with him, but now that he had gone with Tatienne, he could easily see the difference. *Difficult people cause difficulties. They don't even see it. Then they blame it on others.*

That wasn't the way he did things. His clan was collaborative and encouraged each other. It was about the good of the community, not the individual. And Tati understood that.

He turned down Viau Street. "I have a surprise."

She twisted in her seat to give him her best glare. "I don't like surprises."

"It's a good surprise."

"Okay." She sounded sceptical.

"Have you ever gone on the Tour de Montréal?" he asked.

"The leaning tower of Pisa thing? Never."

"Tonight, we are changing that. I've rented it out." He tried not to sound smug. He'd contemplated a lot of options and when he had chosen the Tour, he'd hoped to make a unique experience for her.

"You can do things like that? Oh right, you can."

Thomas grinned. "It'll be fun."

When they got to the parking lot, Thomas pulled up to the front entrance. Isabelle was waiting where he had asked her to meet them. He got out and threw her the keys. She was going to return the Aston Martin to the garage and bring the limo for their ride back to his condo. Since the weekend, he had been dreaming about Tati's desire to undress him in the limo and he didn't want to miss out on that opportunity. That was, if she was game. He hoped she would be.

Thomas walked her to the back entrance, where a security guard was waiting to let them in. He handed the staff member a hundred-dollar bill for a tip—he likely was keeping them from their loved ones tonight.

They walked through to the cable car that would take them to the observatory.

"This is so unusual," Tatienne said.

"Funiculars are more common in Europe. There are cable cars in San Francisco, and probably on some mountains in North America, though."

"I've always loved the word 'funicular'," she mused.

"Really?" He loved her quirky side.

"My mom used to sing that song *Funiculì, Funiculà* by Pavarotti when I was in the bathtub. When I found out there was a real thing called a funicular, I became obsessed with it."

"But you've never come here?" Thomas was curious. *Has she denied herself many things in her life?*

She shook her head. "Never found the time."

He hugged her, breathing in the fruity scent of her hair. "Glad we're here, then."

She smiled up at him and the ice around his heart threatened to melt clean away.

They entered the funicular. He watched her skip around like a school child, looking out from all sides onto the view of the city below. When they stepped out onto the Observation Lounge, he checked his arrangements. A string ensemble played near the entrance. Beside them was a small table set up with champagne, wine and soft drinks, as well as some cheese, nuts and fruit. A uniformed server greeted them with champagne glasses from a silver tray. Thomas took one for himself and passed another to Tatienne. He raised his glass and made a toast.

"What can we see from here?" Tatienne asked. Thomas spent the next hour showing her the city sights. He had often come to the observatory while he was at university. It had given him a space to think.

"Monsieur Ducharme?" Isabelle arrived on the funicular. "You asked me to tell you when it was almost midnight."

"Thanks, Isabelle." Thomas turned to Tatienne. "I turn into a pumpkin at midnight. Time to get me home to bed."

Tatienne blushed prettily as he put his arm around her shoulders and steered her back to the cable car.

As they returned down the funicular, Thomas draped his suit jacket around Tatienne's shoulders. She surreptitiously held the jacket to her nose, just as he liked to hold her close and smell her scent. Maybe she felt it, too? The connection between them?

Thomas helped Tati into the waiting limo, then he got in from the other side. She looked fine in the limo. *I could get used to this.* Was he ready to make a commitment? It was still too early, no matter what his wolf was thinking. But he did want to keep seeing her.

After the limo started moving, Thomas asked if she wanted a glass of water.

"Yes, please. I don't drink a lot usually," she said.

Thomas sidled closer to her and lightly touched her face with his fingers.

She inclined her head and rubbed her cheek on his hand. "This was a magical night."

"There's something pulling me towards you," he replied. "I've never felt like this before." He reached over with his other hand and brushed her opposite cheek. She closed her eyes for a moment and his wolf sat up inside him.

When she opened her eyes, he leaned in and kissed her. Not frantic, but gentle. Like they had all the time in the world. Their courtship had been rushed this week — so many things were happening with his clan — and he hadn't been able to slow down and draw out their pleasure. This time, they had all night. And he was going to make every second count.

She put her hands on his chest and he shivered as she ran her fingers along the hard muscles. He skimmed his hands along her curves, relishing the feel of the soft flesh. As he cupped her thighs and buttocks, she pushed him backwards. His head fell back as he lay down on the seat, his sexy date straddling his waist.

She leaned down to kiss him, her plump breasts pressing against his chest.

Wolf-mate.

Thomas spoke back to his wolf. *She's not ready.*

Mark her.

No.

Thomas ran his hands along her sensuous back, feeling her shiver under his touch. He pushed his wolf down, keeping control.

After he explored every nook and cranny of her mouth, she moaned and broke off the kiss.

"Too much too fast?" he asked. He kneaded her hips and tried not to grind his hard cock against her centre.

She blew out a big breath. "It feels good. Don't stop." She bent down again and settled herself on top of him. When her lips met his, his thoughts fell away, spiralling down as his wolf reached up to meet her.

He ran his hands along her hips and down to her buttocks. As a low rumble went through his chest, she squirmed, panting lightly against his mouth. Her movements set a fire in him. He held her tight and sat up so he could flip her onto her backside. He crouched above her, his wolf growling for release. She gasped then softened under him, reaching for his hair to pull him down into another kiss.

The limo stopped. Thomas raised his head. "We must be at my condo."

Tatienne grinned up at him.

He looked down at her crumpled dress and kiss-swollen lips. "I just want to get you inside and pleasure you until morning. Will you come in?"

She patted his shirt-front and nodded.

As they fixed their clothes, Tati's phone buzzed. Worried it might be Céline, Thomas found her phone and passed it to her.

She frowned at the screen.

"What is it?" he asked.

"Father Andre's trying to get a hold of me." She clicked on his contact and put the phone to her ear. After a moment, someone answered. "Father Andre?" Her face scrunched up. "What?" She looked at her phone. "He said one word. 'Jars.' Then he hung up."

"Does that mean something to you?"

"I don't know. I make him jars of pepper sauce." He could practically see the wheels turning in her head. "He didn't sound right."

"We should check on him," Thomas said.

"Are you certain?" Tatienne bit her lip. "It's been such a lovely evening…"

"He's your family." He used her phone to find the priest's last location, then asked Isabelle to hurry to the parish church. When he turned and hugged Tati, he said, "I'm positive he's all right. We'll just make sure."

She nodded and took a deep breath. Then she took his hand and held it between hers, squeezing a little too tight.

Chapter Nine

Thomas' senses were on high alert. "Tell me about the jars."

"I bring him homemade jars of sauce. After he finishes one, he puts the empty jar in a box in the basement. When the box is full, he returns them to me, and I fill them up again for him." Tatienne frowned. "He won't have a full box yet."

"Is he usually at the church this late?" he asked.

"Sometimes he stays to tidy up or get ready for Saturday programming. But I don't know..." Her eyes filled with tears.

"I'm sorry I'm pressing. I'm just gauging the situation."

"You think he's in trouble?" she asked, wiping at her face.

"We'll just go by the church and see if everything's okay." He took out his phone and texted the security team at their family condos. They'd be on standby just in case, but he didn't want to alarm Tatienne unnecessarily. His driver was a capable markswoman and could assist him in the meantime.

Then he pasted a smile on his face. "I'm sure he's fine. But you'll feel better if we see him." He put his arm around her and pulled her in close. He breathed in her scent. It wasn't the right time, but he couldn't control it when his wolf started panting in his ear.

Mate, his beast said.

No, Thomas replied. *No time for sex.*

His wolf backed down unhappily but stayed at the front to aid in the security check. Wolf senses would be useful.

It was quiet when they arrived at the little church. Thomas asked Isabelle to circle the block. Although he saw no one, the hairs on his neck stood up. Isabelle returned them to the church, then pulled down a side alley and into the dark parking lot behind the building.

He reached over and gently took Tati's arm. "You stay put."

"I don't like being ordered around," she said, crossing her arms in front of her.

"I might not be able to keep you safe if something has happened."

"But you don't know where you're going."

Thomas sighed. "To the basement. You said that's where he keeps the jars."

"I can look after myself, you know," she grumbled.

"I know," he said. "Just let me have a quick look first. Then I'll come and get you."

She pursed her lips but nodded her head. "Be quick."

He left the car, turning to give her a smile he didn't feel and seeing her pale face in the window.

She was worried about her friend and mentor, but it would be easier for him to examine the scene without her. If it turned out to be nothing, then he would come back and get her. But if it were serious, then he would ensure everything was safe before he'd let her in the building.

Isabelle met him at the back door, handing him a pistol and loading her own. They moved with military precision, heads down, traversing the perimeter of the church. They kept the guns low, safeties on.

When they returned to the back door, they opened it and entered single file. Peering down the stairs, he saw the lights were on in the basement. He pointed and the two of them made their way quietly down the stairs.

They reached the basement door. It stood ajar. The only sound was the hum of fluorescent lights. They flanked the door before moving inside.

In the stillness, there was rustling, laboured breathing. He followed the sound to the middle of the room. A large wooden cupboard had toppled over.

Father Andre was pinned under the cupboard. He looked small under the heavy, ancient thing, even though Thomas estimated he was of medium height and build. He pushed the heavy furniture over. Blood pooled beneath the priest's cassock.

"Call nine-one-one," Thomas called out to Isabelle.

She was on the other side of the sizeable room, checking doors and windows. She nodded and pulled out her phone.

Tati's voice rang out from the doorway. "No!" she cried.

Thomas turned to her. "You don't need to see this."

She strode forward and was beside him before he could blink. She knelt down and took one of the priest's hands. Tears fell from her eyes as she sobbed. "Is he going to be okay?"

"He's alive. An ambulance is on its way." He looked at Isabelle, who nodded. "We are still securing the space. I can't guarantee your safety."

"To hell with that. I'm staying with him."

He touched her shoulder and squeezed it, trying to put his strength into her. Not that she needed it. She was the strongest person he'd ever met.

He texted the security team to come right away. While they waited, Thomas and Isabelle checked the exits. They found no signs of forced entry. Perhaps the assailants had been known to the priest.

Soon they heard the sirens announcing the emergency vehicles.

Tatienne wiped her eyes and looked around for the first time. "They're almost here, aren't they?"

Thomas nodded. His heart went out to her. She had already suffered tragic losses in her life. How would this one affect her?

The EMTs arrived and asked them to stand back while they assessed the priest. They spoke little, but Thomas could tell they were worried about him. He was still alive and breathing, though. If Father Andre hadn't phoned Tati and they hadn't come to check on him, the priest might not have been discovered until the morning. He likely wouldn't have made it through the night.

Thomas put his hands on Tati's shoulders. "Are you going to be all right?"

She leaned into him for a moment. Then she looked around the room, as if seeing it for the first time. "What happened?"

"It looks like an accident. But the cupboard could have been overturned on purpose."

"Why would—" Her gaze caught a nearby trunk. It was open, its contents strewn on the floor. Nearby, there were several other drawers open and shelves emptied.

"This is not like Father Andre. He would never leave that kind of a mess." She tried to catch her breath, hiccupping.

Thomas looked up from her, taking it in. "Jars. What were you saying—"

"He kept the jars in the basement." She looked around. After she stood, she went to some nearby boxes that looked like the ones his *grandmère* used for her canning supplies. She peered inside a few, then took out a jar that read "Pepper Sauce."

"Just a few empty jars," she said. "Unless—" She pulled out the containers and looked at the bottom of the box. Thomas came over to stand beside her as the ambulance workers transferred Father Andre to a gurney.

"False bottom. Another piece of cardboard," she muttered. She lifted the barrier to reveal a slim volume and papers underneath.

Thomas stuffed them in his coat.

"Wait, those are mine," Tatienne protested.

"You can have them after we get you out of here safely." He gestured to Isabelle.

"Do you think whoever did this was looking for those documents?" Tati asked.

"We should act under that assumption for now. Did he give you anything else?"

"Yes. He ended up leaving the diary with me before he left. I was making digital copies at home." Her eyes suddenly went wide in fear. "Thomas, what if — "

Thomas' heart sank. Céline and her neighbour were at her apartment.

What if they're in trouble? I should have thought of this sooner.

"Isabelle, stay on the scene. Tell the security team to meet me at Tati's apartment ASAP."

He grabbed Tati's hand. They raced upstairs and out back to the limo. Tatienne sobbed in the passenger seat. He wanted to make her feel better, but all he could do was get to her apartment as quickly as he could.

If Céline was hurt, he would never forgive himself. It was all his fault for involving Tatienne in this investigation. He had put the target on her back — and the backs of her family.

He came to a screeching halt in front of her apartment building, parking beside a couple of town cars from his security team.

A couple of members of the team were fighting unknown assailants on the stairs. He didn't see any firearms. Windows had been broken and he could see smoke.

Before he could stop her. Tatienne opened her car door and jumped out. His team lead, Louis, intervened before she reached the fray. Louis was built like a brick wall, and he was a brilliant tactician — a valuable combination in their clan's security force. Thomas knew he wouldn't let Tati get past him. When Thomas approached, Louis was explaining to her that they were securing the scene.

Louis nodded at Thomas. "We encountered four suspects. They had cut the security alarms and were searching the apartments floor-by-floor. Two of the attackers escaped out through the back."

"Her family?" Thomas asked, steeling himself for the worst.

"No one was hurt. We located Céline and a Madame Bernal in the apartment you identified. There was a small fire there, but we put it out."

"Are they okay?" Tati was practically vibrating with worry.

"A little shaken up, but fine. We'll bring them out as soon as our medics have finished examining them."

Tatienne balled up her fists and hid her face in Thomas' chest. He held her, trying to keep his emotions in check. *If they're hurt, someone will pay.*

Then confusion broke out.

Céline and their neighbour Lynne exited the building.

A gunshot pinged by Thomas' head and landed two feet from Céline. Two more shots fired in rapid succession.

Tati screamed and lunged forward, while Louis pushed her to the ground.

Thomas reacted without thinking, shifting into his wolf form. He could rely on his team to protect his mate and her sister while he found the sniper. The shots came from the building across the street. He sniffed, trying to determine how many opponents they might find. Running on all fours, he was joined by two members of his security team. One in wolf form slipped in beside him, while the other retained their human form to open the building door. The three of them hurried up the stairs, stopping at the third floor, where Thomas smelled gunpowder.

They found the apartment door and the human opened it. There were two people climbing out of the window to flee down the fire escape. Since wolves couldn't pursue the shooters that way, he left the human team member and padded down the stairs to the alley. By the time he arrived, the opponents were gone.

Thomas and his wolf companion took the scent. He recognised the Trois-Rivières Clan's signature, but he couldn't identify the individual. Likely, they hadn't met. They followed the trail to the end of the alley, where the shooters must have had a car waiting.

Thomas cursed. His family was getting close to something, or at least their rivals thought they were. But he had endangered Tati and her family in the process. She was probably going to tear him a new one, especially now that she knew his secret of being a shifter.

He knew he should leave her alone, but he couldn't. His heart was breaking in two. He would have to protect her, find a way to keep her safe. Even if she didn't want him anymore.

* * * *

Tatienne sagged to the ground. There was too much to process.

Her apartment had been burglarised. Attackers had gone into her home when her sister was sleeping. There had been another damn fire. Then, when they were supposed to be safe, someone had shot at them.

Her date had helped save her friend. He'd sent a SWAT team — or something — to her home.

Then he'd turned into a werewolf.

Where should I start with this mess? The world spun around her.

First, she had to make sure Céline was okay. Then she would deal with Thomas.

When the medic brought Céline to her, Tati pulled her into a bear hug. "Are you okay, *mon chou*?"

Céline nodded into Tati's chest then looked up at her. "Everything was quiet until some cars zoomed up. They banged on the door of the building, and I heard yelling."

"Did you see anything?" Tatienne asked.

"Nope. I was asleep. Then a nice woman came and asked me if I was all right and I said yes."

Tatienne hugged her tightly again. "I'm so glad you're safe."

"Thomas looks mad." Céline pointed behind her.

He was back. And in human form again. "He's just worried. We thought something had happened to you." Tatienne released her sister and raised her arm towards Thomas, nodding.

Thomas was beside her in an instant, rushing over to hold her proffered hand.

"Céline, did you get hurt?" Thomas asked, his voice breaking.

"I'm fine. Are you okay?" Céline asked.

Thomas nodded, his eyes shining. "I'm sorry I got you into this mess," he said to Tati.

"We'll talk about the other thing later," Tati said, closing her eyes for a moment. "First, your guys can't find Father Andre's documents in my apartment."

"What about the diary?"

She shook her head. "I have photos of the opening pages on a thumb drive."

"Where is it?"

"In my purse. I don't know why I brought it with me."

Thomas hugged her and Céline close to him. He dragged in a deep breath. "It's not safe for you both here."

"What do you mean?" asked Tati.

He looked at her like she'd grown horns on her head. "Someone just shot at you and your apartment was burgled. Not to mention Father Andre – they must be watching you or they tapped into your phone to know he was involved."

Tatienne knew he was right. Then it hit her. "My dream!" The panic built inside her. "I should have known something would happen."

Céline took her arm. "Don't blame yourself. You couldn't have stopped any of this."

Thomas nodded. "Whatever happened, it's not your fault."

"What do we do?" she whispered, trying not to hyperventilate.

He hugged her, sending his cool energy through her body, tamping down the fire in her gut. Then he looked at Céline beside them. "How would you like to spend the night at my family's condo? We've got a hot tub *and* a pool table."

Céline glanced at her. Tatienne nodded, her shoulders relaxing the tiniest bit. Looking at Thomas, she said, "We still have a lot to talk about, but let's get out of here."

The limo drive to the condo building was very quiet. She clung to Thomas, trying to make small-talk for her sister's sake. When they arrived, Thomas took both their hands, then led them through reception and up the lift to the top floor. In spite of her overwhelm,

Tatienne looked around admiringly when they got out of the lift.

"Is this all for you?" Céline asked, eyes wide.

Thomas chuckled. "I have a big family. We share this when we come to town."

Tati looked down the open hallway flanked by doors on both sides and furnished with sleek and elegant décor. Past the hall was an enormous kitchen and living space, beyond which was a large balcony. The city lights sparkled in the dark.

Thomas spoke. "I'd like to get you both some water and food, to help with the shock." He led them to a fully stocked commercial-grade kitchen, filled with chrome and marble.

"Do any of you cook?" Tati asked.

"I like to dabble," Thomas said. "When I have time."

"Can I have hot chocolate, Thomas?" Céline asked.

"Anything you want." Thomas chatted with Céline while Tati sat on a leather stool at a marble kitchen counter. When he passed her a mug, she drank down the hot, sweet liquid and nibbled on the biscotti he handed her.

Thomas' assistant Frédérique appeared with a stack of papers and a phone. She transferred the items to Thomas and came to speak to Céline. After Céline had eaten some apple pieces and finished her hot chocolate, Frédérique invited her to see the pool table. Tati nodded and Céline happily skipped away after the assistant.

Thomas took Tatienne back to the hallway and opened one of the doors. The suite had three bedrooms and an entertainment space decorated in bold colours and soft fabrics. He led her to one of the bedrooms. There were two queen beds in the pastel-coloured room, with pyjamas and sweats on each bed. They looked about the right sizes for her and her sister. The clothes still had tags on them. She stole a look at the prices and nearly dropped the outfits. She'd never spent a hundred dollars on pyjamas, but they were so soft and looked worn in already. She changed while Thomas unpacked his bag in one of the other bedrooms.

After he'd returned, Thomas asked if she was ready to talk.

She gestured to the bed she had claimed and sat on it. He joined her, sitting a couple feet away from her. That was fine with her. She needed a little space.

She took a deep breath. "We have to sort out the attack, but first I need to ask you. Did I see what I saw? Are you—?"

"*Loup-garou*," he said. "Shapeshifter."

She put her head in her hands and breathed in and out. Then she turned to him. "I'm finding it hard to believe, even though I saw you shift—that's what you call it?"

He nodded and waited.

Her thoughts were swirling. "I was starting to trust you," said Tatienne. "I let you into my life."

"I'm sorry. I didn't mean to deceive you." He looked down at the floor and fidgeted with his hands.

"Why didn't you tell me earlier?" Her voice wobbled a bit. She was protective of her family. Why did she think he would be different with his? She was being unfair, but it still hurt that he had deceived her.

"Shifters have to protect themselves and their clanmates. There is a lot of disbelief and fear about our kind, so it's a delicate matter when we out ourselves."

He ran a hand through his hair. His grey eyes turned towards her briefly, then he glanced away.

"It must scare off dates." She tried to chuckle, but the tension in her shoulders squeezed off the sound.

"We have to tread carefully," he said.

She thought about what he had said. He had to be as private as she liked to be in some ways. He was protecting his family and community. "How did your last girlfriend take it?"

Thomas stared at her.

"You didn't tell her?" Tati's heart skipped a beat. *I shouldn't be happy that he showed me and not her. That's petty, isn't it?*

"She was very judgemental. I didn't think I could trust her."

"That must have been hard on you." She reached out and put her hand in his. *He has to be choosy about who he lets into his life.*

"I couldn't be honest with her. I've been more myself with you this week than I ever was with her." Thomas closed his other hand on hers.

"I can understand why you may be reluctant to open up to humans." Her stomach was still fluttering. "I'm confused, though. I thought we had a connection, and now it feels like a lie."

"Would you have been ready to know this information a few days ago? Or last weekend?" He squeezed her hand.

She considered his question. They had only met six days ago. A lot had happened in those six days, but it was still a very short time. "You're right." The butterflies in her stomach settled. "You need a foundation of trust before you can share this part of yourself with someone. And I'm glad you chased the bad guys who shot at us."

"This can be a step forward for us, if you are willing. Here I am, opening up the two sides of myself to you." He pinned her with his gaze, eyes wide. "Will you trust me? Can I trust you with this secret?"

"I think so." Tati let out a breath. "I'm going to need some time to understand this new world. Will you be patient?"

Thomas moved closer and put his arm around her shoulders. "Take the time you need. Just, please, don't shut me out."

She nodded as the tears started to fall for what felt like the hundredth time that day.

"Do you want to take something to help you sleep?" he asked, handing her a tissue.

"No. Can you stay with me until Céline gets here?"

He pulled her into his lap, cradling her head on his chest, then he moved up to lean against the head of the bed. She sobbed — an ugly cry — but he didn't seem to mind. He just patted her and made soothing noises, humming a little.

As the tears stopped flowing, she wondered when Céline would be ready for sleep. Then she was out.

Chapter Ten

Tatienne woke up in a strange room wearing comfortable but unfamiliar pyjamas. She remembered being safe and warm when she drifted off last night. Thomas had held her, comforting her, and she had relaxed into him like she had never done with anyone before.

She wished for a moment Thomas were still there, but he had an empire — and a shifter clan — to run.

Right. A shifter clan.

She looked over at her sister, who was sleeping peacefully in the other bed. She sighed. In one short week, their world had been turned upside down. She had met a man she liked, really liked. He was rich and successful, and he wasn't intimidated by her. Instead of being annoyingly arrogant, he was appealingly confident. Instead of entitled, he was compassionate.

She was starting to fall for him. Well, she had been starting to fall for him, until he had revealed he was a shifter.

Was their relationship a lie? It was hardly a relationship. They were still getting to know each other. She hadn't told him everything about herself, so she shouldn't have expected him to bare his soul to her right away.

She got up from the bed, and changed into the sweats sitting on a nearby chair. After running a hand through her curls, she followed the smell of coffee out of the bedroom. It took her through the suite and into the shared kitchen area.

Thomas was eating granola and reading on a tablet at the counter separating the kitchen from the living room. There were several heaping platters of food beside him. A few people were drinking coffee and eating in the open-area space set down a step from the kitchen. Past the living space were huge windows out onto a terrace. It was covered with snow — blinding in the morning sunlight — but she could see a place on the right where steam came up. *That must be the hot tub. Too bad we didn't get to try it out last night.*

When Thomas saw Tatienne, he stood and moved towards her, but stopped short of making physical contact. He licked his lips and rocked on the balls of his feet.

He looked relaxed in a lavender button-down, collar open and sleeves rolled up to show his immense forearms. Dark-grey chinos hugged his form. His expensive shoes were casual but elegant.

She smiled and reached out to touch his arm. He grabbed her hand and led her to a seat beside him at the kitchen counter. She sat while he poured her a mug of coffee and brought her a croissant.

"How do you take your coffee?"

"Sweet and light," she said.

He nodded, the corners of his mouth curling up. After he put the coffee in front of her and sat back down, he puffed out a breath. "How are you feeling today?"

"Okay. I'm probably still in shock," she said.

"It takes a while to process big events like that. Are we good?"

She nodded. "I just need some time." When she put her hand on his thigh, his face lit up. He was so handsome when he looked at her like that.

Thomas cleared his throat. "I'd like you and Céline to come back with me to my company's compound in the Laurentian Mountains. That's where my family lives and where we lead our clan. It's the safest place until we sort out this mess."

"Just for the weekend? I can't uproot our whole lives." She knew they couldn't stay at their apartment, but she'd thought they'd just get a hotel room for a few days.

"I'll feel better if I can keep an eye on you. And we have excellent security at the compound. It's a ski resort as well, so there's lots to keep you and Céline busy."

"What about Father Andre?"

"I'll post some guards who can keep us informed as well as protect him. And we can come visit him in a few days."

"As long as Céline's okay with it, then we'll come for the weekend." She took a bite of the croissant and almost moaned. It was a heavenly mixture of crunchy bits and melt-in-her-mouth flakes.

"Think of it as a little holiday," he said. "You can ski or use the pool. We have community programmes for Céline, and yoga and dance classes you could join."

"Have you looked at the documents yet? I'm devastated that they took the diary. I'd only photographed the first third of it."

"It's okay. We'll get it back." He called down to his staff in the living room. A stylish young woman with a severe French-roll hairstyle took a satchel from the sofa and brought it to Thomas. "Here, sir."

He thanked her and opened it, pulling out papers and the red book. "There are some documents relating the allegations made by parish members against the brothers. Paedophilia and the disappearance of some young people. It was usually vulnerable people—just a few—but once the rumours started, the Frères Gris decided to leave the city."

She looked through the original papers quickly, then Thomas passed her a file with copies. Someone had already added highlights and sticky notes for the important passages. Owning a large company had its perks—it would have taken her several hours to go through the documents on her own.

Then Thomas gave her the small book with the red-cloth cover. It had just over a hundred pages, several longer stories and a few shorter pieces at the end. It looked like any number of late-nineteenth-century volumes they had in the diocesan archives. This one was different, though.

The careful lettering on the title page resembled the blackletter fonts used by Victorian folk-tale collectors. It read "*Les Contes Populaires des Voyageurs*. Par Didace et Marie D'Aoust." There was a hand-painted illustration of a canoe with two figures in it, wearing heavy clothing and fur hats. She had never seen it before.

"I need to find out who these people are," Tati said. Her pulse sped up as she considered it might be a rare find.

"My sister-in-law has an interest in folklore collections. I'd like to show it to her." He ran a finger over the book and she shivered as she remembered their intimacies at the archives.

"Is she the one who married Charles? Wait, is he your Alpha? Do you have an Alpha?" She wondered if it was just folklore or true.

"We do. And he is." He nodded. "His wife, Chantelle, has a book of fairy tales made by her Laurentian grandmother."

"Is it like this one?"

"Not exactly," he said. "But I'd like her to see if there are parallels."

"That's a weird coincidence," Tatienne said. *What am I getting myself into? Folk tales, conspiracies, sorcerers? It can't be real, can it?*

"She might call it something else." Thomas flipped through the papers.

"Like, they're connected or something? Is she a witch?" Tati furrowed her brow. She didn't know how the rules for his world worked.

"We prefer the terms Fae or Mage, but yes. She can manipulate energy and air."

"Does your sister-in-law help Charles lead the clan? A Mage and an Alpha working as a team?"

"Chantelle is out front with Charles, and they are finding their own way. The clan is encouraging the Alpha to step back and let the rest of us carry more weight now. He had very unhealthy work habits."

"Do you do that, too?" Tati asked.

"I'm learning. It still takes up a lot of time looking after the clan." He put the papers back in the satchel.

"You have a lot of responsibilities. One day, maybe you can find someone who will help carry your load." She wished it could be her, but that was a scary thought.

He reached out a hand and caressed her face. "One day. For now, we have to solve the mystery of the Grey Brothers and why they are colluding with our rivals."

"And I can help by researching them for you. I'm glad to have something to work on." *This I can handle.*

"Finish your coffee and then we'll get ready to go." Thomas stood and kissed her on the forehead. She smiled and took the last bite of her croissant.

Her phone buzzed and she looked at the screen. It was the archbishop's office. She cleared her throat and answered.

"Tatienne Laflamme speaking."

"Tatienne, how are you?" the archbishop said.

"Good, thanks." Her workplace must be worried about her if Monseigneur Lacroix was calling.

"We are so sorry to hear about Father Andre's fall and the break-in at your apartment. Are you and Céline all right?" His voice held a note of concern.

"Yes, Monseigneur. We're both safe. We had some help from Thomas Ducharme and his employees." She waved at Thomas when he looked over at her.

"What a relief. Listen, we're putting you on paid stress leave for four weeks. No need to come in to work, you've got a lot to worry about right now."

"But, Monseigneur—" she started.

"My child, the decision has already been made. Prioritise your health and spend time with your sister." His voice was firm.

She tried again. "I'm sure I —"

"Nonsense. We'll see you in four weeks' time. Take care of yourself." After he'd hung up the call, Tati was left with silence on the other end.

Tears welled up in her eyes. *What is going on?*

Thomas appeared beside her. "What happened?" he asked.

"I'm on leave for a month. They told me to stay home." She leaned against his solid chest as he put his arms around her.

"You could use some space," he said gently.

"But my job and my family, they're my life. Now my apartment is destroyed, and I can't go back to my job. What will I do?" The tears fell down her face.

"I'll talk to the archbishop."

"But I don't want a knight in shining armour. I can take care of myself." She sniffed. She'd always been independent — she wasn't going to change.

"How can I help, then?" He paused. "You could come and work for me."

"You don't have to solve every problem yourself." She slipped her hands around his waist as he continued to hold her close.

His muscles were tense. "But it's my fault this has happened."

"It's just for a month, and they're still going to pay me." She took a tissue from the counter and dabbed at her cheeks. "I guess it's not the end of the world."

"You've had a lot of surprises this week. It's perfectly understandable that you might feel shattered." He sat on a stool and pulled her into his lap. She resisted the urge to dissolve into tears again.

He was right. A little break might be a good way to gain perspective again.

"Could I ask you to extend your stay at my clan's resort to a week? Then, when the repairs on your apartment are done, you can go back."

She nodded and squared her shoulders. She hadn't had a proper holiday for years, after all. She and Céline could have some fun in the mountains and put all the drama behind them. Then they would get on with their regular lives.

It was only a week.

Thomas knew it was going to take some time before Tatienne felt like herself again. He would help her get through it. Whatever it took.

"Can you see if Céline is awake?" he asked. "After breakfast, we'll take the helicopter to the compound."

Tatienne nodded. Her gorgeous form tantalised him as she walked out of the kitchen. She returned a few minutes later with her sister.

"I've never been in a helicopter, Thomas!" Céline said, rubbing her eyes. "Do you drive one all the time?"

His chest expanded and he chuckled. "Only when I'm in a hurry. And I don't drive. We have a professional for that."

"Okay. Tati says I have to eat something. Then I'll get dressed." Céline's smile brightened his mood.

Tatienne made up a plate with muffins and fruit, put it in front of her sister and poured a large goblet of ice water. Thomas found the teapot and made Céline a cup of hot tea with milk and sugar.

After Chantelle had married his brother, she had explained to Thomas what it was like when she had first arrived at the compound after René and his lackeys had attacked her on the road. It hadn't seemed real at first. Not only because she had just found out her crush was a shifter, but also because everyone in the community seemed so nice and well adjusted. She joked that she had thought they had some horrible secret—like they ate people or something. But the secret was their supernatural heritage, and they had turned it into a strength.

The clan community was not that different from other groups she'd known, yet she had declared it was more collaborative and supportive than most. Chantelle had learned later that it had minor problems, like all communities do, but she was still impressed by the lack of major issues. Everyone worked together for the good of the clan.

Thomas hoped Tatienne and Céline would embrace his clan. And he wanted his clan to like the women in return. His community's opinion mattered. He was getting ahead of himself, but it was getting impossible not to imagine this pair in his life.

Isabelle arrived with warm coats, toques, scarves and mittens for him, Tati and Céline. "The helicopter leaves in fifteen." She showed two black leather duffel bags to Tatienne. "We picked up some things from your apartment. Your neighbour helped us choose."

"Is Madame Bernal all right?"

"Yes. We still have a security team on alert at the building. She's been feeding them coffee and cookies."

"Thanks. We'll go change," Tatienne said.

"Can I wear the pink hoodie I saw in our bedroom?" Céline asked.

Tati looked at Thomas.

His heart caught in his throat. "Of course you can, *mon chou*. Pack the pyjamas as well and we'll wash them when we get to the resort."

Céline pulled Tatienne to the suite while Isabelle trailed behind them carrying the duffels.

A warmth settled in Thomas' chest. Céline was a bright ray of sunshine, a ball of energy, a burst of affection. Tati was moonlight and caresses, soft and sensual, strong and fierce all at the same time. There was no one else like her.

When Céline bounced out of the suite five minutes later, he pulled up the resort website on his tablet to show her where they were going. When Tatienne appeared, Céline was scrolling through photos of the ski village.

"Tati, come see Thomas' resort. This is where we're staying." Céline brandished the tablet at her, pointing to pictures of snow, mountains and trees.

"I have to get out of the city more," Tatienne said. "This looks gorgeous."

Thomas drew a deep, satisfied breath. "You're going to love it."

Frédérique joined them as they went out to the rooftop landing pad. Céline took her hand and asked to sit beside her.

"I get you to myself, then," Thomas said to Tati, his heart beating faster.

She grinned and took his hand as they climbed into the waiting helicopter.

Thomas enjoyed seeing the trip through the two women's eyes. The sunlight on the snow was dazzling, the view of the city outstanding. Céline used her noise-cancelling headphones to pretend she was communicating with air traffic control from the disconnected mike, smiling the whole time.

The trip went smoothly. Tati leaned against him when he put his arm around her, and he relished the closeness even in the noisy, chaotic space. It felt right to be bringing her home.

His wolf chuffed.

Yes, you're right, Thomas told his wolf. *We're getting closer to her.*

Soon, the helicopter circled the mountain on which the ski resort and clan compound had been built. After they touched down and disembarked, Tatienne looked around, wide-eyed and speechless.

Thomas explained the site held not only their company's business offices. It was also the residence of many of the workers and their families. They employed a large number of shifters — and humans who were affiliated with or who supported the shifter community. "It's a company perk for head office employees to live and work in the Laurentians. We have an agreement with the local Indigenous community that our shifters can use the surrounding territories in exchange for our support of their business enterprises."

"The ski lodge looks busy, too," Tati said.

"We have rooms in the main lodge, and we also rent out chalets. The resort is a big draw for humans and shifters alike."

"I can see why. It's gorgeous."

"And we've adapted as many eco-conscious practices as we can," Thomas added. Just as he was about to elaborate, his brothers exited the main lodge and approached them. They hugged Tati and shook hands with Céline, exuding the friendliness he expected from them.

Céline hid her face after the introductions.

Concerned, Thomas stood beside her. "These are my brothers, Charles and Henri. Do you think they look like me?"

The men crouched down to eye-level and smiled at her.

Céline peered at them. "Your brothers do look the same. Except this one" — she pointed at the youngest, Henri — "doesn't have a beard and that one" — she pointed this time at Charles, the oldest — "has longer hair."

All three men chuckled at the same time and Céline laughed. "You sound the same, too."

They all walked together to the main lodge, where the two security personnel were waiting. He had personally chosen Victoria and Émile. They were a strong team, just as able to blend into the background as they were to disarm a small pack on their own. Although Émile was a bear shifter and Vicky a cat, they worked together like littermates. Other members of their security team joked that the pair could communicate telepathically. Thomas was confident in assigning the pair to Tati and Céline while they were here — and he planned to send the guards back to Montréal with the women if they returned before the crisis had been resolved.

Thomas had expected more resistance when he introduced Vicky and Émile. Tati took it in stride. She must have been spooked by the events of the past week — although anyone would be. Also, she had a sister to look after. He was glad she recognised the value of this protection.

Céline took to Émile instantly. In a matter of minutes, she was chasing him around the large reception area. Tati smiled and Thomas knew he'd made the right choice.

His PA Frédérique offered to show Tati and Céline to the suite where they would be staying. It was directly across the hall from his rooms in the main lodge. Frédérique had assumed he would want to keep them close. He was grateful she hadn't pressed about the status of his relationship with Tatienne, since he didn't have answers yet. Nevertheless, Frédérique was always one step ahead of him — thank the Goddess — and had provided a sensible solution for accommodations. Close, but separate spaces.

Thomas took Tati's hands. "I'll see you later. I have to check in with the family. See if we know what happened yet."

She kissed him on the cheek. "Come and find us when you're done."

He waved and joined his brothers for the walk to the executive offices in the lodge. He'd only been away for twenty-four hours, but it felt like twenty-four days. So much had happened, and he still didn't know the extent of the danger Tatienne was facing.

His executive assistant Laurie greeted him. "Clem and your brothers are waiting for you in the north boardroom." She passed him some folders and a tablet. Thomas was glad they had chosen the meeting room closest to his office. He was already exhausted.

He entered the meeting room to find his cousin Clem had already loaded her slides onto the screen.

"What have you found?" he asked, getting right to business.

"Not much yet," Clem replied. "We've scanned the files Tatienne gave you on the thumb drive. We've reviewed the other documents the priest saved for her. But we don't know how to connect it together."

"The Frères Gris were active in Montréal when they first emigrated to New France. They fled the town when they drew too much attention to themselves. We don't know where they moved to, though," Thomas said.

"How many people do we have on this?" Charles asked.

"After last year's attack on the compound, I'm still concerned about information leaks," Clem said. "We've limited access to a small circle. In addition, Chantelle is looking through a digital copy of the folk stories."

"Tatienne will need copies of everything, too. I'm sure she'll have some ideas for us."

Charles fixed him with a stern eye. "Can we trust her?"

Clem spoke up. "Her references checked out and her socials and communication are clean."

Thomas growled low. "We can trust her."

"How do you know?" Charles asked.

"She's not involved. We are the ones who put her in danger." *Why can't they see it?* He clenched his fists.

Thomas' younger brother Henri asked, "What if she's bait or a lure?"

"Don't talk about her like that!" Thomas exploded.

"Whoa!" said Henri. "You like her, don't you?"

He counted to ten and nodded. "It's irrational, but my gut tells me I—we—can trust her."

Charles looked at him. "Listen to your gut. We'll let you oversee her research—you can be her liaison with us."

Thomas nodded.

"And we'll have to invite her and Céline to the next family game night," Henri added.

Warmth spread through Thomas' chest. His family understood and supported him. "Absolutely," he said. "We'll kick your asses in the trivia competition. Just you wait."

They closed down the meeting. Thomas hurried to the accommodation wing to see how Tati and Céline were getting settled.

Chapter Eleven

Thomas reached Tatienne and Céline's suite. He smoothed down his hair. After he'd knocked on the door, Tati opened it.

"It's good to see a friendly face," she exclaimed, inviting him in.

"How are you two doing?" he asked.

"Céline is over the moon. She has a large-screen TV in her room and Frédérique gave her a tablet and some board games."

"I've got a tablet for you, too." Thomas passed her the device. "I've programmed my personal contact information into it. You can reach me straight away through the messaging app. You can message me any time—day or night—and I'll get back to you right away. If I'm in a meeting and can't get out, then my executive assistant will respond. She'll have one of my family contact you. My staff knows you are a priority guest."

"Vicky and Émile said we can also ask them to use their comms. Céline wants her own wristband, but Émile said he has a pair of old walkie-talkies at home he can bring for her to use."

"Your sister is going to love that," Thomas said. He was glad Céline was settling in well. New environments were not always an easy adjustment. "Émile and Vicky can also help you find anything you need or take you wherever you want to go. This is a big compound."

"Will we see you?"

"Yes. I live right across the hall from this apartment."

"Then we'll see you after work at least."

"And if you need a late-night booty call, just knock." He loved to make her blush.

"I don't want to seem ungrateful," she said, "but when can we move back to our apartment?"

"The building is a mess. We have to install a new security system, replace windows and do some other upgrades."

"I thought it was just some broken windows," she said.

"We're planning to make the building safer for all the tenants. I don't know how long it will take us to find the perpetrators, and I'll be damned if I let you move back unprotected."

"Why do you think you're in charge of this?" She fixed him with her patented glare.

"I bought your building." He'd had to do something to ensure her welfare.

Her eyebrows shot up. "You what?"

"We fast-tracked the sale this morning. My lawyers made the owner a very tempting offer."

She put her face in her hands. "You rich people think you can solve everything with money."

"Are you angry? I can't protect you otherwise."

"This oversteps the bounds of our relationship," she said firmly. "It's not okay to buy your girlfriend's apartment building and renovate it without her permission."

"It's my fault that you're a target for this Frères Gris Consortium. I want to make it right."

"I get that, and it's sweet. But you're not responsible for everything."

"Let me do this for you," he said. "Please?"

"There have to be parameters. You have to consult me in the plans. You can't walk into my apartment whenever you want just because you own the building."

"That's fair. In return, will you let me choose the upgrades and the security enhancements — as long as I show them to you first?"

"I can live with that," she said. "But you should have asked me first before you did any of this."

"I'm sorry," he said. "I messed up."

She looked at him, her brow furrowing.

"What's wrong?" he asked.

"Why are you smiling?"

"You said we are in a relationship. You said you're my girlfriend." He tried to stop smiling, but he couldn't. Instead, he put his arms around her.

"Yeah, I know." Her voice was a little too loud still, but she forgave him.

"In the meantime, I'd like you to relax and enjoy yourself this week. What do you want to do?" he asked.

"Ummm, that's a good question." She walked over to the fridge in the kitchen area and took out two bottles of water. She held one out to him and he took it.

"You're not used to making yourself a priority, are you?" he said.

"No time," she said, waving her free hand.

"Are you being honest with yourself?"

She ran a hand over her face. "I spend so much of my time running from one thing to the next."

"Now you have a whole week to slow down. What do you want to do first?"

"Curl up with a good book by a fireplace and drink coffee."

"That sounds wonderful!" Thomas said. "Does Céline like to swim? I could take her, and you could have the afternoon to yourself."

"I couldn't ask you to do that," she said.

"You didn't ask. I'm offering. I like to do laps a few times a week and I missed the last couple of days."

Tatienne thought it over. "She doesn't have a swimsuit."

"I'll take care of that—the gift shop by the pool sells suits." He held up a hand when she looked about to interrupt. "I won't let her choose a bikini. Just the kind the women wore on the swim team in college."

"Were you on the team, or just an admirer?"

His face grew hot. "On the team. I have my lifeguard qualifications, so your sister is safe with me."

She laughed then nodded. "Okay, but if she's not having fun, please bring her back here and we'll do something together."

"Deal. Do you have a book to read? Do you want to stay here and enjoy the small fireplace in the living room? Or would you like to sit in front of the giant roaring fire in the lobby?"

She smiled. "No, this is perfect. It's quiet and peaceful. And I've got my reading app on my phone."

"Okay. I'll go talk to Céline and see if she'll come with me." Thomas left for a moment and returned to confirm Céline had said yes.

"She just needs a few minutes to get ready," he said, clearing his throat. "So, am I changing your mind about rich people?"

"You are different than I expected. More down-to-earth. Not as full of yourself as I imagined a Monsieur Ducharme would be."

"And you're sexier than I thought a nun would be."

She laughed and hugged him.

"So if you're my girlfriend," Thomas said, "can I take you on a date tomorrow? Our last one got cut short. I didn't get to take you home."

"Here I am at your compound, though." She raised an eyebrow.

"I guess I got my wish then. But I didn't plan it this way. I'd like a do-over date."

Tatienne studied him. "The last date was a beautiful night—until it wasn't. Dinner was fantastic, then the funicular ride. It's going to be hard to beat it."

"I was thinking of something that won't end in gunshots and fire."

"That's a great idea. What do you have in mind?" she asked.

"There's a dance tomorrow night. Would you like to go?"

"I don't have anything to wear, but I'd love to."

"I'll get you something. Also, let me know what you and Céline might need from the city. Some of our guys are going there tomorrow and they can pick up your stuff from your apartment."

"Oh, that's right, you can gain access because you own it." She gave him a look then chuckled.

"Only with your permission."

Céline came out of her room. "Thomas, I'm ready."

"Great. Tati, just relax in the room and enjoy yourself. We'll be back in a couple hours."

"Don't you have a job to do around here?" she asked.

He grinned. "I have a staff and I know how to delegate. They'll survive for a couple hours."

Céline started tugging Thomas to the door. They said goodbye to Tati and walked down to the pool.

Tatienne sighed as Thomas closed the door behind him and Céline. Her head ached. She wished everything would slow down.

Did she just agree to be a billionaire's girlfriend? Was he her sugar daddy now? She shook her head. *That's not for me.* But being Thomas' girlfriend was appealing.

She was looking forward to having a date with him tomorrow night. They could learn more about each other. He was kind and warm... He brought her peace. But the shifter side was an unknown for her. What could it mean? Was he a different person? He didn't seem to be, since he'd shifted to protect her and Céline. He was a good person, whether he was hairy or not.

But he lived in this different world—not just of shifters but of money and privilege. How did that influence him? So far, she'd seen him be good to his employees, an ethical businessperson and responsible.

He wanted to serve his community and help others. He was a lot like her, after all.

So, she would be open to dating him and not worry about all the other stuff. See if they had a connection. He was right, they did have a lot in common. But were they compatible? That is, were they compatible in other ways than in the bedroom? Or the limo, or the record office... They had a lot of time to find their sexual compatibility.

They'd had fun on their date Friday, before they'd gone to check on Father Andre. And she'd enjoyed the time they had spent in the archives — it hadn't felt like work at all. He also respected her boundaries and didn't press her to open up. She was the one who had invited him into her life and introduced him to her family.

Tomorrow night, she could learn more and see if it might lead anywhere.

For now, she should just relax and read her book.

She sighed. When was the last time she'd had a couple of hours to herself? She lived her life and fulfilled all her commitments, but maybe she needed to give herself some downtime. There was so much pressure today for everyone to stay busy and be "productive" — whatever that meant. Folks couldn't just be, they have to be doing, buying and snapping selfies.

She got out her phone and opened her reading app. Just then, her phone buzzed. It was the landline at Father Andre's church.

"Hello?"

"This is Father Genette. I'm taking over Father Andre's parish while he's in hospital." The priest spoke in a deep timbre, but there was something in his voice that put her on edge.

She didn't know what to say. "Oh, how is Father Andre?"

"He's resting comfortably. He won't be going home for at least another week, and then he'll need some time to recuperate before he can come back to work."

"Please give him my best," she said.

"I will, my child."

She hated it when priests patronised her like that.

"Father Andre mentioned something to the archbishop about finding some old papers. Did you hear anything about this?"

"Uhh…" Tatienne hesitated. She didn't know this man, but he was part of the Church. Could she trust him? "Yes, he told me about this, too. He mentioned an old journal."

"That would be quite a find, Miss Laflamme. Did he show it to you? Or any other papers?"

Tatienne wondered why he was asking these questions. Was he trying to piece together what had happened to Father Andre? Or was there another, more sinister reason for his questions?

"He told me they were in the basement, but I didn't have a chance to look at them before…" She broke off.

"Yes, of course, my dear. I understand you found him in the church?"

Tatienne started. Why was the priest asking her this question? She knew Thomas had kept her name out of things when he contacted the police.

"I was at the church, but I didn't see him." She closed her eyes. *I'm going to hell for lying to a man of the cloth.* But something felt wrong. "They said he had slipped and a cupboard fell on top of him. Do you know anything else yet?" She tried to sound casual.

"Yes, that's what we know too. Such a shame."

"I'm praying for him," she said.

"Will you be coming back to Montréal soon?"

"I've been having some time off. I'm out of town for at least a few days."

"Oh, are you staying somewhere nice?"

The nosy question made the hair on the back of her neck stand up. "Just with friends. I'll probably be back in the city by the weekend."

"Could we meet up then? I could use your advice on the parish while Father Andre is ill."

"Sure," Tatienne said, even though her gut told her to say no. She needed to find out what was going on. "Can I call you after I've made my plans?"

"Please do."

After they'd signed off, Tatienne still had a queasy feeling in her stomach. She thought about going to find Thomas but shrugged it off. Nothing was going to happen in the next two hours. She would talk with him when he brought Céline back to their suite.

Instead, she decided to look over the documents from Father Andre, the partial journal copies and folk tales included. At least she could get a start on it, even if she couldn't read through it all before Céline and Thomas came back. The papers had been tabbed already, so she skimmed through them, then turned to the copies of the books.

Taking them over to the sofa, she put them on the coffee table and turned on the gas fireplace. Then she made a pot of coffee and brought a big mug to the living room. She sighed with satisfaction and started in on the documents.

Chapter Twelve

The next day, Tatienne and Céline were eating breakfast in their suite when there was a knock on the door.

Tatienne opened it to find a kind-faced woman with long black hair and medium-beige skin. She was dressed casually, in elegant clothes of muted colours.

"My name is Chantelle. My brother-in-law Thomas asked me to talk with you about the documents you discovered." Warmth emanated from the woman.

Tatienne stepped to the side and gestured for her to come in. "I was hoping you'd come by. I looked over everything yesterday and I have some questions."

Chantelle set her tablet and briefcase on the kitchen island and stretched out her hand to Céline. "You must be Céline. I'm Chantelle. Pleased to meet you."

Céline shook her hand. "You're nice. You know Thomas?"

Chantelle smiled. "Yes, I do. I married his brother."

"I met his brothers. They're nice," Céline said.

As Chantelle chatted with Céline, Tati offered her a cup of coffee.

"I'm a tea drinker," Chantelle said.

"I have tea in the mornings, too," said Céline. "We can make you a cup." Céline helped Tatienne get the mug ready. While Tati poured the hot water, Céline brought the milk and sugar over to Chantelle. Once Chantelle had her tea, Céline said goodbye and went to her room to play on the tablet Frédérique had given her.

Chantelle said to Tatienne, "There is a group for families who have children with Down syndrome. They get together a couple times a week for family activities. They're meeting tomorrow night."

"They don't mind visitors?"

"It's a very welcoming group."

Tatienne nodded. "Thanks. Now let me get my notes."

Chantelle followed her to the living room area, where she had left her copies of the documents.

"I'm mystified as to why shifters would steal a diary and be looking for an eighteenth-century book of tales. It's not as if they're classified government documents," Tatienne said.

"That's why I'm interested. My granny made a collection of folk tales which held some clues to the history of the shifter communities in this area. I'm wondering if this book does the same."

"Maybe if you told me some more about shifters?"

"The Alpha of the neighbouring Trois-Rivières Clan is cruel and controlling. They have a very authoritarian organisational structure. They're also involved in some shady businesses. And there's bad blood between them and the Ducharme's clan," Chantelle said.

"That doesn't explain why they'd want some books and papers. I mean — wait." Tatienne started. "Unless they were hired by somebody else."

"We haven't been able to tie them to the Frères Gris organisation. But we think they have been working together."

"The brothers are using the shifters to do their dirty work."

Chantelle nodded. "We don't know if the Frères Gris are simply trying to erase the evidence of their past wrongdoings. Although it would be ideal to find a link between the two groups, what we really need is evidence to help us find where the Frères Gris are living."

"In that case, the diary and the book of tales might be helpful. Bernadette's journal details her account of travelling from Montréal through the Laurentian Mountains. She met some 'brothers dressed in grey' on her journey. They were building a shrine to Saint Valeria in the mountains. There were rumours that the brothers were practicing blood sacrifice and fertility rituals, but nothing was substantiated. Bernadette said the brothers were dangerous and she was warned to stay away from them."

"Hmmm, they might be sorcerers," said Chantelle. As the woman flipped through the pages, something niggled at the back of Tati's mind. It was something about sorcerers. A conversation? One of the books they'd read? She couldn't figure it out.

"How do you read this handwriting? It's like chicken scratches," Chantelle said.

"Practice. I took a course on settler colonial documents from the university when I started working in the archives."

"That's cool. What about the folk-tale collection?"

"I'm not sure about them. I'm hoping you can help me."

Chantelle looked over the copies. "My granny's folk tales reworked Breton and Québécois sources. She combined her beliefs with stories she had heard to adapt them for the clan."

"Do they provide details of shifter communities or specific individuals?" Tatienne asked.

Chantelle shook her head. "They're mostly re-imaginings of traditional motifs. There are stories about leaders of communities and another one about three fairy princesses who unite the tribes when they find their mates."

"There is a similar story in this collection." Tatienne looked through the pages until she found it. "In this tale, three princesses fight three sorcerers and save some children who have been kidnapped. The sorcerers travel up the Rouge River. They make a deal with the Devil to fly over the rapids, but seven sisters try to stop them. The bad guys take one of the sisters hostage and then they join the Devil at his lake. They erected a Red Chapel for their demon worship, and they lived evilly ever after."

"There is something similar in my granny's collection. It's a story about sorcerers who fought the Devil and kidnapped a Mage. They had killed children for blood sacrifices and the shifter clan defeated them.

"Do you think this has any basis in fact?" Tatienne asked.

"I've never heard of a church like that, but I think there's a Devil Lake and Rouge River in the mountains. We could look at some of the local maps."

"That's a good idea," Tati said.

Chantelle's phone dinged. "I've got another meeting in fifteen minutes. Can we meet again tomorrow?"

Tatienne nodded.

"Before I go, can I ask how is Thomas?" Chantelle asked.

"Good. I think. We haven't talked much since Céline and I came to the compound."

"He's been trying to find your attackers."

"I'm still processing that he's a shifter. He told me you're a Mage?" Tati asked.

"I didn't know about shifters — not really — until I met Charles. When I got ambushed outside the village, he came to help in his wolf form."

"How did you deal with the revelation?"

Chantelle shrugged. "It was probably different for me. My granny had always told fairy stories and I knew in my mind somewhere shifters were real. But there had been an incident when I was younger, so she had wiped my mind of the knowledge of shifters."

"And then you found out."

"Don't worry, it was still a shock. But he had helped me, and his family was so kind."

"Did you know you were a Mage, or had your granny hidden that from you, too?"

"She had suppressed my powers, because something dangerous had happened and she was trying to protect me. But when I started dating Charles, my powers came out."

"I've had a couple of weird experiences around Thomas, too," said Tati.

Chantelle put out her hand but paused. "May I touch you?" When Tatienne nodded, Chantelle put her hand on Tati's head. She hummed for a moment, and Tatienne's body tingled.

"What was that?" Tatienne asked.

Chantelle removed her hand and smiled. "Just checking. You do have magical tendencies. Not sure what your specialty is."

"Premonitions. Images in my mind."

"Will you meet with me tomorrow at the Mage offices? We can have you tested."

"I might as well. Thomas seems to bring something out in me."

Chantelle laughed. "Those Ducharme boys do. Has he gone into protective Alpha mode on you?"

"Yes!" Tatienne said. "He bought the building my apartment is in so he can update the security and put in more levels of protection."

"Security and protection are one of the Ducharme boys' love languages. They feel responsible for the people they love, and they want to look after their mates."

"Oh, we're not mates," said Tatienne. "We only just started dating."

"That's another thing about the Ducharmes. There are these stories in their family about Fated Mates. That they will have a one and only love."

"You don't believe that, do you?"

Chantelle looked at her. "I didn't...until I did. Charles and I, we had a powerful attraction when we first met. It seemed like something was pushing us together. And together, we can weave some powerful magic."

"What about being leaders together?"

"It's true. We make each other better. We complement each other."

"Maybe we could talk about this another time?" Tati asked. "I have a lot of questions."

"I'd love to. We'll have coffee and tea soon, okay?"

Tati nodded and said farewell to the Mage. She felt more hopeful than she had since she had arrived at the compound.

* * * *

Thomas wondered if he had gone overboard for his date with Tati. He couldn't help himself. He loved seeing a smile light up her face. And tonight was not as extravagant as their last time in Montréal. He wanted to show off his clan — and his personality — tonight.

He knocked on the door of her suite.

Tati opened it, wearing the midi-length dress with the handkerchief hem he had given her.

"You look great," he said.

She twirled. "I love the dress. It's perfect for a community dance."

He smiled.

"I haven't seen you in regular clothes very much," she said. "Either business wear or fancy date clothes."

He looked at his short-sleeved button-up shirt and designer jeans. "I plan to do a lot of dancing. I want to be comfortable and cool."

"You are very cool," she said, stretching up to kiss him.

Céline came to the door. "Hi, Thomas. I'm having a movie night with Émile. You should go to the party now."

Thomas chuckled. "Yes, *mon chou*."

He offered his arm to Tati and folded her hand against his biceps. Céline closed the door behind them, and they walked down the hall. The dance was being held in the Wolf Room at the lodge — a little joke, as it was often the site of clan gatherings in the winter, when it was too cold and snowy to use their outside spaces.

"I hope you'll have fun tonight. I arranged for a Montréal-based Cuban band to come and play."

"You did this for me? Did Diego tell you that's his dance specialty?" She had that special sparkle in her eyes she reserved for him.

He nodded. "Usually we just have a DJ, but I wanted to make it special for you. A taste of your home. And I thought our clan would enjoy the music, too."

"It must be nice to snap your fingers and make something happen."

"We're a tight-knit community. The Alpha family looks after the clan and the clan reciprocates."

"That sounds very traditional, like the way the French colonists had something like feudal lords in the districts," she said.

"It does come from our settler roots, but it's changed since then. We have a clan council that meets with the Alpha family to discuss community concerns and projects. We've also instituted a new Elder Council to advise us."

"It seems too good to be true." She rested her head against his arm as they reached the lift.

He chuckled. "In some ways it is. But we have our problems, and we have our conflicts with other communities."

"The Trois-Rivières Clan?" Tati asked.

"Our values are very different than theirs. We've worked hard to make things equitable for all folks and not have the clan benefit just a few at the top."

"I appreciate that."

They exited the lift. Putting his hand on the small of Tati's back, he steered her down the hall to where the band was playing and people were talking. Tati stopped for a moment when they reached the doorway of the small ballroom.

"This is going to be so much fun!" Her dazzling smile made the extra effort worthwhile. She dragged him onto the dance floor, and they started dancing to a Cuban beat.

After a couple of songs, the band stopped playing and the dance instructor at the clan's community centre took the microphone.

"Time to practice the salsa," the instructor announced.

Amid whoops and hollers, the partygoers arranged themselves on the dance floor facing the instructor.

Tatienne hung back, watching the scene unfold.

"Do you want to join in?" Thomas asked.

"I don't want to embarrass the learners. This is one of Diego's specialties."

"It would be great to show them how it's done," he said, making a sign to the instructor.

The dance leader clapped his hands. "Everyone, we have a special demonstration for you. Our Lieutenant Thomas will show us the steps with his beautiful date, Tatienne."

Tati shot him a look, but he smiled. "I know you aren't shy about performing. Sorry to put you on the spot, though."

"It's okay," she said. "I'll do it for you."

Thomas took her hand and led her in front of the small stage where the dance instructor and the band were situated.

The band started the beat and Tati moved with rhythm. Thomas took her right hand in his left and held her upper back with the other hand. They slipped into the salsa steps effortlessly, moving as though they had danced together a hundred times before.

For once, he was grateful for the ballroom dancing lessons Aimée had made him take. She had been too uptight to master the more sensual moves, but he had loved the rhythms and beats of the Latin dances.

Dancing with Tati was how it was supposed to be. A sexy give and take, his body responding to hers, paying attention to the subtle nuances of the communication between them.

When the song ended, the whole room erupted into applause. Thomas and Tati took a bow, her face colouring slightly. Thomas was breathing heavy – in part from the dancing, and in part from Tati's presence.

As the applause died down and the band started another song, Tatienne turned to him. "You underplayed yourself. I didn't know you could dance like this."

Thomas said, "I have never danced like this. My previous partner was more mechanical and not in tune with me."

"That is what the salsa is supposed to be. But you need a good partner and a good connection."

They walked to the side of the room and watched the instructor going through the steps.

"Is that what you have with Diego?" Thomas asked.

"Yes, but not in a romantic way."

He pulled her in tight against him. "Is it different when there's a romantic connection?"

She looked up into his eyes. "Yes. You can tell, too."

He smiled and kissed the top of her head.

The instructor led the partygoers in a few more pieces while Thomas chatted with Tati.

Then the band struck up a *danzón*, a quieter, gentler style than the salsa. Thomas took Tati onto the dance floor, and they held each other as they went through the sequence. When the other dancers broke off for the stroll section, he continued to hold her close in his arms. *This is what it should be like.*

He pulled up her chin and kissed her on the lips. She melted in his arms, and he pulled her closer, trying not to grind his hard erection against her front. Then she grabbed his ass and pulled him in, sighing in his mouth.

"*Calisse*," he muttered. "Do you want to go back to my place?"

She looked up at him, eyes shining. "Yes."

One word. But the only word he wanted to hear.

He took her hand and led her out of the Wolf Room, back up the lift and to his suite.

"Do you want some water?" he asked.

She nodded and he went to the kitchen and filled two glasses. He returned to the living room and put the glasses on the coffee table.

She sat on the couch, openly admiring his form. When she beckoned him over, he knelt in front of her. She loosened his shirt buttons and ran her hands down his torso. His skin tingled where she touched it.

He pulled her close to him and kissed her again. As she eased off his shirt, he skimmed his hands from her calves to her thighs, finding her bare skin underneath the handkerchief hem of the dress. She snaked her hands around his torso, teasing him gently along his lower back. Sighing, he gripped her thighs and pulled her centre against his aching cock. She squirmed against him.

Reaching towards her curvy bottom, he explored the outline of her panties. He grumbled his approval. "Black?" he asked.

She shook her head and pushed him back on his haunches with a smile. She reached down and pulled her dress over her head, throwing it to the side.

The panties were dark red. The matching demi-corset pushed her breasts together in a way that made him salivate. "*Merde*," he swore. "My cock is as hard as a rock."

"Can I ask you not to rip this set, please?"

"I will be gentle," he replied. He proceeded slowly and delicately, enjoying the feel of her skin under his hands. He took his time running his hands up and down her body, kneading her breasts, playing with her nipples. He had to turn her over to pay proper attention to her backside, feeling the curves and nipping her skin as she trembled.

By the time he had undressed her, she was humming with pleasure, and he was drunk on her scent.

She turned herself around so she could explore his chest and run her hands along his shoulders. Kneeling on the couch, she unbuttoned his jeans and pulled them down, while he ran his fingers up her thighs. When he reached her glistening centre, he took a finger and traced the outline of her pussy lips. She shivered and reached for his aching cock. As she ran her fingers over the smooth hardness, a droplet of pre-cum seeped from the tip. She wiped the liquid onto her index finger. Then she brought it to her mouth and sucked it clean.

"Fuck me," he said. "I mean, *calisse*, that makes me hot."

"But I want to fuck you," she said, kneeling on all fours on the couch.

He growled and grabbed a condom from his jeans pocket. After putting it on, he knelt on the couch behind her, and explored her folds with his fingers. When she moaned and wiggled her hips, he couldn't wait any longer. He took one hip in his hand and squeezed gently while positioning his cock at her pussy entrance. This time, he didn't go slow. He thrust in deep and fast, groaning at the delicious feel of her walls around his cock.

She gasped and started to rock forward and backward. He reached down and felt her breasts swinging with their rhythm. "God," she moaned.

He thrust in and out, losing himself in their frantic fucking.

"Almost there," she breathed.

He reached forward and found her clit, rubbing the button back and forth as he got ready to come.

His cock grew rigid and he pulsed inside the sheath. "Come for me," he said. Tati was there with him, squeezing his cock with her pussy as she moaned. They finished and he rested his head on her back for a moment before sitting down and pulling her into his lap.

She rested her head on his chest, panting. When she slipped her arm around his waist, he hugged her.

"Will you spend the night, Tati?" he asked. He breathed in her scent and nuzzled her hair with his nose.

"I should be back in my suite for the morning." She sighed.

"Can I stay with you in your bedroom? Just for cuddles and sleep, not sex."

She looked at him, her eyebrows raised. "Nobody has ever asked me that before."

"I mean it."

"Then yes," she said, a small smile on her face.

Thomas changed into sweats and Tati put her dress back on for the walk across the hallway. When they got to her room, Thomas stripped to his boxers and Tati put on his T-shirt.

"Do you mind?" she asked.

He shook his head. *She looks better in it than I do.*

"Now come here. We should get some sleep," he said.

They lay down and quickly nodded off, curled up in each other's arms.

Chapter Thirteen

Thomas woke up more refreshed than he had in a long time. He looked over at Tatienne, still sleeping beside him. *I could stay like this forever. But I'd better make her some coffee.*

He slid out of bed and put on his sweats. Tati stirred, then opened her eyes.

"Good morning," she said.

He came over and kissed her forehead. "Good morning. How did you sleep?"

"Very well." She grinned and her sparkling eyes hit him straight in the heart.

"Do you have a busy day?" he asked.

"Yesterday, we met the group of families who have children and youth with Down syndrome. We made some friends and we're meeting up with them today for a hike."

"That sounds fun," he said. "There should be snow pants in your closets. Be sure to wear them and the heavy boots."

She sat up and swung her feet over the edge of the bed. He'd forgotten she was wearing his T-shirt. She looked so hot in it that he wanted to jump back in bed with her. But they had stuff to do.

"I'll go make some coffee," he said, and, humming, left the room before he changed his mind.

Tatienne arrived first in the kitchen and her sister a minute later.

"Good morning," Céline said. "Thomas, what are you doing here?"

Thomas looked at Tatienne, eyebrows raised. "I stayed over."

"Okay," said Céline.

Thomas opened his mouth, then closed it. The corners of his mouth twitched.

"Tati, don't forget we have the hike today," Céline said. "And Samantha wants me to go shopping with her tomorrow. Is that okay?"

"How long will you be gone?" Tati asked her sister as Thomas passed her a mug.

"We're just going to the village. We'll look around and have lunch. They said to tell you we'd be back by mid-afternoon."

Thomas filled the kettle and put tea bags in a nearby pot.

Tati smiled. "That sounds great. We're going to need a way to contact you."

Thomas spoke up. "I forgot—I have something for both of you." He left their suite for a moment and went to his apartment. Near the door were two small boxes. He picked them up and returned to the women.

He handed one box to Céline. She opened it up to find a purple cell phone—the latest model, with all the bells and whistles. "Thomas, this is so great! I've always wanted one of these!"

Thomas gave the other box to Tati. "These phones can't be hacked or traced. You can keep your other one, Tati, but we should also have it checked for bugs or tracking apps." He turned to Céline. "Émile and Vicky will be with you most of the time. But if you ever need me or your sister, just call. I've programmed our numbers in at the top of your contacts."

"Thank you," said Tati. "But it's too much."

"It's a gift," he replied.

"You've given us so many things already," she said.

"What's the use of having money if you can't spend it on the people you l—you care about?" he said. Was he ready to use the l-word? He didn't want to scare her off.

She stood and hugged him. "You're a very generous man. Thank you."

"Now sit down and drink your coffee," he said. "And, Céline, your tea is almost ready."

The two women sat at the kitchen island and chatted away while he busied himself in the kitchen. The warm feeling inside his chest expanded. *Life can't get any better than this.*

When Céline left to get dressed, he sat beside Tati.

"My sister didn't mind that you were here," she said.

"What usually happens when you bring someone home?"

"I don't." She took another sip of coffee.

"You don't what?" he asked.

"I don't bring people home. I keep my family life private." She looked at the kitchen counter.

"But don't your boyfriends wonder when they don't meet your family?" He didn't feel jealous, exactly, when he thought about her other boyfriends. Just glad they weren't around.

"I don't have boyfriends." She picked up a spoon and stirred the dregs of coffee in her mug.

"What do you mean?" He went stock still and held his breath.

"I keep my dating life separate, and I don't get involved in serious relationships."

"Except now?" he asked, and he could breathe again.

She flashed her eyes at him and grinned. "Except now. This is new territory for me. And for Céline. But we're both taking it pretty well, I think."

He put his arm around her. *I'm a lucky S.O.B.* "So, you're free tomorrow. Will you spend the day with me?"

"Don't you have work or something? Aren't you in the middle of a feud?" She leaned her head against his arm.

"My family's worried I'm going to turn into Charles and not take time off. They'll be happy."

She gave him a big hug. "Yes, I'd love to spend tomorrow with you."

"And on the weekend, there's a big gala in the city I have to attend. Will you come with me? We can visit Father Andre in the hospital, too."

"Sure." She scowled. "I don't have anything to wear to a gala."

Thomas thought. "I might have some people who can help you with that." He smiled and hugged her back.

* * * *

Two days later, Tatienne was sitting in their suite when there was a knock on the door. Céline answered it and showed two women into their apartment. It was Chantelle and a woman with short hair who wore simple athletic separates. She looked a lot like Thomas.

Chantelle said hello. "This is Clem, my cousin."

"Thomas told me about you and your brothers." Tati shook her hand. Calm radiated from the woman, like a comforting blanket.

"I'm sorry I haven't welcomed you yet. How are you settling in?" Clem asked.

"Fine, thank you. I haven't had a vacation like this…well, ever." Tati said. "It's a gorgeous place."

"We like it, too." Clem smiled.

Chantelle spoke up. "Thomas is happy to have you here."

Tati's face grew hot. "He's been so kind and helpful. To me and my sister."

"Thomas said he's taking you out for a big night in the city," Clem said.

"He told you about that?" Tati ducked her head.

Clem chuckled. "He's told the whole compound."

Tati's stomach twisted into knots. "That's a lot of pressure."

"Don't worry!" Chantelle patted her shoulder. "It's just a date. A chance for you to get to know each other better."

"I don't know. What if it doesn't go well?" Tatienne realised she was getting emotionally involved. Her heart raced.

"I think you two are getting along just fine so far. A fancy night out won't be that different."

"I guess it feels like we're getting more serious." Could she do it? Take a risk and get closer to him?

Chantelle took her arm. "Relax, it's going to be fun. And we're going to take you to the Clothing Depot to find a dress for your date."

"If you look good, you'll feel good," Clem added.

Tati put her shoulders back. *Time to be brave, I can do it.*

Chantelle turned to Céline. "Do you want to come?"

Céline shook her head. "I hate dress shopping!"

Clem spoke up. "Thomas said you could go swimming with him instead. What do you think?"

Céline nodded and went to get her swimsuit.

"How does Thomas do it all?" Tatienne shook her head.

Chantelle laughed. "He's better at delegating than Charles is. And he likes his routines—including exercise and relaxation. It's partly his personality, but it also comes from watching Charles and from losing his brother and father. He learned the hard way that life is precious."

"I feel the same," Tati said. "Losing my parents changed the way I live my life."

"We all felt the loss of the Alpha and his oldest son," said Clem. "It was so sudden, it messed with everyone. But Charles and Thomas stepped in and helped everyone through their grief, all the while dealing with their own. They kept the whole community together."

"That's a big deal," Tati said.

"Thomas likes to stay in the shadows, work behind the scenes. The Lieutenant position is good for him. It lets him take a leadership role that also supports his brother as the Alpha," Clem said.

Céline came out in her bathing suit and a cover-up. She was carrying her bathing cap and goggles with a towel. "I'm ready," she exclaimed.

The women walked Céline to the pool and waved to Thomas, who was waiting at the entrance. Céline hurried over to him. He beamed at Tatienne before he headed into the pool area with Céline.

Tatienne's heart warmed to see her sister's smile.

Clem said, "The Clothing Depot is on the other side of the compound. It won't take us long to get there."

"I could use a walk," said Tati.

They made casual conversation as they strolled past large A-frame chalets as well as some smaller cabins. Everything was made from sustainable lumber and other eco-conscious materials. They walked through a large open space to a cluster of buildings on the far side of the compound, some with shop signs over their front doors.

Chantelle pointed to one of the small buildings in the middle of the group. "It's called the Depot but it's not that sketchy — it's a consignment store. Sunita, who runs it, is an artist, so it's very creative and welcoming."

When they walked through the door, Tatienne was immediately impressed by the bright colours and soft fabrics used in the casual décor.

A stunning woman — black hair, brown eyes and mahogany skin — approached them, smiling. "You must be Tatienne. Clem told me you were coming." She shook Tatienne's hand. "I understand you'll be helping us with some research?"

Tati nodded, thinking it was a simple and useful explanation. "Yes, I'm reviewing some historical documents and papers."

Sunita nodded. "And what can we help you with?"

"I've got a formal date tomorrow night. I don't have any suitable clothes."

"She's going out with Thomas!" Chantelle said in a high-pitched voice. "Sorry, I'm just really excited."

Sunita grinned. "That *is* a big occasion. All the straight women and gay men will be jealous of you."

"Tatienne can handle it. If she can go toe-to-toe with Thomas, then she can take care of herself." Chantelle chuckled.

"I'm glad to hear it." Sunita gave Tati a once-over. "You have a killer figure. I'm sure we can find you something that will make him wolf-howl at the moon."

Tatienne didn't know what to say.

Clem called Tati over to a rack with several muted colours of dresses. "There's a nice mauve one here. Or a plain grey one."

"Pretty," said Tati.

"Pretty plain," pronounced Sunita. "They're comfortable, but they remind me of sweatpants. Maybe something to throw on when you're watching TV before bed."

Tati's heart sank. It wasn't going to be easy to find something.

Sunita looked at her. "No, that's not what I meant. It's just you are such a beautiful woman. I want to see you in something that makes you shine."

Tati raised her head. *Maybe this is going to work.*

Sunita found a few formal gowns to try. There was a hideous floor-length orange gown, and a simple black dress that was too small.

Tatienne was sceptical when Sunita passed her a slinky, dark-purple dress. "This isn't my style," she said.

"Just try it. For me?" her new friend asked.

She went into the changing room and slid it on. It fit like a glove. But she didn't usually wear body-con dresses. The slim skirt went to the floor, with a long slit up to her mid-thigh. And the bodice had a sweetheart neckline that showed off a lot of cleavage.

"What do you think?" asked Clem from the other side of the dressing room curtain.

"I'll come out if there's nobody else in the Depot." The dress was growing on her, even though it was more form-fitting than her usual style. But it had a touch of that old Hollywood glamour that she loved.

The women gasped when they saw her in it. "The colour really sets off your skin tone. It's gorgeous," said Chantelle.

"I feel too exposed. The colour is beautiful, though." She looked in the mirror again.

"Be bold! You have a sexy body. You should show it off," Sunita encouraged. "I have a gauzy wrap that might make you more comfortable." She bustled off to the front of the shop.

"Clem?" Tatienne asked. She would have an ally in this sensible, no-nonsense woman.

"Thomas is going to love it. You have to wear it," Clem said.

Tatienne raised her eyebrows. "You too?" She sighed and put her shoulders back. "Okay, nothing ventured, nothing gained. You're right—it'll be fun." She returned to the changeroom before she could chicken out. *It's only one night.*

Chantelle and Clem picked out some casual clothes for Tati while she changed out of the dress and tried to imagine Thomas' reaction when he saw her in the gown. Her heart raced in anticipation.

When she came out of the change room, Sunita showed her the shawl and took the dress. She leaned over conspiratorially. "Thomas is a catch."

"He's a wonderful man." Tati smiled. "I'm looking forward to spending more time with him."

"His last girlfriend was a hot mess. I'm glad he's dating again."

"He's been a little shy and weird about the girlfriend," said Tatienne, as she searched her purse for her wallet.

"She really hurt him." Sunita scowled. "Cheated on him and then dropped him when she thought she found someone better. Not that anyone could outclass Thomas."

"She sounds like a real bitch." Tati couldn't imagine treating anyone like that, especially someone as warm-hearted as Thomas.

"She didn't appreciate him for who he was. Always tried to change him and make him into a little doll." Sunita shuddered. "It was awful."

Chantelle and Clem joined them at the front of the shop.

Tatienne unzipped her wallet. "How much do I owe you?" There weren't any prices on the clothes. She hoped she could afford the dress, that the second-hand rates in the luxurious shop were affordable.

Sunita shook her head. "This is a consignment shop. And Clem has a lot of unused credit — she's one of our best donors."

"I'd be thrilled if you could use up some of it for me, Tatienne." Clem squeezed her shoulder.

"Really? I feel like I'm taking advantage..." Tati said.

"Nonsense!" said Sunita. "We aren't a for-profit shop. I take pride in our ability to recycle and upcycle clothing so that we can decrease our carbon footprint. That's what matters to me — oh, and finding the right outfit to make someone shine." She handed Tati a dry-cleaner bag with the gown inside. Tati thanked her and the others, her face growing hot.

As they left the shop, Clem asked Tatienne if she was nervous about the date.

"Not exactly nervous," she said. "We've already gone on a date. But this feels different. There's a lot of expectations — from him, from everybody. What if it's a disaster?" Tati's stomach flip-flopped again.

"You won't know unless you try. That's what a date's about, right?" Clem said.

"Yeah, but it's weird to be dating someone so publicly. And Thomas has made his intentions very clear that he wants us to have a serious relationship." Tati's thoughts swirled around in her head.

"Forget about Thomas for the moment," Chantelle said. "What do you want?"

"I don't know. I haven't really thought about it." She paused. "I don't want to be lonely. I want to find someone to share my time with. Who respects and loves me."

"Good," said Clem. "That's what you deserve."

"Do you think you could have that with Thomas?" Chantelle asked, searching her face.

"Yes, I think I could. But it scares me to think about the future." *Maybe it's time to deal with my commitment issues.*

Chantelle put her hand on Tati's arm. "So, you like him as a person, as a friend?"

"I like Thomas. Maybe a lot." She frowned. "But what am I doing getting involved with some rich, glamorous man? That's not me."

"He's not about his money. He's looking for someone real, who will care for him."

Tatienne closed her eyes. "It just feels wrong, like he could do so much better."

Clem poked her, quirking an eyebrow. "Girl, you are a queen. He's lucky to have you."

"So, it's me? I'm holding myself back?" Her heart caught in her throat. *It's not that simple, is it?*

Chantelle nodded. "You can do this."

"I've had all these emotions from my parents' death and looking after my sister. Maybe the unresolved issues have been stopping me from—from living my life." Tati stopped in the snow as the wind whipped around them. "It's been easier to stay away from people and hide. But now with everything that's happening..."

"You can't stay detached? You aren't an island anymore?" Chantelle asked.

Tati nodded, tears in her eyes.

"Welcome back to the world. We've been waiting for you." Chantelle hugged her, and Tatienne hugged her back.

Chapter Fourteen

Tatienne looked around the hotel lobby. *Fancy-shmancy!*

She was equal parts nervous and excited. The Opera Gala was a big event in the city and she had always wanted to attend. Now here she was with a dashing gentleman at her side, wearing a dress fit for a princess. Sunita had fixed her hair—Céline had helped, of course—and added a silver fascinator with a purple feather to match the lipstick she had loaned her.

She clutched Thomas' arm. "Is everyone going to be talking about designer shoes and luxury vacations?"

"Not everyone is focused on status. Some people are down-to-earth, if you know where to find them."

"Your family is, that's true. We'll see about the others." Tatienne pursed her lips.

There were photographers, servers with trays of champagne and gorgeous people everywhere. She just needed to relax and enjoy herself. Spending time with

Thomas was the goal, not mingling with the rich and famous.

"Did I mention how hot you look in your tux? I could eat you right up," she said.

Grinning wickedly, he leaned close and said, "I thought we'd eat each other up later."

Her core heated at the thought. "Can we skip the gala and go right to dessert?"

"Nice try, but you're not getting out of it that easy. I'd love to have someone to take to these events. I don't go to them often, but our family has to put in appearances, and I do my fair share."

She nodded. It warmed her heart to hear him talk about their future. Although she wasn't sure there would be a future yet—it was still too early in the relationship—she was glad she was taking a chance on Thomas. He was a wonderful man and he deserved for her to take them seriously.

He took her arm and led her into the ballroom. She couldn't believe how luxurious it was. The large space was decorated tastefully with giant vases of cascading black and white flowers and matching gauzy panels draped around tables and on the walls. It was a classy scheme, with touches of gold scattered in the decorations.

They looked at the seating arrangement and found their table in the middle of the room.

"The other people at our table are fine. You don't need to worry. Mostly artist types who married bankers."

She laughed. "Is that like us?"

"I'm not that staid, am I?"

"No. You've got your intellectual side, but you're also athletic and a leader in your community." She put her arms around him. "It shouldn't work, but it does — all of your amazing qualities are wrapped up in one sexy package."

He kissed her then, a hint of citrus on his lips.

Tatienne sat beside a lovely woman who owned an expensive art gallery downtown but was very easy to talk to. Thomas kept his hand on the back of her chair. Every time he brushed it along her skin, she shivered in anticipation of when they would be alone. The seven-course dinner was over sooner than she expected. It hadn't been as boring as she thought. And the food had been exquisite. She was glad Thomas had invited her.

After they cleared away the plates, Tatienne excused herself to get soft drinks for the two of them. When she returned from the bar, Thomas was talking to a very skinny, very white young woman. This person stood above him, staring down her nose, while he sat in his chair. She was very animated but her eyebrows were turned down into a scowl.

Then it hit her. *That's Thomas' ex, Aimée.* She wondered if she should be jealous. Aimée was stunning, in an ice-princess kind of way. Tatienne could see why she was popular in society circles — perfect hair, perfect clothing, elegant in all ways. Thomas had told Tatienne about Aimée's perfectionism and how she had constantly criticised him. Nothing was ever good enough for her. She should pity the woman, but her anger at how Aimée had treated Thomas overshadowed her good will. He deserved unconditional love and respect from his partner. Certainly, he treated his family and friends that way.

Then she reconsidered. Thomas' ex-girlfriend deserved to be happy, too. Aimée hadn't been a good fit with Thomas, and she had treated him poorly, but he had moved on. It didn't matter anymore.

She walked up to Thomas and put the drinks on their table. Then she leaned down, put her arms around him and kissed him on the cheek. "Hey, sweetheart. Who's this?"

When Thomas turned his gaze up to her, it was clear only she mattered to him now.

"This is my ex, Aimée. Aimée, this is Tatienne."

Tati stood at her full height, a head taller than Aimée. "Pleased to meet you." She held out her hand. After a moment, Aimée shook it, her nose crinkling up and lips puckering.

Tatienne cleared her throat. "I just want to thank you for breaking up with Thomas. You hurt him, but you did him a favour. He's much happier now."

The woman looked stunned. "I—I'm glad," she spat out.

"Did you marry the other guy?" Tatienne asked.

Aimée nodded her head, turning even paler.

"Then I wish you two all the best." She looked at Thomas. "Will you dance with me?" she asked.

He nodded. "Always."

They said a quick goodbye to Aimée, who stomped off. Then they went to the dance floor and held each other to the strains of Mozart.

"Thank you," he said, sweeping her around the room.

She kept forgetting how smooth a dancer he was. "Thank you. For making this a special night. For inviting me into your world. For not being afraid to open your heart again."

"You're damn near perfect," he rumbled.

"I don't want to be perfect. I want to be real. I want to be with someone who appreciates all my imperfections."

"But you don't have any," he replied, tracing his hands along her lower back.

"I guess that's what I mean, then." She placed her head on his shoulder and revelled in his strength. She felt calm and happy. "I could stay here all night."

"But I booked the presidential suite here."

"You didn't, did you?" Her heart raced. "I brought extra pairs of panties in my purse, in case you want to rip them off while we're here."

He squeezed her waist. "Do you think I'm a perv?"

"Never! It's a pretty mild kink. You're passionate and fierce. You appreciate beauty and sensual enjoyment."

"Good, because I bought you something to wear tonight."

"You didn't have to do that! I'll only wear it for a few minutes, knowing us."

His eyes sparkled. "It'll be worth it."

She smiled. *I've never been this happy before.* He took her hand and led her through the ballroom to the lift.

Thomas escorted Tati into the lift. He wrapped his arms around her as she turned to face him. When she leaned her whole body against him, his cock stood at attention, desire coursing through his veins.

It was moments until the lift door opened into the Presidential suite and he whisked her inside. He skimmed his hands down her sides, relishing the feel of her curves in the body-con dress. She kissed him, then pulled off his suit jacket and started unbuttoning his shirt.

"You are killing me," he moaned.

"In a good way?" She nipped at his lips and ran her hands down his arms as she removed his shirt. He planted kisses along her neck before scooping her up in his arms and carrying her into the bedroom.

He sped her to a large four-poster bed. It was handsome...dark-grey satin sheets, grey paisley covers and shiny shams. He placed her in the middle of the duvet, then found the remote to turn on the gas fireplace in the bedroom's seating area.

"Wait here for one moment," he said. He found his bags and grabbed a large box with a bow. He brought it back to Tati, still lying on the bed in the sexiest dress he'd ever seen.

When she smiled up at him, his heart swelled. She sat up and ripped open the package. The lingerie set he had chosen was his favourite yet. Dark blue and lacy, it had garters and a bustier as well as the sweetest little thong. There was also a negligee she could wear later.

"Thomas, this is beautiful! Thank you." Her face turned an adorable shade of pink as she pulled out the pieces to admire them.

She stood and he helped her out of her gown and shoes.

"We can't just throw this dress on the floor," she said, placing it carefully on a nearby club chair. She turned back to Thomas and removed her undergarments to stand naked in front of him. She was gorgeous...and it was all for him.

He held up the panties first and gestured for her to sit on the bed. After she took a seat, he caressed first one leg, then the other with soft, gentle touches up and down her outer legs. Lifting her feet one by one, he eased the panties up her calves then her thighs. She sighed, relaxing into his touch.

He lifted her buttocks, growling with desire. After the panties were in place, he picked up the bustier. Running his hands over her stomach and breasts, he thanked his lucky stars he had found her.

He corralled her ample breasts into the fabric and reluctantly fixed the closures. He trailed his fingers along the lines of the bustier, murmuring his appreciation.

"Now, up." He knelt in front of her to put her garters in place. She was breathing shallowly, and he could smell her arousal. "Your stockings are last."

"I don't need them," she said.

"I want to see the whole picture," he said. "I've been thinking about it all day." She held his shoulders as he helped her into the lace-topped stockings and clipped them to the garters. Their silky feel enhanced her soft skin.

Growling, Thomas picked her up over his shoulder and brought her to the seating area. He lay her down on a faux-fur rug placed in front of the fireplace. She put her hands behind her head, eyes dark, and posed for him. After stripping off his trousers and finding a condom for later, he looked her over and stroked his cock, enjoying the friction from the thin layer of fabric of his boxers. Then he sat down and caressed his woman from top to bottom.

"Such a beautiful sight," he said. "Can you turn over for me? Feel the softness of the faux fur against your skin."

She flipped over and wiggled against the rug, sighing. "I want one of these for my apartment."

"Done. We'll get one for every room in your apartment—and my place, too."

She chuckled. "Come here."

He straddled her and unlaced the bustier as slowly as he could. He rose on his knees and turned her to the side so he could pull the fabric out from under her. Her breasts sprang free, and he massaged them, playing with her nipples. She moaned and moved her hips under him. He couldn't resist rubbing his hard cock against her skin. Their undergarments still separated them, but he loved the feel of the thin fabrics between them.

He traced his fingers from her breasts down to her hips and thighs. "*Belle*, I want you to kneel so I can get a better look at your pussy."

She wet her lips and he almost came in his boxers. She scrambled into a kneeling position and a low rumble came out of his chest.

He caressed her backside. Then he pushed her knees farther apart. She whimpered as he ran a finger along the edge of her thong, from the top of her ass down past her hot crevice to her pussy and clit.

"You are nice and wet already," he growled. "Stay just like that for me."

He played with her garter, running his hands along the curves of her cheeks and down to her thighs. Holding the strap with a finger, he licked down to the top of her stockings. He unsnapped the stockings, one by one, and pulled them down, taking his time to kiss a line down her legs. He could hear her little moans. After the stockings came off, he grabbed the garter belt and snaps in his mouth and pulled them down her legs, taking care to nip gently along her skin.

He skimmed his hand along the edge of her panties, and she shivered. He ran his fingertip along her folds.

"Is all this cream just for me?" he asked. "I want to taste it."

When he trailed his tongue along the inside of her thighs, she shuddered. Blowing his breath on her mound, he reached out his tongue for a light flick on her bud. She gasped, urging him on. He decided not to rip these panties, and instead quickly pulled them down and off her legs.

He touched a finger to her clit then whispered in her ear. "What do you want me to do?"

"Thomas." She shivered.

"Tell me."

"I want to come all over your hands and mouth."

"I'll lap all your sweet juices up." He moved his head down and breathed in her delectable scent. He lapped at her folds as he eased a finger in her channel.

"Oh," she whimpered. "You make me so hot and needy."

He moved his hand back and forth, two fingers deep in her pussy. She pushed back, riding his hand while he sucked her clit. When she began to pant and sigh, he kept up the pace until she went over the edge in wave after wave of pleasure. She held him tight as her cream gushed over his hand and mouth. He lapped her up, sucking greedily, as she crested the wave.

Tati lay down and rolled over on her back, whimpering. He straddled her. While she was still pulsing, he put on the condom. Then he took his hard cock and rubbed it against her slit.

She cried out. "Fuck, yes!"

He put her ankles over his shoulders and slid his cock deep into her pussy. He groaned as he reached the hilt, then he dragged his length out and thrust it back in. After a few slow strokes, he pistoned fast and hard, slapping his balls against her ass.

"Thomas," she cried.

When she said his name, he went to the edge.

"Come for me," he said.

She milked his cock with her pussy as he spurted deep inside her. He had never had a release like that. It was total and complete.

Spent, they collapsed in a heap on the rug. After their breathing slowed, he rolled them to their sides to spoon, his half-hard penis nestled between her beautiful, sexy ass cheeks. He kissed her neck and snuggled in behind her.

Chapter Fifteen

In the morning, Thomas ordered coffee, eggs and bacon — the works. He didn't know what she preferred to eat for breakfast. But he would know soon.

As she continued to sleep, he'd left a fluffy white robe on a chair near her on the bed. She'd put on her new negligee after they had exhausted each other and decided it was time for rest.

In the main open area of the condo, a server wheeled in a large trolley covered with a pristine white tablecloth. Thomas had already had a shower and put on his robe, not ready to get dressed and return to the real world after their magical night. He tipped the server after they laid the silver platters on the dining table.

Tatienne appeared a moment later, pulling the robe over her shoulders. Even when she had just woken up, she was the most beautiful woman he'd ever seen.

"Good morning," he said, kissing her. "Hope you're hungry."

"Famished! We burnt a lot of calories last night."

He grinned and pulled her close for a moment before they took their chairs at the small table.

With a flourish, he pulled the silver cloches off of the platters, revealing an assortment of breakfast delicacies. Offering Tatienne a plate, he piled it high as she held it. Then he served himself and sat as she poured them coffee. *This is what they mean by domestic bliss.*

"When is your appointment to see Father Andre?" he asked.

"Ten o'clock. Will you come with me?"

"I won't be in the way? He hasn't met me before."

"I'd love it if you joined me. I'd like to introduce you to him."

He basked in the smile that lit her face. He took another sip of coffee and said, "I'll have to check on the building repairs before we return to the compound. Shall we do that after lunch? I'll have Isabelle pick up another basket for us if you like."

"I'd love that."

He thought about their first lunch together at the diocesan archives. So much had happened in a short space of time. Life was better with Tati in his life.

After they finished breakfast, they dressed and took the town car to the hospital. Thomas was relieved that Father Andre was awake in his bed when they arrived. Tati would worry less about her friend. When the priest shook his hand, Thomas assessed his kind eyes. He was one of the good ones.

"I don't remember much about that night," Father Andre told them, lying back on his pillows.

"It was scary seeing you on the floor like that." Tati shuddered. "It looked like someone had pushed the bureau over on you."

"That's what they told me. I don't know why someone would do that to me. I don't have any enemies."

Thomas cleared his throat. "I'm afraid it is related to my family and those documents you found."

The priest shook his head. "Who would do something like that for old papers?"

"I know it sounds unbelievable," Tati said. "If anyone asks you about it, can you please keep this information to yourself? We don't know who to trust yet."

"Did you find anything useful, at least?" Father Andre asked.

"We think so," Tatienne said. "I don't want to get you involved any more than you already are."

"Always protecting others, Tati. Who looks after you?" The priest's gaze strayed to Thomas.

Thomas put a hand on Tatienne's shoulder and nodded.

"I can look after myself," Tati said, her jaw setting.

"I'm not saying you can't," said the priest. "I'll feel better knowing someone is helping you out."

"To tell you the truth, Thomas has been a big help. And Céline adores him."

Father Andre smiled at her, his eyes flickering.

"We should go and let you rest," Tatienne said.

The priest nodded. "Thank you for visiting. Thomas, take care of her for me."

"I will."

As they left the hospital room, two men in cassocks came down to the hall towards them. Thomas' wolf stood on alert.

Are they friend or foe? Thomas looked behind himself at a large man in a dark suit who stood outside the priest's room.

"I'm glad you're having him watched," Tatienne whispered.

The men stopped in front of Tatienne and Thomas. "Excuse me, Mademoiselle Laflamme?" They sized Thomas up and he resisted the urge to knock them to the ground.

"Yes," Tatienne said.

The shorter one spoke. "I'm Father Genette. We spoke on the phone. I wasn't expecting to meet you here. This is my assistant, Deacon Brébeuf."

"I'm sorry, I forgot to contact you," Tatienne said. "This is Thomas Ducharme, a friend."

The hairs on the back of Thomas' neck stood up. Father Genette's eyes lit up for a moment before he smoothed his expression into a neutral one. "Pleased to meet both of you. Would there be a time we could talk, my child?"

Thomas put a hand on her back. He didn't like the priest's tone of voice. "We have an appointment shortly. Could we do it another day, perhaps?" he asked.

"Ah yes." The priest's lips twitched, and he felt Tatienne's back tense up. "Was Father Andre in any trouble? Is there anything I should know about?"

Tatienne shook her head.

"He had some documents, I heard. Were they recovered?" Father Genette stared at her intently.

"No."

Thomas spoke up. "We could come by the parish church later this afternoon. Would that be convenient?"

The priest looked at his assistant briefly before nodding. "Yes, my children. Come, Deacon Brébeuf, we have matters to attend to."

The two men inclined their heads, turned and strode down the corridor towards the lifts.

Tati frowned. "What was that all about?"

"You're not talking to them alone," Thomas stated.

"I don't think I want to." Tatienne put her hand in Thomas'. "Is Father Andre safe?"

Thomas squinted. "I'll double the guards, if that will make you feel better."

"I'm sorry for all the trouble." Tati squeezed Thomas' hand.

"No trouble at all." Thomas rubbed his free hand over his face.

"It's not your fault, Thomas," Tati said. "We need to find the people who hurt him and stop them."

"You're right. Let's get through our meetings today and then we can concentrate on our search."

He put his arm around her and they left the hospital. Isabelle brought the car around and they drove back to his condo for a break. They were going to need their energy for the afternoon's tasks.

* * * *

Tatienne arrived at the church, grateful Thomas was coming with her. This was the first time she had returned to the site of Father Andre's "accident" — that was what church officials were calling it. It made Tati's blood boil. Thomas had assured her it was better not to draw attention to what she might or might not know.

Calling it an accident meant she was safer. But it didn't seem right.

How strange it would be to talk with Father Andre's replacement. She had bonded with her parish priest over many things — first it was their love of hot sauces inherited from their grandparents, then it was navigating the system for support for Céline. He had been a sympathetic ear and a champion when they had needed him. He was the one who had told her not to give up on the world when she felt so tired and alone.

Thomas opened the door. Tatienne blinked as they went from the sunny exterior to the dark vestibule of the church. The lingering smell of incense and flowers was soothing, but her nerves were still jangling. They walked through the front hallway to Father Andre's office.

She knocked on the door. Father Genette's assistant, Deacon Brébeuf, opened it. She hadn't looked at him too closely when they ran into them at the hospital. His green eyes were mesmerising. The deacon ushered her and Thomas into the main office.

Father Genette sat behind the desk — Father Andre's desk. It looked wrong, disrespectful. The priest rose and shook her hand.

"Mademoiselle Laflamme, so nice to see you again."

Her hand was damp from touching his, so she wiped it surreptitiously on her skirt. Her stomach lurched as they sat down in stiff wooden chairs across the desk from Father Genette. The deacon stood behind the priest and fixed them with a glassy stare.

"I'm trying to get to know the parishioners who were close to Father Andre," said the priest. "What do you do for work?"

"I'm on a short leave. I work at the diocesan archives."

"Ah, yes. Monseigneur Lacroix told me, I forgot. Do you like it there?"

"Yes. We help a lot of people with ancestry research and folks studying Montréal's religious history."

Father Genette narrowed his eyes, but he kept a smile pasted on his face. "Do you have many people digging into the city's past?"

"Reporters come sometimes, and community members who are looking to make exhibitions. Things like that."

"Is that where you met Monsieur Ducharme?" His gaze flicked to Thomas as Tati's pulse sped up.

Thomas shifted in his chair and spoke for the first time. "Yes, we did. She was helping me with an ancestry project for my family. It's a surprise for my grandmother."

Tatienne hoped the priest would buy it. Father Genette paused then smiled unctuously. "Of course. Your grandmother, Marie Ducharme, lives in Lac St Patrice, doesn't she?"

Thomas' knuckles grew white as he gripped the arms of his chair. "My family is very close, and we work together to look after her. She's rarely alone these days."

Her heart beat faster.

"And you were the ones to discover Father Andre in the basement?" The priest's eyes narrowed again.

When she nodded, the priest stood up. "Monsieur Ducharme, would you be so kind as to show me what you saw in the basement? We won't make the pretty lady live through that experience again."

Tati added another strike against Father Genette. *A misogynist, of course.* Father Andre had restored her faith in the clergy after his predecessor had been arrested on public indecency charges, but she knew there were still some bad apples in the vocation.

Thomas looked to her and she nodded. She could feel his strength and calm reaching her.

Thomas followed the priest out of the room.

After the pair had left, Deacon Brébeuf sidled over and sat on the edge of the desk in front of Tati. She shifted back in her seat to make more room between his legs and her knees.

"You must have been very upset to find Father Andre like that. Did anything look strange to you?" he asked.

Tatienne's back stiffened. "I don't remember much. I think I was in shock —" She broke off.

"Of course, my dear." The assistant patted her on the shoulder, and she tried not to react in disgust. Tingles shot down her arm at his touch. They were similar to when Chantelle had examined her, but while the woman's touch had been comforting, the deacon's numbed her arm. It reminded her of anaesthetic.

She struggled to keep her eyes open while the deacon murmured softly to her. *What is he saying? Something about Father Andre?*

"Do you have the documents? Where are they?" he asked.

She tried to shake her head. It was like something had her brain in a vice grip. The assistant's hands were on her shoulders. She tried to push them off, but he held her tight. As he continued chanting, her consciousness floated. She was awake, but she couldn't move.

The deacon's words faded as she slipped into a dream.

Images of Father Andre swam past. Lying on the basement floor, the cupboard on top of his prone form. Papers and boxes swirled around her in the dream. She tried to grab them, but they danced out of reach. She opened her mouth to scream, and nothing came out.

Wisps of grey smoke swirled around, obscuring her view. The deacon's voice became strangely deeper and inhuman. She caught a glimpse of him through the fog. He was wearing dirty grey robes, his face hidden under a hood. There was something in his hands — some kind of light or purple fire, maybe? She struggled to set it in her memory. She didn't know if she would recall any of this, but it seemed important to try.

The deacon approached her through the smoke. When he reached for her shoulders, she tried to back away, but couldn't move.

Then something rose in her mind, fighting against this psychic assault. She felt prickles all through her body, a mixture of fire and ice that lifted her out of the fog. The deacon's hands were manipulating something that looked like fire. The flames surrounded her, immobilising her. She fought the invasion in her mind, reaching out and grasping at the ribbons of fire encircling her.

Then he was beside her. Thomas. He looked fierce, cloaked in furs like something out of a movie. His love enveloped her, reaching through the flames that choked her. Could she stop the deacon with Thomas' help? Chantelle believed she could harness her magical abilities, that her gift of seeing fire could be expanded to control the element.

But how could she do that?

She reached out to Thomas. She had always believed she had to do everything herself. She couldn't depend on anyone else.

But that was a lie. She wasn't dependent on Thomas. He was like her family. They loved and supported each other. It was a bond that fed them both, making them better both individually and together.

She could use his support—his love—to fight against the sorcery. She leaned her back against his chest and he put his arms around her waist.

As she reached out with her hands, Deacon Brébeuf snarled, his eyes glowing green. She scooped up the flames and made a circle of fire around her opponent. She pinned him in place while he struggled helplessly.

Then everything went dark.

Chapter Sixteen

Thomas surveyed the dark basement, Father Genette by his side. The old cupboard was right side up. The papers had been tidied and placed on a nearby table. His people had put the trunk and jar boxes back where they belonged. Everything was in its place.

The priest's glittering eyes narrowed. "Where did you find Father Andre?"

"He was trapped under this." Thomas gestured to the cupboard.

"Do you know why he was down here?"

Thomas shook his head. "Tatienne said he liked to keep things neat. He was probably cleaning."

Father Genette sniffed around the cupboard then shuffled the papers on the table, Thomas glanced around the room. There wasn't anything out of place, was there? They had taken the significant papers to the compound.

After another minute of silence, the priest turned back and peered at Thomas. "Lead me through what happened after you saw him."

Thomas began a sanitised rehearsal of calling 9-1-1 and examining the scene. When he heard someone calling his name, he cocked an ear. There was only the priest beside him.

When he heard it again, he looked around. *Where is it coming from – inside my head?* It was different than communicating with his pack mates when he was in wolf form. His family connection with his brothers allowed them to communicate emotions and simple thoughts to each other as humans – especially in emergency situations. The call reminded him of this.

Suddenly, a series of disconnected images and feelings bombarded him. Getting into the car with Tatienne on the day Father Andre died. Arguing with Tatienne at the lodge, waves of fear and desire and death. And their bond, burning like a beacon in a smoky landscape. He felt the outside world slipping away.

When he opened his eyes, they weren't his eyes anymore. The deacon was perched on the edge of the desk in Father Andre's office. He was seated in the chair, too close to the man's legs. The deacon reached forward and put his hands on his – no, her – shoulders. He – no, she – was afraid, in pain. He heard the word she whimpered. *Help.*

Tatienne. She was in trouble.

He sprinted for the basement door. The priest followed, but he was too slow to catch Thomas as he ran up the stairs. When Thomas reached the office door, it was locked.

Three kicks. The door frame splintered at the same time Father Genette reached him.

Tatienne was lying on the floor of the office, unconscious. She was breathing, thank the Goddess. The voice in his head was still there, though faint. Behind her, the deacon moaned, his arms covered with bubbling blisters and burns. There was no fire, no smoke. Just the burns on his upper limbs.

Father Genette pushed past Thomas and bent down to check on his colleague. Then, he swivelled and stood, reaching into a pocket in his cassock. He pulled out a gun and pointed it at Thomas.

"Get back," he snarled.

Thomas took a step away from Tatienne, ensuring the priest's aim was still on him. "I'm not leaving without Tatienne."

"Put your hands behind your back."

Thomas did as Father Genette ordered, fighting his instincts to ram into the priest and knock him over. He didn't want to put Tatienne in more danger if he could help it. He'd have to wait for the right moment.

The priest transferred the gun to his left hand while he opened a desk drawer. He pulled out a pair of handcuffs, shuffled over to Thomas and secured the cuffs around his wrists. Thomas' stomach churned. How was he going to get out of this situation?

"These are spelled so you can't shift."

The priest dug in Thomas' pocket for his phone, then retrieved Tati's phone as well, securing the devices in the pocket of his robes.

"Leave her alone," Thomas growled.

Father Genette pulled the groaning deacon up from the floor. "Did you get what we needed?"

The man nodded, wincing.

"We don't need the girl," Father Genette said to Thomas. "The two of you can stay here." He pushed Thomas over to a chair, found some rope and tied him up. The priest nudged Tatienne with his toe. When she didn't move, he retreated and put the deacon's arm around his shoulder. The deacon gasped but clung to the priest.

Thomas listened for Tati's breathing and was relieved it was steady. He didn't want her to wake up in the middle of the priests' retreat.

Still holding the gun on Thomas, the priest checked the front door to the office and locked it. He propped up the deacon and went to the other side of the room, a sheen of perspiration on his face. As they left through the back door, he turned the key behind them.

The room was quiet. They were locked in.

And Tatienne was still unconscious.

It was a long thirty minutes until she woke. Thomas shifted his chair a little at a time until he was beside her, but that was all he could do. The spelled cuffs dampened his strength as well as his shifter powers and he was unable to break his bonds. While he tried to get free, he concocted plans to torture and kill the priest and his companion.

After slipping off his shoes, he nudged his toes under her calves. The physical contact eased the hurt in his chest.

When she stirred, his heart lurched. Her eyes opened and she looked around.

"Hey there, sleepyhead." He put a smile on his face while his pulse raced. "I can't tell you how glad I am to see you're awake."

"What happened?" she asked, her eyelids flickering open and closed.

"You tell me." He waited. All he wanted to do was scream and laugh and cry, but he held it in.

She sucked in a few breaths. "It felt like magic. How could that be? He's a member of the clergy."

"The Frères Gris were—are—clergy, too. They might have contacts all through the Church." He had to consider that possibility when they got out of this situation. It would change their strategy.

"Do you think the archbishop is involved?" Tatienne's eyes were wide.

"Can't say. I hope not."

"What did the priest say to you?" she asked.

"He was digging for information about the documents and Father Andre. Then I saw these images—you were there. And I heard your voice."

"I thought I was hallucinating." She closed her eyes for a moment

"How did you reach me?"

"When the deacon attacked, he tried to invade my mind to access my memories. Somehow, he put me under, and I reached out and found you."

"That's when I came up from the basement." Thomas took in a deep breath. "Father Genette held a gun on me and tied me up."

Tati stood up slowly and came to inspect the ropes and handcuffs. "I can untie you. I don't know about these cuffs."

"They are magic dampeners. And they prevent shifting." He tried to sit still.

She started on the ropes. When he had been released, Thomas checked the building and found it empty. Tati found a working phone and called Isabelle at the number Thomas gave her. Isabelle sent a security team to look for the priests.

Thomas shrugged his shoulders. "I expect they've gone to ground or disappeared, but it's worth searching the area."

"They won't come back, will they?" She put her arms around him and he ached to do the same.

"Their cover's blown. They won't be able to."

"Will they go after Father Andre, do you think?"

"I don't think so." He kissed the top of her head. "I'll make sure his guards know what happened."

"Thank you," she whispered.

"Isabelle will be arriving shortly. Let's get you back to the compound."

"I don't want to stay here any longer." She shivered and led Thomas out of the office.

* * * *

That night back at the ski resort, Tatienne relaxed and spent time with her sister. Céline had kept busy while Tati was in Montréal. Vicky and Émile had taken her to an art class, and she had gone swimming with her new friend Samantha.

After Céline went to bed, Thomas came over. They watched a movie in the living room of her suite. She was so exhausted that she fell asleep ten minutes after the film started.

An hour later, she woke from a dream of smoke and sorcery. Thomas was holding her while she kicked and thrashed.

"What happened?" she asked.

"You had a bad dream."

She sat up and took a deep breath. "There were some figures in grey robes. They were trying to get me to do something. They shot flames at me when I resisted."

"You're awake now. It's not real."

Thomas checked her forehead. "Let me get you something to drink." He left the couch and returned a moment later with a glass of water.

She took a sip and rested the chilled glass on her cheek. "It's probably just my subconscious processing the weekend."

"I want you to rest tomorrow. Then on Monday morning, I'll take you to see Chantelle. She can work with you to recover your memories of the incident."

She snuggled back into his arms. His presence, just his touch, could calm her down. She hadn't expected this kind of intimacy would make her feel safe. After resisting getting close to anyone for years, she couldn't imagine doing without it — without him — anymore.

"How are you feeling now?" He brushed the hair from her forehead.

"What if the deacon did something else to me after you left the room with Father Genette?" she asked, shuddering.

"I am so angry with myself for letting them separate us." He let out a little growl and held her closer to his chest.

"I was raised to trust the clergy." She ran her fingers along his arm. "Though something seemed off the first time I talked with Father Genette."

"We need to trust your instincts more. And your powers, too. You can access supernatural experiences on a different level than most humans can understand."

"I've spent so long being afraid of my dreams. I don't know if I can accept my powers the way I should." She rubbed her face against his shirt, trying to soak up strength from him.

"You can do it. When I look at you, I see a warrior princess."

She glanced up at him. The acceptance in his eyes soothed her aching heart. Maybe she could be strong.

"You just need to develop your skills. Most Mages in the clan start training when they are young, but others come into their powers later." He kissed the top of her head. "Chantelle didn't know about her abilities when she arrived here. There had been an accident and her grandmother had hidden her skills to keep her safe from the Reynards."

Tati had heard most of the story from various sources. She knew Chantelle had dealt with the past and grown confident in her abilities by training with the Head Mage, Gwen.

"I would like to understand my abilities as a blessing and not a curse. The visions have terrified me for so long," she said, reaching for his hand.

"They are there for a reason." He kissed her palm.

"I know you're right." She sighed, the butterflies settling in her stomach.

"Do you want me to stay with you?"

I could stay like this all night. Wrapped in his arms, safe and content.

"Yes," she said. "Come to my bed."

She led him to her room, and they pleasured each other until both of them fell asleep, exhausted.

Chapter Seventeen

Tatienne twisted a lock of hair around her finger as she made her way through the main lodge. What if the deacon had done something damaging to her while she was unconscious? Worse yet, what if they couldn't find out what he'd done? She took a deep breath.

Buck up, there's only one way to find out.

She couldn't believe what they had gone through in the past week. Father Andre had always told her she was tough, but she'd never really believed him. He said it was her inner strength that kept her going when everything was changing around her. *More like stubbornness*, she thought. Either way, she was a survivor.

Thomas had surprised her at every turn, supporting her like she was family. She had never let anyone get close like she had with him. But nobody was like Thomas. Maybe she had been waiting for him?

She found the wing of the building that contained the staff offices. Consulting the list on the wall, she walked down the hall towards the Mage offices, where Chantelle was expecting her.

Thomas had been unable to join her this morning. She didn't mind. She needed to do this. Face her fears and embrace this part of herself.

Thomas had asked her and Céline to stay another week at the ski resort and she had agreed. Everything was still too unstable and it would give her more time to train with the Mages.

In addition, the new building manager had called to say Deacon Brébeuf had been lurking around Tatienne's apartment building last week before they met up with him. They had caught him on the CCTV footage. Tati didn't want to go back home if there was a danger of running into him or Father Genette again.

She missed her friends, though. It felt strange not to be in constant contact with her found family, but she knew they would always be there for her. Besides, she would be home soon enough, and life would go back to normal. Whatever normal was when she was dating a billionaire shifter.

She found the room where Chantelle had said she'd meet her. She knocked on the door and it swung open.

"Welcome! Did you have trouble finding me?" The petite woman smiled, and Tati's worries fell away. Although she knew Chantelle had mighty powers, she just looked like a girl next door in jeans and a long ponytail.

"No problem at all," Tati said.

They sat down in leather office chairs near a small table. The spacious room contained a larger desk set against the far wall, with an open space in the middle. Quiet, muted colours made it look like any millennial office space. The magical implements on a corner table also fit the aesthetic—bright crystals, dried herb branches, simple bowls in earth tones. If she didn't know better, she'd think they were just "for the vibe," as her sister would say.

"So." Chantelle leaned forward and looked deep in her eyes. "You had an experience when you were in Montréal."

"I was attacked—somehow—by a priest and a deacon at my local church. We think they're part of the Frères Gris Consortium, or else they were hired by them. The deacon used magic on me and I fell unconscious." She shrugged. It still didn't sound like it could have happened to her.

"And you'd like my help to figure out what happened?"

Tati nodded. "I can remember some flashes. It felt like one of my visions, but they usually happen when I'm sleeping."

"My powers tune in to physical and emotional energies. I can do some work with memory recall as well." Chantelle smiled reassuringly. "Don't worry, we'll figure it out."

The woman's soothing presence helped calm Tati's frayed nerves. Thomas' whole family—his pack—had this effect on her. She was confident she would find answers with Chantelle's help.

"Relax and take a deep breath. I'm going to make contact." The unassuming woman reached out and touched her forehead with her cool fingers.

Tatienne sucked in some air and willed her heart to slow down. Chantelle's touch was featherlight on her skin. There was a nudge in her subconscious, like a knock. Concentrating on connecting with the presence, she let it slip into her memories.

The presence led her back to Father Andre's office on Saturday afternoon. She saw the scene unfold like a movie in front of her.

Thomas and Father Genette left the room. Deacon Brébeuf came over and stood near her, leaning against the desk.

She remembered that part. But what had happened afterward?

The deacon touched her arm. Suddenly, everything felt like it was under water — everything moved more slowly, and light and sound warped around her. It looked like the deacon was speaking to her, but she couldn't make out what he was saying.

She jumped when she felt the presence beside her. Chantelle. When the woman put her hand on Tati's shoulder, the underwater feeling disappeared. The deacon's words rang clearly in the small office.

"Tell me what happened when you found Father Andre," he said.

She explained how they had found the priest on the floor, then discovered the documents in the bottom of the canning jar box.

Tati struggled against the memory, trying to stop it from happening. Chantelle placed her hand on her forehead and whispered, "Just observe. We will unpack it after."

She settled back and took in the scene.

"Who has the documents now?" the deacon asked.

"They're at Thomas' head office. We're going through them."

"Who is helping? Who knows?"

Tatienne heard herself listing off Thomas' family members and the other people on the team. She tensed as she realised what the man had done.

Then the deacon placed his hand on her head and began chanting.

Mind's Peace

"What's he doing?" she whispered to the calm presence beside her.

"Removing your memories of this exchange," Chantelle replied.

"What about the nightmare images I saw? Did he plant those?" There was something else going on, she knew it.

"Hold on." Chantelle shifted, moving her hands to the back of Tati's head and neck.

When the woman spoke some ancient words, Tatienne relived the conflict with the deacon in the smoky landscape he had created. She saw the sorcerers, the cauldron and the flames. She fought back, harnessing her powers to stop the deacon. His arms burst into flames, and he pulled her out of the dreamscape.

"There's something else," she whispered to the soothing presence by her side.

"Let go," Chantelle said. Humming, the woman ran her hands down Tatienne's arms.

Tatienne relaxed and fell further into the vision.

Several nuns dressed in red danced at the edge of a river.

"How many nuns?" a voice asked. Her guide. She couldn't remember who it was, although the reassuring presence felt familiar.

She counted. One, two, three, four, five, six, seven. Seven nuns. Dancing at a river.

There were purple ropes – maybe pipes? – in the ground beside the river, going up, up, up. The sisters danced above them until a canoe drifted to them.

It was the men in robes again. The nuns scattered, but the brothers reached out with their magics and pulled them down. The women fell, crying. The colours of their clothing faded, leached out by the robed figures, who swirled the tones together with quarry stones and leaded glass. A red building emerged from their magics, nestled beside a lake that churned with blood.

190

The purple ropes snaked through the river to the chapel, pulsing. Tati followed them, her guide trailing along. Beside the church, buried underground, were many bones, sad and forgotten. Little ones and big ones, children and women who had been sacrificed to the robed ones, the Grey Brothers.

The flames grew inside Tati. She called out, but there was no one there. The flames swept out of her hands. They cracked the windows, the stones of the little chapel. The place burnt, incinerating the evil inside. As the flames subsided, so did her raging emotions. Everything dwindled, turning grey and silent.

Tatienne opened her eyes. She was back in the Mage room with Chantelle. "It's always fire."

"Pardon?" Chantelle asked.

"There's always fire in my dreams."

"Fire?"

"My parents died in a house fire." Tati dragged in a deep breath.

"I'm so sorry," Chantelle whispered.

"I had a dream about fire a few nights before it happened. I didn't understand what it meant."

"You think you could have stopped it?" Chantelle asked.

Tati nodded, her sight growing blurry.

"You would have needed proper training to prepare for a premonition like that. An unskilled young Mage is never to be blamed for experiences they have."

Tati wiped at the tears on her face. "I had another dream about a fire a couple of nights before Father Andre was attacked. If only I'd listened, I would have known something bad was going to happen."

Chantelle touched her hands. "You already know your Mage tendencies—premonitions and fire affiliations. Now we will work on accepting them and learning how to use them."

"I don't want anything to do with fire!" Tatienne sobbed.

"If your visions have some basis in reality, then you can harness the fire element. And you may be able to learn how to predict fire incidents. With time and training."

"If only I wasn't terrified by them." Tatienne bit down on her lip and swiped at her cheeks.

"We've got Mages here with experience in each element. We can find someone to help you learn how to use your gifts." Chantelle smiled at her. "You're in the right place."

"It seems like I was destined to come here and meet your family." Tatienne knew it sounded silly as soon as it had left her mouth, but Chantelle only nodded.

"The legends you have been reading, and the ones my granny recorded, tell of magical connections through the generations," Chantelle said. "They take a different view of time. It's cyclical, regenerative."

"So, the past repeats itself?" Tati asked.

"There are stories and events that are destined to happen again and again. For example, there are myths of couples who are born to mate and help their communities defeat their foes."

"Like you and Charles?"

"My partnership with Charles contains a magical bond that is deeper than the usual mating. There's a connection that transcends the two of us."

Tatienne didn't know what to say. But her heart told her Chantelle was right. She knew there was something special between her and Thomas too. Could it be connected to the shifter clan's past, or to her magical heritage?

"I know it sounds impossible. I just ask that you keep an open mind as we continue your training."

Tatienne nodded. "You've done so much for me. Your whole family has."

"Family is everything," Chantelle said.

"I'll try my best." Tati asked, "Do you know what it's like to fear a part of yourself?" She was afraid to look at Chantelle, but when she did the woman simply nodded at her. "I would love to overcome that fear. Learn to love myself. Help others."

"We can get you there. I promise."

* * * *

The next day, Thomas took Céline and Tati swimming at the pool.

It was Tatienne's first time joining the pair for a swim. Thomas had to cajole her into it, promising her a massage afterwards.

Céline had called it a bribe, but Thomas countered that it was a negotiation tactic. They had all laughed about it.

As they walked through the lodge to the pool, Tati talked about the support she'd had from everyone in the pack and clan. What a godsend. She wanted to make sure her sister was safe and happy. And Tati herself said she was feeling pretty good about things, too. She was more rested and content than she had been in a long time.

Thomas was happy Tati was getting to know his pack mates and friends. They were an important part of his life. He was pleased she was integrating well with his family and community.

The entire clan loved Tati and Céline. Elders greeted them, wide smiles and open arms as they walked past. Céline was such a loving person that it was natural to care for her, to show her affection. Tati had been closed off for so long that he had wondered if she would find it difficult to be in the clan. Many of the clan members could be nosy and interfering – they felt strongly about every voice mattering, which was true, but that meant they would voice their opinions loudly and without being asked for it. But Tati thrived with the attention.

They had scared Aimée off the rare times she came to visit the clan compound – she preferred instead to stay in the city with her friends. In contrast, Tati appreciated the closeness and community of the clan, blossoming under their care and love for Thomas and the pack. For everyone. She said it was such a different way of belonging and she appreciated it.

As they entered the pool area after changing, Céline approached Thomas, her brow furrowed.

"I need your help," she said.

"Sure. What do you need?" Thomas asked.

They walked down the stairs into the pool's shallow end while Tati grabbed a flutter board.

"You know my friend Samantha? Her family invited me on a ski trip next weekend. But Tati won't let me go."

Thomas frowned. "I don't want to get in the middle of you two."

"I know." Céline sighed and swished her hands through the water. "But I really want to go. Will you talk to her?"

"You know I can't say no to you. But I can't promise anything." Thomas' heart was so full it threatened to burst.

Céline said thanks and splashed off on her own as Tati swam over. Thomas took her arm and pulled her close for a kiss, feeling her smooth skin under his hands.

"Céline wants me to talk to you about the ski trip," he said.

"That imp!" Tati shook her head and put her arms on his shoulders. He snuggled her onto his lap, the water gently bouncing them together. "What did she say to you?"

"Not much. Just that she really wants to go. What are the details?"

"Samantha and her family are going with some other clan members to Mont Tremblant for a weekend ski trip. They got a good deal through a website."

"Sounds fun. Are there enough adults to chaperone the youth?"

Tati nodded. "Samantha's moms and her grandpère are going. There are also two other families."

"So, you're not worried about Céline being neglected?"

"No. And Samantha is a great girl. I like her family, too," Tati said.

"Then what's the issue?" Thomas asked, running a hand down her arm.

Tati sighed. "When you put it like that, I don't know why I said no."

"It's a big deal to entrust your sister to another family. You have Lynne and Diego, and Father Andre. But it's been just that small group for a long time."

"What if something goes wrong?" Tati said, biting her lip.

Thomas stole a kiss. "Can we send Vicky and Émile with them? Would that make you worry less?"

"Is that okay?"

"It's their job. Of course it's okay."

"Can we go and visit them for an afternoon, too? It would be nice to see the mountains there," Tati suggested.

"Of course. That would be fun." Thomas hadn't gone skiing all season.

Tati thought about it. "Okay. I will tell Céline she can go. Logically, I know nothing is going to happen. I'm anxious because we're still in the middle of a crisis with the Frères Gris and there's the border incursions with the Trois-Rivières Clan. I can't help but worry about everything."

"Let me help you shoulder the worry." He pulled her close.

"But you have your whole clan to worry about."

"That's the beauty of clan living." He nuzzled her cheek. "We support each other. We all have a lot of responsibility, but we help each other where we can. It's a labour of love."

"And what can I do to help with your responsibilities? Those broad shoulders of yours don't have to carry everything."

Thomas chuckled. "Be here for me. Keep bringing me peace."

She smiled and twisted out of his arms. "Let's go play, then."

He chased her as she swam away, content to forget his troubles for an hour or two.

Chapter Eighteen

Thomas had been working in his office for a few hours when his executive assistant Laurie buzzed. "Monsieur Ducharme, Miss Laflamme is here to see you."

"Send her in, please."

Tatienne strode in, wearing a simple but elegant red maxi dress, the flowing fabric showing off her gorgeous curves. He resisted the urge to pull it off and take her right there.

"Did Céline leave for her ski trip already? I'm sorry I couldn't see her off," Thomas said.

"They left an hour ago. You said goodbye to her last night, don't worry." She held up a picnic basket. "I thought I'd bring you some lunch." She grinned.

Thomas got up from his desk and came to kiss her. "This is a treat." She smiled and looked around his office. He loved using his father's oversized antique desk, but it didn't suit the modern look of the rest of the office.

When she turned around, she gasped. "The view!"

The corner office had floor-to-ceiling windows on two sides, facing straight into the Laurentians. He could look at the mountains and trees whenever he needed inspiration.

"I can't believe how gorgeous it is. How do you get any work done?"

Thomas tracked her form as she walked over to the windows, then sidled up behind her. "If you keep showing up, it's going to be difficult." He lifted up her hair and kissed her on the neck. After putting his arms around her, his chest against her back, they both stood together taking in the scenery. A feeling of bliss settled over him.

"Mmm, this is nice," she said. "But it isn't getting you to eat your lunch."

"I can think of other things I'd like to eat," he murmured, skimming his hands down the soft jersey fabric hugging her sides.

"You are naughty." She turned around, stood on her tiptoes and kissed him. "But you have to eat your lunch before you can have your dessert."

"I'm a grown-up. I can have dessert first." His whole body tingled.

She slipped out of his arms and pulled him back to the desk, grinning wickedly. Handing him the picnic basket, she led him to the seating area facing the bank of windows.

After she sat down, she said, "I still can't get over the view."

"Me too." He waggled his eyebrows. He loved making her laugh.

She opened the basket and pulled out the wrapped lunch items. He arranged the sandwiches and cut veggies and fruit on their plates. They chatted as they ate—nothing consequential, just easy conversation between lovers.

Once he had demolished the food on his plate, he asked, "Have I eaten enough yet?"

"Here, have some of this." Tatienne handed him a pastry in waxed paper.

He unwrapped it and took a bite. "Chef's butter tarts are out of this world." After he had eaten the treat, he took everything out of Tati's hands and placed it all on the table. "Okay, what's for dessert?" He licked his lips and kissed her lightly.

She stood and he pushed the coffee table out of the way. When he looked back up, she had pulled off her dress to reveal a dark red bra with a strappy high neckline and plunging cups that barely held her breasts in place. The matching panties had string details running along the top.

His wolf rumbled appreciatively. He liked this side of her. Both parts of him did.

"*Calisse*, I'm glad you're mine," he said. He unzipped his trousers and stroked his suddenly throbbing cock.

"And you're mine," she said, cupping her breasts.

He stopped and looked in her eyes. "Are you sure?" he asked.

She nodded, her eyes shining. "It might not be forever, but I want us to be together."

"Oh, *ma belle*."

He pulled her close to him and devoured her mouth, losing himself in her berry and hibiscus flavours. He played with her lingerie, following the strings along the waist of the panties to cup her cheeks. He wanted to touch her all over. Mark her with love bites.

She unbuttoned his shirt and ran her hands along his torso. He shivered at her touch. Growling, he lifted her up in his arms and carried her to the large conference table in front of the second bank of windows.

"Can everyone see us?" she asked.

"No, they're mirrored windows." He licked his lips.

She lay back on the table. After pulling off his shirt and trousers, he climbed up beside her and knelt over her, licking and nuzzling her breasts.

His skin tingled as he bit down on the straps of her bra, snapping each one in turn. When she moaned and wrapped her legs around his waist, his cock strained against his boxers. He skimmed a hand down her waist to the straps of her panties. With one pull, the thin strings broke and he bunched the fabric in his hand. Moaning, he pulled the ruined panties out from under her hips and returned his attention to her mouth-watering chest. She squirmed underneath him as he unhooked the fastener between her breasts. She sighed and he crawled forward to pull his cock from his boxers and rub it between her soft mounds.

When she squeezed his ass cheeks, pre-cum dribbled from the tip of his cock and he growled, deep and low.

He bent down to plant a soft kiss on her mouth, then he trailed his tongue between her breasts and down to her navel. She shuddered in pleasure as he licked and nibbled her skin. When he sat up to climb off the table, Tati whimpered and reached for him.

"Scooch forward to the edge," he murmured, pulling her forward. Her legs dangled off the table and he spread her thighs, kneeling in front of her beautiful pussy. A growl came from his chest as he admired her glistening lips. "This is going to be the best meal I've had at this table."

"Better than stale sandwiches?" She giggled.

"I've had some delicious gourmet meals prepared by Chef, but they are nothing compared to you."

He nipped playfully at her belly before moving his head down towards her centre. Blowing his breath on her mound, he reached out his tongue for a light flick on her bud. She gasped, urging him on.

He spread her folds with his fingers and nuzzled her sweetness. He drew his tongue along the labia, making long licks up and down. She ran her fingers through his hair and moaned. He moved to short strokes while he circled her button with the tip of a finger.

As he explored her pussy, moving his tongue in and out, he played with her clit until she was moaning in ecstasy. Then he brought his mouth to her button. He inserted a finger into her channel, looking for the sensitive spot as he thrust inside. When he touched the wall and she arched her back, he inserted another finger. He thrust his hand back and forth, using his fingers to bring Tatienne to the edge of a climax.

"Thomas," she gasped.

He wanted her to come. He loved the feel of her surrender, the way her eyes glazed over and she quivered in ecstasy. He thrust faster, sucking her button. She began to pant, her sighs getting louder and more urgent. He kept up the pace, her hips bucking in rhythm, until she went over the edge in wave after wave of pleasure. She held him tight as her orgasm gushed over his hand and mouth. He licked greedily, moaning his pleasure as she crested the final wave, then brought her hips back down to the table.

When he stood, she took his hands and pulled herself up to a sitting position. Once she had wiggled off the table, she took two steps to reach the window and turned around, her flushed and naked body framed by the snowy mountains. He took off his boxers and found the condom in his trouser pocket. He closed the distance between them, his cock rock hard. Taking another glance at the gorgeous creature in front of him, he put on the condom.

"That's mine," she said, reaching for his straining member.

"Is it?" He lifted her right leg and rubbed his cock against her wet slit. She moaned and her head fell back against the window. Then he inserted his throbbing tip inside her pussy and lifted her other leg, hooking his arms under her knees. He thrust in hard, and she bounced against him, her breasts jiggling and sending him closer to the edge.

After a dozen quick thrusts, he pulled out. "Turn around," he growled. She moved quickly, planting her hands on the glass and tipping up her buttocks. He spread her legs and reinserted his hard member from behind into her hot pussy, groaning as he slipped inside. With every thrust, he pushed her exquisite breasts against the glass. Tati moaned and gyrated her hips. He took her hands and extended them above her head while he picked up their rhythm. Her hot breath on the window nearly undid him.

He reached his mouth to her neck and grazed his canines lightly on the spot where her neck met her shoulder. His wolf urged him on, but he didn't bite down, instead enjoying the exquisite combination of pain and pleasure from being so close to claiming. One last thrust and he came as her pussy walls clenched around him. He sucked lightly on her neck. A love mark, but not a claiming yet.

They sank down to the floor against the windows, panting and clutching each other breathlessly.

"You are so sexy. I can't believe you're here with me." He kissed her and ran his hand down her side. "Will you visit me every lunch hour?" He grinned mischievously.

"You'd never get any work done!" She smiled. "You are perfect."

"No, I'm not." He laughed.

"You are perfect for me." She hugged him. "Now I have to go for my lessons with Chantelle. I don't want to be late." She stood up and threw on her dress. When she pulled out a pair of lace panties from her purse and waved them around at Thomas, he chased her around the office with a fake growl. He insisted on another kiss before she put her panties on.

"I love that you're going to smell like my sex all day. I want everyone to know you're mine." He found his clothes and started to dress.

"Everybody already knows," she said, shaking her head at him.

He pulled her into his arms. If only they could save this moment forever.

"Okay, I give up. Maybe we can have a bubble bath tonight together when you get home?" She waved and left the office, humming.

Home, he thought. *That's what it is, isn't it?* He started humming as he went back to work.

* * * *

The next evening, Tati heard a knock on the door of her suite. She answered and saw Thomas holding a pack of cards.

"Game night," he said.

Tatienne tried to calm herself. She smoothed down her favourite mocha jersey dress.

Thomas looked her over and a rumble came out of his chest.

"Nice to see you, too." She laughed. "Do you do this every month?" she asked.

"Chantelle instituted family game night as a new Ducharme family tradition when she married Charles," said Thomas.

"What kinds of games—Monopoly, Risk, Trivial Pursuit? All the ones I hate?"

"We've got all types of tabletop games."

"But what if I lose all the games?" Tatienne put her arms around him.

"You won't. And the games don't really matter." He hugged her. "Now, let's go!"

Thomas kissed her on the top of her head as they left the suite. They took the short walk through the main lodge and out to the row of chalets behind the building. Tati put on a cloak to ward off a chill wind blowing the snow around. Spring didn't come until June in the mountains.

They were last to arrive at Charles and Chantelle's chalet.

Tatienne looked around, gasping in admiration at the floor-to-ceiling windows at the front of the log cabin. She looked out at the compound. Everyone left their seasonal lights up all winter to brighten up the long, dark nights. It was a cheerful message that the dark of winter couldn't take their hopes away.

Henri and Juana were carrying bowls of snacks into the living room. Thomas' cousin Bertrand was introducing his date, Aasir. Aasir's dark-brown skin was set off by a red T-shirt.

"Have they been dating long?" Tatienne asked Thomas.

"Just a couple of coffee dates. It was brave of Aasir to agree to come tonight. But Bertrand says he grew up in a big family in Kenya, so he's used to noise and chaos."

Tatienne smiled and went to shake his hand. She was glad Thomas had a large family. She was proud of his kindness and loyalty, and she couldn't stop the feelings she had for him. All of them. The respect, the affection, the desire — everything.

Also, the fear. Opening up her heart had been scary. She was afraid for his clan's conflicts, and that she had put Céline in danger by pursuing this relationship. She worried she was selfish. And she was scared he would reject her after she had taken a chance with him. If he broke her heart, she didn't know what she would do.

Chantelle called the rowdy group to order for the official start to family game night. They began with a couple of crowd-pleasers — charades and a picture-drawing guessing game. Then they broke into smaller groups for some tabletop games.

Céline teamed up with Thomas in a round of Euchre with Bertrand and Aasir. Thomas joked around with the couple. He had told her his youngest cousin often chose serious partners, which left his fun side out of the equation. Aasir seemed like a better fit. And Bertrand was only eighteen years old. He needed to have fun and enjoy himself.

After they finished a couple hands of cards, Tatienne went to the kitchen.

Thomas was laughing with Bertrand as Tati grabbed a glass and turned on the faucet. It was so nice to hear him having fun, too. She was sorry Céline had missed the party, but maybe she could come next month. If they had moved back to the city by then, they could drive up for the weekend.

She filled up her glass of water and turned off the tap. Euchre wasn't her favourite game, but she didn't mind playing it with this group. Nobody was very competitive. They were just having fun. She took a sip of water as her head started to ache. It felt like a spike piercing into her left temple. Probably a migraine. She didn't get them often, but since they had been working on her magical powers, she had noticed some side effects.

Another spike in her forehead. She turned to the fridge. Perhaps some ice would ease the pain.

As she reached for the freezer compartment, the glass slipped from her hand and smashed on the floor. She opened her mouth, but no sound came out. Instead, she slumped to the floor and landed sideways, narrowly missing the corner of the fridge. She couldn't move. She saw shoes running into the kitchen, but she couldn't hear any noise. Then the lights went out as her eyes closed.

She opened her eyes. *How many minutes have passed?* Long enough for Thomas and Chantelle to be kneeling beside her. Long enough for the blood to drain out of Thomas' face. Charles was herding everyone else out of the kitchen and shushing them. He was right. It was too much noise.

She closed her eyes for another minute, then forced them open again.

Thomas was the first to see she was awake. He reached down to put his arms around her shoulders, but Chantelle stopped him.

"We need to examine her before you can move her."

Thomas clenched his jaw before nodding. Chantelle put a hand on his shoulder. Tati wanted to say something, but she was too dizzy.

Gwen, the Head Mage, appeared beside Chantelle and checked her pulse and shone a small light in her eyes. "You're right. It was magic-induced," She said to Chantelle.

"She's going to be fine," Chantelle said to Thomas.

"She has to be," he said, looking down at the floor. "I don't know what I'd do without her."

Tati held out her hand to Thomas and he took it, squeezing it gently.

"Was it another dream?" asked Gwen.

"More fire," she said, blinking to focus her eyes on the imposing woman. "A cauldron—I think it's a focal point for the men in robes."

"Frères Gris?" Thomas asked.

Chantelle flicked her gaze to him. "Likely. What else?" she murmured to Tati.

"They were chanting and making fire ropes. Does that make sense? I saw big lines—like hydro lines—threading through the mountains. And one of the sorcerers was on a computer. Why were they doing that?"

"Could you see the computer screen?" Chantelle asked.

"Not well."

"Concentrate," Chantelle said, resting her fingers on Tati's forehead. "Close your eyes and look back at your vision."

"They were flipping through files. There were photos of handwritten letters, old books and things like that."

Chantelle drew in a sharp breath. "Tatienne, look closely. Do you recognise any of the documents?"

Tatienne relaxed her shoulders and breathed deeply. Then her eyes snapped open. "Father Andre's books. But how could they —?"

Chantelle reached for Thomas. "Security breach. Did they access our server?"

"*Ostie!*" Thomas swore. He called his brothers and told Juana to get their cousin on comms. Tati remembered Michel hadn't come to the party because he was supervising the monthly server maintenance.

As the door closed behind them, Tati struggled to sit up. "What do we do?" she asked Gwen and Chantelle.

Gwen answered. "We wait for further instructions. If it's a cyberattack, then our security and IT personnel will take care of it."

"But if it's magical, then we will be called in," Chantelle said. "In the meantime, I want you to rest and see if there's anything else you remember."

Tati nodded. They helped her stand and move to the living room, where she could lie on the leather couch.

She hoped everyone would be okay. The bad guys might have gotten the electronic files, but she didn't want more blood on her conscience.

Chapter Nineteen

Thomas and Henri made it first to the server room. Juana arrived ten seconds later with weapons and passed handguns to the two men.

Heart pounding, Thomas threw open the door.

Smoke wafted into the hall. Thomas and the others coughed. He held his breath and entered the dark room. The employees were slumped over their desks, some lying on the floor.

Henri bent down and checked one. "They're alive."

Thomas let out a sigh of relief.

Juana went forward to the bank of machines at the far side.

Beside the servers, Michel was knocked out on the floor. That meant someone on the inside had helped. Maybe that was where the gas had come from, too.

After another security team arrived and evacuated the staff, Thomas, Henri and Juana looked at the machines. All their experts were unconscious. having been called in for the server maintenance. The Frères

Gris had chosen the time for their attack very strategically.

"Should we just close everything down?" Juana asked

"Let's get Bertrand over here," Thomas said. He'd been working with his older brother, Michel, and had gotten top marks in his computing classes.

While they waited, Thomas wondered if Tatienne needed him.

Henri bumped his shoulder. "Tatienne will be okay. Chantelle will look after her."

"I've got it bad for her." Thomas rubbed a hand over his face.

"I know, bro." Henri put his arm around him. "That's how I know she'll be okay. She's your Fated Mate."

"I thought you didn't believe in that," Thomas said.

Henri chuckled. "I see you with her and it's just like Charles with Chantelle. I believe in them, so I know it's true for you."

Thomas stood straighter. "You're right. We'll get through this."

Bertrand and Aasir showed up a few minutes later and got to work looking at the servers. Aasir was studying cybersecurity and helped Bertrand look over the connections. "We're having trouble getting through. The Frères Gris used magic to protect their incursion." The combination of technology and magic was a powerful force.

"What do we do?" Thomas asked.

"We'll have to shut the whole system down. It could take a few days to sort it out. By then, Michel and his staff should be able to help," Bertrand said.

Thomas contacted Gwen at Charles and Chantelle's chalet and gave her an update. Gwen said it would be better for her and Chantelle to stay with Tati at the chalet for now.

"Do you need anything else?" Thomas asked.

"Everyone's fine, don't worry," Gwen said.

When he got off the phone, Juana touched his shoulder. "I'll go and check on them since I can't help with the tech."

Thomas hugged her. "Thank you."

She shrugged. "I'll feel better being there. I can't do anything here."

He waved as she left the room, then turned to check on Bertrand's progress.

* * * *

Tatienne sat with Chantelle while Gwen spoke on the phone with Thomas. Gwen told them Juana was heading back to the chalet and Charles was coming with her, since they were getting the server room under control. Gwen would stay for an hour and confer with her colleagues, Gavin and Gareth. They would try to help with the magical side of the cyberattack.

"Could I help?" Chantelle asked.

Tati knew Chantelle was powerful, but Gwen shook her head. "For now, just rest up in case we need you later."

Chantelle nodded.

Tati still didn't understand why the computers were important, though it was likely the clan held a lot of private information in their databases. Her eyes filled with tears.

She felt so awful about being the one who had revealed the file information to the deacon. She should have known how to fight back and stop them from using her like that.

Chantelle asked, "How are you holding up?"

She wiped her cheeks. "I feel so guilty. It's all my fault."

"The Frères Gris are users. They exploit people."

"Still, I should have stopped them." The tears kept falling.

"You were compelled by a powerful Mage. You're not responsible."

Just then, Charles and Juana came through the door. Charles gave Chantelle a hug and nuzzled her hair. Such an intimate gesture–it showed they cared for each other, and they would look after the clan just as well. Charles was a lot like Thomas — caring and responsible, leaders who supported their loved ones and had learned to be supported in return. Her heart filled as she thought about extending her found family to include Thomas, then to his family and pack as well. What a bounty!

There were extra security personnel in the chalet, so someone started making tea and coffee.

"Why are there so many people here?" Tati asked.

"In the fall, the Trois-Rivières Clan marched into our compound and slaughtered several of our people," Chantelle said.

"The Alpha's residence — this chalet — was targeted and Chantelle and her security team almost died," Gwen said.

Tati drew in a sharp breath. "What happened?"

When Charles sat down behind Chantelle and folded her in his arms, he looked like Thomas. "My mate turned into a Fae Queen and knocked them on their asses — literally."

Chantelle shook her head. "It wasn't as impressive as it sounds."

Charles looked at her in disbelief.

"We were trapped in the basement, and I pushed my powers out. I knocked out all the attackers in the room," Chantelle explained.

"How did you do it?"

"It was in the heat of the moment," Chantelle said. "I didn't even know what I was doing. I just had to save my people." She rested her head against Charles' shoulder. "You are already further along in your training than I was."

Charles kissed her on the top of her head. "Do you remember how worried I was that night? Thomas is probably feeling the same about you, Tatienne."

Tati twirled a lock of hair in her fingers. She hoped Thomas was all right.

"Don't worry," Chantelle said. "He knows we'll take care of you."

A warm feeling spread through Tati's chest. This was how Céline and she operated, too. It was nice to have a group of people looking out for each other.

* * * *

Tati tried to close her eyes for a few minutes, but there was too much going on.

Juana had set up comms and a monitor in the den area on the second floor. Tati sat up when Juana came down the stairs with an update. Their people had shut down the network and disabled the Frères Gris' entry points. The IT staff would still have to work out how much information the attackers had taken and where they had broken through.

They had confirmed there was a mole. Someone on the maintenance team had left the room shortly before the gas came in and they didn't come back. Security was trying to locate them, but they weren't on the property. Tati was glad to hear the rest of the IT staff were recovering. They were experiencing some nausea and vomiting, but they would be all right in a day or two.

Tati sighed with relief.

Juana passed her a cup of tea. "If you hadn't alerted us to the cyberattack, things could have been a lot worse. The gas could have fatally poisoned the staff. And if the attack had gone too far, then we could have been locked out from our own systems."

Tati fidgeted with her hands on her lap. "What do we do now? Can I do anything to help?"

Chantelle said, "I'm going to wait on Gwen for an hour and then go to bed."

Charles said he would check in with Thomas. "He might need to stay up later. You can stay the night here. Your mate will feel better knowing you're with us."

"It's still weird to hear you guys talking about mates. I know it's part of your culture, but it makes it seem so permanent."

"I felt the same way after I met Chantelle. I had commitment issues." He laughed. "I coped by focusing on the present and not worrying about the future. I know it's not easy. If it feels right for now, then that's all that matters."

"Trust your instincts," Chantelle added. "Don't let the fear win."

Tati thought about that. "I can stay with you two. Will you let Thomas know I'm here?"

Charles nodded and excused himself, going to the den area to talk with Juana and make the call.

Chantelle said, "He'll be awake for a while, too. He finds it hard to sleep during a crisis. I could sleep through anything." She patted Tati's hand and Tati immediately felt calmer.

After a moment, there came a ruckus from the den. Juana and Charles were talking in raised voices.

"What's going on?" Tati said.

Chantelle stood up, but Charles reached them before she had left the seating area.

"There's been an incident," Charles growled.

"Incident?" Chantelle asked. "What do you mean?"

Charles looked at Tati. "It's at the ski lodge where your sister is staying."

Tati shot up out of her chair. "Is Céline okay?" Her heart bounced around her chest.

"We don't know any details yet."

Tati couldn't breathe. Chantelle put her arm around Tati's shoulder and gently sat her on the couch.

Juana joined them. "Vicky and Émile just called in. It's a hostage situation. They were attacked by a pack from the Trois-Rivières Clan."

"Do you have any cameras or anything there?" Tati asked. "Can we find out what's going on?" She tried to release her death grip on Chantelle's fingers.

Juana shook her head. "We don't own the lodge. We only have the reports from the people on the ground. And they aren't able to contact us continuously."

Tati's heart sank and she dissolved into tears in Chantelle's arms.

Thomas burst into the chalet and ran straight to Tati, his eyes wild. Chantelle stood so Thomas could take her place on the couch. When he sat, he hugged her like his life depended on it.

"I'll get her back. I promise." He pulled away, fire in his eyes, and growled, "I'm going to rip the Trois-Rivières Clan apart with my bare hands."

Charles tried to calm him down. "We need you to be our Lieutenant, stay alert and use your brilliant mind to bring everyone home safely."

Thomas took a deep breath. "Okay. Give me a minute."

Tati held his hand and sent her warmth to him, his coolness looping back to her. They offered their strength to each other and she knew it was going to be all right.

Thomas spoke. "I'll take two teams to the lodge. We'll land far enough away that we won't be detected. I'll try for a peaceful resolution but I won't hesitate to kill the other pack if they have hurt our people."

Tatienne stood up. "I'm coming with you."

Thomas shook his head, his lips in a firm line.

Chantelle stood as well. "I'll come too and stay with Tatienne."

Tati took Chantelle's hand again and whispered, "Thank you."

Thomas nodded, eyes still dark.

"I'll coordinate with you, Thomas," Juana said. "We'll bring them all home safe."

Tati's vision grew blurry as she hid her face in Thomas' chest.

Chapter Twenty

Tatienne could hardly sit still in the helicopter. "I shouldn't have let her go."

Thomas folded her hands inside his. "You didn't know this would happen."

"What's the use of having premonitions if I can't help my family?" She started sobbing.

He squeezed her hands and kissed her.

Chantelle spoke up. "It won't do any good to use up your energy in this. Let's see if we can get you focussed so you can help me on site."

Tati took some calming breaths. She was worried about Céline's friends and the other clan members. "How do you do this all the time?" she asked Thomas. "It's so much responsibility."

"It is," Thomas said, "But there is so much love in the clan that it's worth it."

Juana listened on her comms. "We got another call from Émile. A couple people have been injured.

They've got Tommy guns—two of them—and some handguns."

"Is Céline okay?" Tati's breath caught, but she had to know.

"Yes," Juana said.

A tide of relief surged through Tati.

"Here's the plan so far," Juana said. "We've got another team setting down about a half mile from the site. They'll go through the woods and come up the mountain side of the building. They'll wait until we give the word—we've got a Mage on the team, so if Chantelle needs to communicate telepathically, there will be someone to receive her messages. They'll be prepared for anything."

"What about us?" Tati asked. She had to do something. She couldn't just wait around.

"Thomas and I will go inside. The outside team will wait for us and make their plan based on our assessment."

"We are planning to negotiate," Thomas said. "Juana and I will start out alone."

"I want to come in with you," Tati said.

"I don't want the situation to escalate. If just the two of us go in, it's less likely to overwhelm the kidnappers. We can find out what they want and attack if necessary–and I'll make sure Céline is okay."

"I don't know if I can stand it." Bile rose in her stomach.

Thomas looked at her. "You are strong. Reach deep down for that part of you that protects your sister, the part that would do anything for her family."

She squeezed his hand.

Juana cocked her head and listened on the comms. "Okay, the other team is landing. We are five minutes out. Everybody, take a moment to clear your head and get ready."

"You can do this." Chantelle reached across to Tati and put her hands on her shoulders. "We don't need to be in the same room like the warriors do. We can work our magic from another location, even."

Tati remembered the ropes of purple light from her premonition. And the cauldron and cavern. Maybe she could reach beyond her physical place and find out more information at the ski lodge. She could help get her sister and their clan members to safety.

Soon, the helicopter was touching down in a clearing beside a traditional ski lodge. She was so nervous she wanted to vomit. When Thomas laid a hand on hers, his coolness helped to calm her. She gave him a tentative smile and nodded her head.

Someone with a machine gun came out of the lodge. Only Thomas and Juana got out. They went over and talked with the solitary figure. He was gesticulating but didn't point the gun at them.

Another greasy-looking man arrived. Then the two escorted Thomas and Juana into the building.

She breathed out.

"Now we let them do what they do best," Chantelle said, "You can trust your mate."

Tatienne wondered if she and Chantelle could do anything about the situation at hand.

"I could try and connect with Thomas like you can do with Charles. We did it that one time at the church."

Chantelle nodded. "Take it slowly."

She closed her eyes and reached out. She couldn't sense much, just general feelings of anger and fear. Nothing that felt like Thomas.

Her eyes snapped open when the helicopter door was yanked open. Tati and Chantelle didn't have time to fight back before they were picked up and dragged into the lodge.

When they were pushed through the foyer and into a large reception room, Tati saw Céline and her friends. Her sister looked scared, but she wasn't hurt. Hope bubbled in Tati's chest.

Thomas sensed Tatienne before he saw her.

Two Trois-Rivières Clan members who had brought him and Juana into the lodge had disappeared for a few minutes. He felt some impressions, not as strong as last time — a ripple of surprise from Tati in the helicopter, then anger as she started moving. Thomas didn't know how, but he could tell that she was coming towards him.

He braced himself. He would know if she were hurt, wouldn't he? But what if this connection was unreliable? They hadn't claimed each other as mates yet. For now, their bond could be patchy.

The missing kidnappers reappeared, pushing Tatienne and Chantelle in front of them. Thomas breathed out a whoosh of air. They both looked unhappy, but not injured.

Juana reached a hand to his arm. He tried to stay calm. Tatienne glanced at him. She was doing the same.

Then the Trois-Rivières Clan members murmured and made a space by the door. Thomas' people looked around.

Their rival clan's Lieutenant, Louis "The Thunder" Lalonde, entered the room, a dark hoodie and black jeans on his enormous frame. He had been an amateur boxer for some years before joining the Reynards' security team and rising to Lieutenant. His broken nose and the asymmetry of his face were matched by his usually dark expression. But today his features were arranged into a nasty smile.

"You're here," he announced, looking at Thomas. Flicking his eyes to his people, he snarled. "Gather up the Ducharmes. And those two." He pointed at Tati and Juana.

Growling, Thomas leapt towards the Lieutenant. Louis stepped back, allowing his guards to form a barrier between the two. Thomas lunged and they held him back.

The Lieutenant smirked. "The one with the tits is yours, isn't she?" Louis looked at Tati and leered. Tati stood her ground and threw him her meanest glare.

Thomas wanted to kill Louis.

Chantelle caught his eye and shook her head almost imperceptibly. What was she up to?

Thomas and Juana kicked at the guards, breaking free and bloodying some noses in the process. Their weapons had been confiscated, but they used hands, teeth and feet to inflict damage and keep the guards busy.

When Chantelle hugged Tati and whispered to her, Thomas hoped nobody else noticed their exchange. Fighting was a good way to get out his pent-up emotions, using his anger and fear about Tati and her sister as fuel. He could see Céline with Samantha's family. Vicky and Émile flanked her and the family, doing their best to protect them. Thomas knew they'd defend them with their lives. They all would protect their family and their pack. Céline was safer where she was—it wouldn't do any good to draw attention to her connection with Tati and Thomas. She was safer in the group.

Then Louis "The Thunder" uttered the words that made his heart sink. "Get those ones together. And don't forget the sister." He inclined his head towards Céline. "Kill the rest."

Tati cried out and made a run for Céline. The kidnappers grabbed her and forced her back.

Vicky and Émile stepped out in front of Céline. Their weapons were gone, but they were ready for hand-to-hand combat. The kidnappers stepped towards the two guards. In the blink of an eye, they tasered Vicky and Émile, who crumpled to the ground. Tati screamed and struggled against the people holding her.

Chantelle took advantage of the chaos and nodded at Thomas and Juana. Juana made a sign and the remaining security people quickly fanned out, trying not to be detected.

A moment later, Thomas spoke to their people. "Get down!"

Most of the clan members turned and looked at them, sinking to the floor as realisation dawned on their faces. Samantha and Céline grabbed each other and they crouched down.

Another moment and Chantelle acted, closing her eyes and reaching out her arms. The energy pulsed from her hands and the Trois-Rivières Clan members collapsed to the ground. Even the Lieutenant was down.

Two more beats…then the outside team broke in through the large picture windows overlooking the mountains, landing on the floor. They cocked their guns and looked around at the rival clan members on the floor. Several other guards filed into the doorways.

Some of them started triage for first aid with the Laurentian Mountain Clan community, while others started tying up the hostage-takers. It was chaotic, but the worst of the crisis was over. His people were safe.

Thomas found Céline at the same time Tati did and gathered them both in his arms. His heart stuttered in his chest.

"Are you okay?" he asked them.

Céline nodded. "How about Samantha and her family? And Vicky and Émile?" she said.

"I'll check on them in a minute," Thomas said. He held them close to his chest.

Thomas took Céline and Tati over to Chantelle, who was resting on a couch in the corner of the room. One of the medics brought over several bottles of water. Thomas thanked her and distributed them.

He crouched down in front of Chantelle and Tati. "Can I leave you here for a few moments? Should I bring a medic?"

Chantelle said, "We're fine. Go take care of things and I'll stay with Tati and Céline."

Thomas nodded and sought out Juana. Then he talked to the families who had been held hostage. There were some minor injuries, but nothing that couldn't be healed.

His shoulders sagged. It had been a long day and it was going to be even longer before they were done here.

Chapter Twenty-One

Tatienne clutched at Céline, trying to calm her heartbeat. "I was so worried."

"We were fine, Tati," her sister said. "I knew Vicky and Émile would look after us."

"You were so brave," Chantelle added, looking at both of them. "Did the kidnappers say anything to you, Céline?"

"They asked me about my sister. And about Thomas. I didn't tell them anything."

"I know you didn't," said Tati.

Juana approached them, her mouth set in a hard line. "Are you okay?" She knelt and checked Céline over.

"A medic already looked at me," Céline protested.

"*Ma chouette*, that's true." She looked in her eyes. "But Thomas has been like a brother to me since I was a teenager and you and your sister are very dear to him. I would never forgive myself if anything happened to you."

"I like you, too." Céline gave her a hug.

Juana wiped at her eyes. When she rested her hands on Tati's and Chantelle's knees for a brief moment, a spark like electricity zinged through Tati and into the other women.

"What was that?" Tati asked as the tingles subsided.

Juana stood up, wringing her hand. "I don't know. Probably just static electricity."

Chantelle looked at both of them, not speaking.

Thomas approached. "Juana, we've got several hostage-takers in restraints. I need your advice on their Lieutenant. I may have broken his hand."

Juana excused herself and hurried away with him.

"What do we do now?" Tati asked.

"If you're up to it, you and I can examine the seized weapons for traces of magic."

"Sure." Chantelle called Vicky and Émile over to sit with Céline. The guards moved slowly but smiled when they saw Céline. "I'll be back soon," Tati said.

Chantelle found Patti, the magic-user from the security team that had gone around the front of the building. She took them to the weapons they had taken from the Trois-Rivières Clan members. Chantelle showed Tati how to hold her hand over top of the item first, gauging if anything emanated from the weapon before putting a hand on it. It took Tati a few tries, but soon she could get a reading from the guns.

An old knife with a wooden handle looked out of place with the modern weapons. The blade was made of iron and inscribed with runes. Purple power — it had a colour and feel — flowed from the blade. Trying to get a better sense of its magic, she rested her hands on its handle.

When Tatienne touched it, she found herself in a dark cave with a fire glowing red at one end. She looked for distinguishing marks, but it was empty except for a large metal cauldron sitting over the fire and some chains on a wall.

By the chains was an old door. Tati walked over for a closer look. It was rusty and heavy, but Tati managed to heave it open. She stepped through it and into the night.

Three women stood in a dark clearing, lit only by the flames of a large bonfire. They held hands, their simple white dresses stained with blood and dirt. The fire glowed behind them, lighting up like auras around the figures. Their heads were held high, reminding Tati of the pictures in her children's Book of Saints.

Men in dark robes circled the women, chanting. One of them took a knife from beside the fire – the knife Tati was holding. He went to each woman in turn, grabbed her wrist and made a small cut with the knife. Another dark figure followed behind him and collected their blood in a black bowl. The women wailed and the dark-robed brothers tied their hands and bound them to large wooden posts set in a semicircle around the fire.

Tatienne was caught up in the women's feelings, as if they were her own. Fear, anger and determination coursed through her.

The men poured the bowl of blood into the simmering cauldron and stirred the fire. One man left the circle and returned carrying a bundle. A cry issued from his arms.

It was a child.

"No!" the women shouted. Tatienne's heart broke when the child gave a keening wail.

Then the impossible happened.

One of the women broke from her bonds and flew – flew in the air – to the child.

Fire crackled around them as she flung out her arms. She pointed at the robed sorcerers and they fell to the ground. The flames rose higher as she freed her sisters. They embraced and moved quickly to the child.

As the sorcerers remained motionless, the woman picked up the child and led the others into the forest.

When Tati returned from her vision, she still clutched the knife. "Whose weapon is this?" she asked.

"Louis, the Lieutenant," Patti said.

"Where did he get it, I wonder? There's a connection to the Frères Gris from it."

Chantelle looked at it. "It's powerful. These markings relate to blood rites."

"These robed figures were taking blood from Mages. And they were going to sacrifice a child." Tati shuddered at the memory.

"I'll tell Gwen right away," Chantelle said. "We have to get this weapon back to our Mage lab."

Tati sighed. At least one good thing had come from this horrible day. After Chantelle left with the knife, she sought out her sister. A wave of relief coursed through her that Thomas was sitting with her. He stood and hugged her, sending the cool stamp of his reassurance straight to her soul.

"If you're done, we can take Céline back to the compound," he said.

She nodded and took their hands. Together, the three of them left the building and boarded the helicopter. As soon as they were in the air, exhaustion overtook Tati and she fell asleep.

* * * *

A few days later, Thomas knocked on the door of Tati's suite. He adjusted his gi, feeling foolish, even though his swim trunks were more revealing than the karate uniform. He preferred workout clothes, but Tati had asked him to go to the gym so they could practice self-defence.

They travelled through the lodge to the gym. When they reached the double doors, he showed Tatienne through to a large open space. The gym was simple and workable — workout machines to the one side and mats for hand-to-hand combat on the other. Time was set aside for team sports in the evening, while during the day, individuals practiced and experts gave group lessons.

Juana, the Clan Defender, was in her happy place, her glossy black hair French-braided in a long queue down her back. She moved quickly through the motions of their clan's specialised grappling techniques. After the demonstration, she circled through her class to observe and correct the students' movements. Thomas admired her skill. She was a fine asset to the clan.

"There's Henri." Tatienne pointed to the back of the gym.

His younger brother was working with a small group of new recruits in white uniforms tied with white belts. Henri walked them through the first set of techniques. He was one of their best fighters, when he was focussed.

Juana approached Henri's group and offered some pointers while Henri sparred with a partner. Then Juana gestured and the recruit stepped back to the far side of the mat.

"We should watch this." Thomas took Tati's hand and they walked over to Henri's group.

Juana picked up a pair of fighting sticks and threw Henri one. He and Juana bowed and circled each other on the mat. Henri feinted, then pulled back. Juana advanced a step, flicked her stick and stepped out of range. Thomas smiled. She was looking to throw Henri off-balance. Henri advanced and swung. She jumped backwards and he missed. They began a complicated dance around the mat, a series of steps forward and backward, with their long sticks weaving in and out between their bodies and arms.

Tatienne breathed, "They're good."

"Henri will be a strong tactical leader. He has the combat skills to best almost anyone in the clan, but he needs to mature a little still."

"I think he's going to be ready sooner than you think," she said.

Juana was smiling. She was light on her feet, muscular and fast. Henri had a heavier build. He was already sweating from the exertion.

Thomas chuckled. Juana was toying with Henri.

As Henri got more aggressive, he started to make some mistakes. Juana got her stick in close enough to sweep behind his knees.

Henri tried to jump, but it was too late. He landed on his back. Juana knocked the stick out of his hands. Moving lightning fast, she pounced and pinned him on the mat.

Juana's face was inches above Henri's, and both were panting. She smiled. As she looked in his eyes, the energy changed. Crackling, it sparked through the room. Murmurs broke out across the gym.

Thomas squeezed Tatienne's hand. That hadn't happened before — that electricity. *What is it?*

Juana was the first to break, moving back to straddle Henri and put her stick to the side. Breathing heavily, she spread her hands on Henri's chest and leaned over. Thomas could have sworn she sniffed his neck and shoulder. Henri lay motionless under her, eyes closed and a low rumble radiating from his chest.

Tatienne moved closer to Thomas, running her hand along his arm as if she sensed it, too. Whatever it was.

The combatants pulled away at the same time — Juana jumping to one side and Henri rolling the other way. They stood and bowed to each other, Henri's eyes glued to Juana's. But the spell was broken.

Thomas called to the pair. Juana turned, saw Thomas, waved then walked over. Henri watched her go, eyes trained on her like a lovesick puppy. He shook himself, took one last wistful look and turned back to his group of recruits to continue their lesson.

Juana patted Tati's arm. "Thanks for coming." She led the pair to a nearby mat. "Let's see what you know already."

She led them through the fundamental defensive movements used by their clan, explaining that all clan members received basic training to help them develop discipline. "Those who are interested move on to offensive training," she said. "Those who choose to join the security teams also take weapons training."

"Tatienne, you seem to be a natural," Thomas said. "I'm impressed." She moved through the techniques effortlessly.

"Some of the postures remind me of the martial arts my grandmother taught me when I was little. She said it was a special form of self-defence her family had brought from the old country."

Thomas wondered what it was. He had questions, but Juana stopped him.

"Show us," the Clan Defender ordered.

Tatienne moved into an upright position and closed her eyes for a minute, taking deep breaths. After she moved through several forms, he looked at Juana. Her eyes were wide, taking it all in. The techniques looked familiar.

Tatienne finished the first sequence and looked up. "What?" she asked.

"That's a form of the ancient *Duvell Hud*, with a few variations," Juana said. "I've seen it performed at international gatherings by Mage historians. Our clan traditions combine them with modern Mage arts and other spiritual traditions. It's rare for transmission of the original to be passed down by living family tradition."

"Oh," said Tatienne.

"Your grandmaman's family came from Brittany?" Thomas asked.

She nodded. "It feels right to practice a piece of my grandmother's heritage. Granny went through the movements every day together when I was growing up."

"Show us some more," said Thomas.

Tatienne went through a few more movements, while Juana adjusted her stance and refined some gestures. Then the Defender showed her how to adapt a couple of the movements into fighting techniques. They worked together for a few minutes before Juana called a halt.

Juana asked Tatienne to come back the next day for some more lessons. "You've got a great foundation and we can build in some more fighting techniques so that you'll feel more prepared in the battle."

Tatienne nodded, her confidence shining. Thomas thought she was a wonder. How many more secrets did she have?

* * * *

Tati walked with Thomas back to her apartment. She invited him in for hot chocolate. "Céline's out with friends until after dinner."

While she got out the mugs, Tatienne asked, "Has Juana been in the clan her whole life?"

Thomas shook his head. "She showed up at our compound when she was about fourteen or fifteen. Kicked out of her pack. She had travelled alone all the way from New Mexico."

"Does that kind of thing happen to shifters?"

"More than I'd like. Especially to women and children in certain packs. Some Alphas require submissiveness and can be cruel to those who refuse."

"That's horrible!" Tatienne shuddered to think not all clans were as equitable as the Laurentian Mountain Clan.

"My brother Henri took a shining to Juana—they became good friends. The three of us got into a lot of trouble when we were young. Nothing serious, just having fun and not thinking about the consequences. Those two are adrenaline junkies."

Tatienne passed him a mug, then sat on a stool beside him at the kitchen island, their legs touching. When he leaned on the counter, she watched the muscles flex in his forearms. He was quite a specimen.

"Juana has been like family ever since. It took her some time to trust us, but now she's her cool badass self." Thomas took a sip from his mug. "Her wolf is beautiful. Dark brown with yellow eyes."

"Why haven't you dated her?" Tatienne asked. "She's gorgeous."

"Gross! Too much like dating a sister or cousin." He put down his mug. "Besides, Henri's always had a crush on her."

"That's so cute! I saw the way he was looking at her."

"Henri has some growing up to do before he could take her on. But I keep hoping one day…" He smiled at her, and she melted.

Thomas reached over to brush her hair over her shoulder. His hand rested gently on her back, making small circles and setting her skin on fire.

She relaxed her shoulders. "When I first met you, I didn't know what to think. You were rich, smart and way out of my league." He stopped moving his hand. "But you're so sweet and kind—not at all like I expected." He let his hand drift down to the small of her back.

"You are everything I hoped for and more," he said hoarsely.

He looked up and she stared into his grey eyes. He moved to perch on the edge of his seat, pushing his legs up against hers. Reaching forward, he took the cup from her hands and placed it on the table. He kissed her roughly, invading her mouth, reaching into her hair and pulling her closer.

Tati pulled him off the stool and dragged him to her bedroom. They quickly undressed and he put on a condom. Thomas trailed his mouth from her neck to her breasts. He brought her nipples to attention, the buds snapping up—one in his mouth, the other in his hand. He pressed his torso against her centre and she rubbed herself on him, sighing.

They lay on the bed, hands roving across naked skin. She couldn't get enough of this man. She braced her elbows on his chest and manoeuvred so she could push him onto his back.

"Oh, *chérie*," he sighed.

She straddled him, bringing her hips down and rubbing the tip of his cock on her clit. She moaned as he thrust upwards, his wolf rumbling beneath her hands.

She moved her centre up and forward to position his thick cock at her pussy. He groaned and swivelled his hips, seeking her entrance. After a moment of exquisite anticipation, she bore down — slowly — until she had enclosed him to his hilt. She liked seeing his eyes half-closed with desire, his teeth biting his lower lip. When she put a finger to his mouth, he sucked on it greedily.

They began moving together, slowly at first. Soon neither could hold back as she bucked and gyrated on top of him, bracing her hands on his hard chest. Panting, he grabbed on to her hips as though they were a life raft. She climbed higher, seeking release. When it came, it was earth-shattering. She tossed back her head and arched her back in ecstasy. She looked down and his dark eyes glinted with yellow flecks as he whispered, "*Caradec.*" Then he was coming too, filling her up with his desire, riding her through the waves of ecstasy only he could bring her.

She collapsed on top of him, her body like jelly. She was happy. She hadn't worried about the past or the future — she'd just focussed on the two of them together in the here and now. Something inside her eased and she fell asleep in his arms.

Chapter Twenty-Two

A few days later, Tatienne strode through the Mage Wing. She stopped at Chantelle's office. After pushing her shoulders back, she knocked and entered the half-open door.

"Can we talk?"

"Sure." Chantelle smiled and gestured Tatienne to the chair in front of her desk.

Tati sat down, her heart pounding. "I think I know how we can stop the Frères Gris. And I need your help."

"What can I do?"

"I've been thinking about what I saw when I touched the knife," Tatienne explained. "It must be connected to the Frères Gris Consortium."

"Needing sacrifices for blood rites would explain the disappearances you read about. The ones linked to the Grey Brothers. We've tracked more recent examples, too," Chantelle said.

"Blaming the missing people on superstition or other groups would be in line with sorcerers trying to hide their actions," Tati added.

"We had assumed the Trois-Rivières Clan was involved in human trafficking. They may well be, but it's likely they are supplying humans and shifters to the Frères Gris for their rituals."

"Their sorcery feels wrong...evil? Oily? I don't know how to describe it."

Chantelle nodded. "I know what you mean. Likely they use it to extend their lives and work their rites. They think they are above law and justice."

Suddenly nauseous, Tati folded her arms around her stomach. "What do we do?"

"We have to find them. Stop them."

Her heart pounded again. *I can do this.* "I think I can find them. If I go back into my dream vision state, then I can try and trace their location."

"I don't know." Chantelle raised her eyebrows. "It's dangerous."

"The other option is I let them capture me. Then you contact me psychically and trace my location."

"No way," said Chantelle. "Thomas would never agree to that."

Tati raised her hands in surrender. "I know. That's why I'm suggesting we go through the alternate plane."

Chantelle drummed her fingers on the top of her desk. "If I asked some other Mages to work with me, we might be able to do it."

"The cauldron is a focal point. My goal would be to home in on that. It's in a cave or something like that."

"Do you sense anything else about this place?"

"I think the red church and the nuns I saw in my vision are part of the answer. Yesterday, I found references to a group of Grey Nuns performing a miracle on the bank of the Rouge River. The story is associated with a section of the river called the Seven Sisters Rapids. Seven sisters, seven nuns — just like in my dream."

"We need to look into that area. Is there anything else?" Chantelle asked.

"I'm not sure if it's important, but I've seen these purple light strands, sometimes thin and sometimes big as ropes."

"Connections between people can appear this way."

"They're like telephone lines, or something underground."

"That sounds different. More like ley lines."

"Maybe they are a connection or a way to track them."

"Okay," said Chantelle. "I'll bring this information to Gwen and see what she wants to do. I expect she'll want to be involved in the experiment attempt."

"How long will it take to set it up?" She wanted to get it over with as soon as possible now that she'd made the decision.

"Maybe a day, maybe two. We'll have to make sure we're ready and we can minimise the danger to you."

Tati nodded. "I'll go talk to Thomas." She twirled a lock of hair in her fingers. She wasn't looking forward to the conversation.

* * * *

"No way. *Tabernak!*" Thomas paced in the living room of his suite. "Have you lost your mind?"

"I am perfectly aware of what I'm suggesting."

"You can't be. Otherwise, you wouldn't have suggested it." He turned around and came to stand in front of her. "I couldn't deal with it, knowing you were in danger and not being able to do anything."

"I'm the one who can access the dreamscape. It's my connection we need."

"Can't they find somebody else? You've just started learning about your powers."

"I've already picked up some clues in my visions. And with our research on the Frères Gris, I think I can interpret their whereabouts."

"Don't do this to me!" Thomas scrutinised her face, his eyes shining.

"You got me into this mess," she replied. Her stomach churned as she looked at his anguished expression. She reached out for his hands. "I didn't mean it that way. I'm involved. I want to help."

He squeezed her fingers and brought them up to his mouth. "I feel guilty enough already. What would happen if I lost you because you risked yourself for the clan in this way?"

Tati straightened up, jutting out her chin. "Thomas, *mon loup*, my wolf. Risking yourself for your clan is literally your job as Lieutenant of the clan. Why would you think your mate wouldn't feel the same way and do the same thing?"

"Don't play the mate card on me." He growled low, pulling her into his embrace. "That's a dirty trick."

She smiled into his hard chest, snaking her arms around his torso. Then she looked up at him. "You have to trust me. I want to help save the clan, just as you do."

"Tati." He sighed. "I wouldn't want to be with you if you weren't brave and strong."

"You have to grant me the power to make my own decisions."

"I don't like it." He released her and started pacing again. "What if something goes wrong?"

"Chantelle asked some other Mages to participate. I'm sure they'll keep me safe."

He stopped. "I can't do it. I can't say yes."

"Thomas?" she whispered.

"I just found you. If you — if you didn't make it, I wouldn't survive." He buried his face in his hands.

"Thomas," she said.

"It's too dangerous."

"Thomas, don't make me choose between saving the clan and being with you." The tears fell on her cheeks.

"You're breaking my heart!" He ran out through the door, leaving Tati alone with her sorrow.

Chapter Twenty-Three

When Tatienne entered the Mage training room, she made out two figures in the darkened space. Chantelle and Gwen were lighting candles in the corners of the room. The hum of protective energies swirled around her.

A pang of grief stabbed through her when she thought about Thomas. *He should be here with me.* Instead, she hadn't seen him for two days. Céline told her Thomas would get over it. She hoped her sister was right. Tati sat on the floor, in the middle of a pentacle enclosed in a full moon circle. She tried to tamp down the fear in her chest. Gwen and Chantelle joined her.

Two Mages entered and Gwen introduced them. "I believe you've met my friends, Gavin and Gareth. They'll complete our set of five Mages for the session."

The men grinned at her with watchful eyes. Like most of the Mage presences she had met in the clan, they radiated peace and calm. As they sat down, the circle clicked and the pressure of the magics increased. She felt energised. Nervous, excited and…powerful.

Chantelle had told her she would be working with the dominant Mages of the clan. It was true.

As all five joined hands, Gwen spoke up. "We're going to help you access the dream vision-scape. Then we'll figure out how to connect with the sorcerers."

Tati nodded and closed her eyes.

"Just like we practiced. Feel yourself falling into the vision state," Chantelle said. "When you're comfortable, look around and describe what you see."

Tati took her time breathing and counting backwards from one hundred. *It's just like a regular meditation. Don't be afraid.*

She wished she had consciously accessed the dream vision-scape more often. It controlled her more than she controlled it. But maybe that would change today.

As she relaxed, she opened herself up to her psychic surroundings. Eyes still closed, she used her other senses, hearing the hums of energy, feeling the warmth of her fire spirit course through her limbs, smelling the herbs Chantelle burnt There were whispers on the perimeter. Opening her eyes, she caught faint presences on the smoky horizon. A faint purple glow of fibres swished in undulating lines in the background.

As she got used to her surroundings, she cast out feelers. Chantelle had told her to visualise them as tendrils extending from her centre. They allowed her to extend her senses out in several directions at once. She had learned not to rely only on sight in the visions, although it was a powerful aspect of the experience. But the tastes, touches, smells and sounds were also important.

The whispers got louder as she extended her tendrils. She chased them, moving slowly so as not to startle them. She couldn't pick out words very well, but it sounded like dozens, maybe hundreds of voices.

She stood up in her psychic body, gliding through the space. The whispers led her over the mountains, to a river, churning red. *Rouge River*. She lifted her body up into the air and followed the river's course upward, flying against the current.

She followed the river past a set of rapids — the Seven Sisters. She could make out the voices of Deacon Brébeuf and Father Genette. What were they saying? She followed their voices to a lake, where a little chapel painted red was set on the mountain side.

She landed on the ground and opened the chapel door. It looked like a small church from the pioneer times — like the one in the diary the Trois-Rivières Clan had taken. She walked through the church to a small, wooden door behind the altar. Passing through it, she stepped down a narrow wooden staircase into a stone tunnel.

The purple lines lit her way into the mountain.

She followed their glow through the tunnel until it opened into a large stone cavern.

There were three shadowy figures in dark-grey robes chanting by the fire. She stepped on a piece of kindling and it snapped.

"Ahhh, there you are," one of the brothers spoke in a raspy voice. "I thought I sensed your presence."

"Come over and see us," another brother crooned.

She stepped backward, shaking her head. Although her physical body was still at the Laurentian Mountain Clan compound, she was certain they could keep her mind — or was it her soul? — there if they chose to do so. She had to find a way out and back to her clan.

"You can't stop us," the first one said. "We are ancient. We will live on and you will die."

The third figure stepped towards her. "So much power. We could use her."

She tripped and fell, fear gripping her throat.

The three sorcerers closed in, placing their hands upon her.

She felt the pull of their magics and fought to keep them at bay.

"This will hurt," one cackled. "But it will be worth it to have you here with us."

"No," she cried. *How can I escape? If they trap my consciousness there, then it won't matter that my body is elsewhere, will it?*

The brothers talked to each other about how they wanted to keep her with the others. One of the children was growing weak and she could replace him.

She tried to reach out to find Chantelle—anybody. But she was too weak.

The sorcerers chanted and held her hands to her sides. As they continued their spell, she became immobile and slipped away into oblivion.

* * * *

Thomas felt Tati's fear as he was swimming laps. He had come to clear his mind and stay away from their dangerous plan. But he couldn't stop their connection, even if they were fighting. As he stopped and listened, his stomach churned.

She needs me.

He swam to the edge of the pool and got out. Throwing a towel around his middle, he rushed through the lodge to the room where his mate's presence called to him.

He hadn't prayed since he was a child. He thought now might be the time to start again. Anything to help his mate.

When he reached the working room, he pushed open the door. Chantelle cradled an unconscious Tati while the others chanted. He could smell the fear in the air.

"Thomas, I'm glad you're here," Gwen said. "We'll try to follow your connection to her, like Chantelle and Charles can do."

"Anything it takes." Thomas came forward and took Chantelle's place. His heart stuttered as he looked down at Tati's blank face.

What have I done?

"They must be using some sort of magical force to sedate her or keep her mind there," Chantelle said, her voice trembling.

"I can get to her," Thomas said. He had to. Their bond was strong — it would be enough for him to reach her.

The Mages resettled in the pentacle on the floor, while Thomas held Tati in the centre. "What if they find out how powerful she is and they've already killed her?" He squeezed his eyes shut.

"You would know if that happened. You can still feel her, can't you?" Chantelle said.

He stopped and concentrated on their bond. It was still there. He nodded.

"Okay, then let's help her." Chantelle's voice grew steady again.

They settled down again and quickly formed a link. Gwen traced the threads and called on the others' powers to follow the lines.

Gavin said, "That leads to Céline." Chantelle said two more lines led to Montréal. "But there's another one over here."

"Thomas, I need you to concentrate. Can you close your eyes and try to visualise your connection with Tati?"

Thomas closed his eyes and reached for Tati with all his love. He sought her presence, looking for his mate, the one who made him whole. The Mages poked and prodded. Then he heard it — a light and airy whisper. The slight tug of his Fae princess pulling him towards her.

"I found it. But is it real or a trap?" he asked.

Gavin said, "It could be a trap, but we're only going to know if we go in. Here, let me see if I can get through." The Mage poked at the thread, but there was a barrier preventing them from reaching the other end.

Thomas followed him, desperate for a connection with Tatienne. She was waiting at the end of the thread, he knew it.

Then she reached him and suddenly he was flying through the mountains, over the trees and up the river in the dreamscape.

He landed beside his mate, overwhelmed by emotions. She was groggy and slow to put her arms around him. But he didn't care. He'd found her.

"Tati," he whispered. "Come home with me."

She nodded and clung to him.

Thomas surrounded her with his devotion as he followed their link back to the Mages. As they got closer, Chantelle added her powers, helping to lead them back. He hurried then, his strength renewed. Then all the Mages reached up and pulled them back into the room.

He opened his eyes, heart pounding. Tati was staring back at him, pale but conscious. He was shaking. "Don't ever leave me again."

Their tears mingled as they held each other tightly.

Chapter Twenty-Four

Tatienne finished the bottle of water and the protein bar Chantelle had given her. Her head spun and she held on to Thomas. He led her to a chair, sat down and put her in his lap. His body was solid, warm and comforting.

"Do you want to rest before you talk about it?" Thomas asked. He held his arms around her possessively, and she didn't mind one bit. He was here.

"I figured out how we find them. It's simple, really." She squeezed his hand.

"What did you see?" Gwen asked, pulling up a chair beside them.

"There's three of them. They're very old — we should look at those illustrations from the archives again."

Thomas nodded. "Do you think they're the same people?"

"The blood magic rituals keep them alive. They need the blood to convert to magical energy. After they drain their victims, they must renew their sources."

"Like magical energy vampires?" Thomas asked.

Tati shrugged. "Since they don't drink the blood, I guess so."

"How do we locate them?" Chantelle asked.

"I was right about the river and lake. We need to look at our territory maps and identify potential sites for the cavern. I think they transformed a mountain cave into their lair."

"We should concentrate on the Rouge River, right? Near the Seven Sisters Rapids."

"And I saw a lake," Tati said.

"That gives us a great start," said Gwen. She glanced over at Gavin and Gareth, and they left the room.

"I think the cauldron is the key to their power. We need to find a way to disrupt it," Tati said. This was a big step. Could they succeed?

Chantelle scratched her chin. "We can look at the knife again. It seems to act as a focus. The technicians think it allows the sorcerers to shift through the realms, too."

"How do they do that?" Tati asked. She hadn't heard about there being more than one realm.

"Ancient Celtic legends described the worlds of humans and Fae as separate. This isn't true anymore since most of the Fae migrated into the human world when dark wizards took control of the Fae realm. Perhaps the sorcerers have found a way to access the other world and take power from it."

"They could be using it to hide their residence," Tati said.

"And store their power," Gwen added.

"But how will we find them, let alone get a hold of their cauldron?" Tati asked, dread catching hold of her chest.

Thomas said, "You're not on your own. We will figure it out together."

"We need to get this done as soon as we can. There are people—women and children—who are being exploited by the sorcerers. We have to stop the Frères Gris." Tati squeezed her eyes shut, trying to block out what she had seen.

Thomas held her close. She rested her head on his shoulder, taking in the comfort of his presence.

Gwen spoke up. "We need time to plan."

"I get it. It's just hard knowing what's going on."

"Being a leader means making tough decisions," Thomas said. "Sometimes that involves waiting for the right moment to act."

"I'm glad you found me," she said, her vision blurry. He had saved her.

"Chantelle helped me follow our bond, and then you broke out of the cage they were keeping you in."

Tati's pulse raced as she remembered the sorcerers controlling her. "I was afraid I would never get out. Then I sensed you were near and I knew you could help me escape."

"You really scared me," Thomas said. "But I know why you thought you had to do it."

"Thanks for coming when I needed you." Tati had been raw, exposed, in the lair. Now she was surrounded with love and support. She would re-energise. Then they would work together to defeat their enemies.

* * * *

Thomas knocked on Tati and Céline's door the next day. He held a down parka in his other hand.

Céline opened the door. "It's your big date, isn't it?" Thomas nodded.

"I've never seen you in jeans and a T-shirt. You look cool," she said and let him into the suite. "My friend Samantha is here for a sleepover."

"Frédérique said she was invited too," Thomas said, putting his leather duffel bag and coat on the floor.

"Yep. And Vicky and Émile. We're going to watch movies, eat popcorn and have a pillow fight." Céline grinned from ear to ear.

"Sounds fun." He fiddled with the stubble on his chin. *Maybe I should have shaved. No, Tati likes my facial hair.*

"I'll go get Tati." Céline ran off, calling her sister's name.

Tatienne appeared a minute later with an overnight bag slung over her shoulder. He rumbled low as he took in the way her dark red sweater and medium-wash jeans hugged her form. Her high ponytail accentuated her elegant neck.

"You look good enough to eat," he said, sweeping her up in her arms for a long kiss and enjoying the taste as much as the sight of her.

"Ewww!" Céline said. "You two get going so we can start the sleepover." She shooed them out of the door after Tati put on a heavy coat and he grabbed her stuff.

Thomas took Tati's hand as they sauntered through the lodge towards the ski centre. His heart was full. He couldn't imagine his life without Tati and Céline in it. He thought she felt the same, but since their argument, they hadn't spoken about it. Tonight, that was going to change. He wanted to tell her how he felt. Let her know how much she meant to him.

They reached the ski lifts and Thomas helped Tati into one of the chairs before hopping up himself. It was dark — night came early in the winter mountains — and the lights along the chair lift cast a warm glow on the snow.

As they made their way up the main peak, Thomas put an arm around her shoulders. "It's not a funicular, but it was the best I could do."

"This is wonderful. I love it." She rested her head on his shoulder before sitting up again to take in the scenery below them.

When they got to the top of the mountain and jumped off the lift, Thomas led Tati to a sleek snowmobile. They tossed their bags onto the connected sled and drove to a small chalet on the other side of the peak.

The location was very private. The resort used it as a special VIP location. There were no bookings this week, so Thomas had arranged to use it for the night.

Tati squeezed his middle when they pulled up beside the log cabin. After stepping off the machine, she twirled around, her mouth opened wide. "This is gorgeous!"

He tried to look at it through her eyes. A small bungalow constructed with certified-green timber logs, large picture windows looking out at the mountains, twinkly lights hung around the windows. It looked like Santa and Mrs Claus should live there.

They crunched through the snow to the front door. Upon entering, they found a roaring fire in the fireplace and delicious smells coming from the small kitchen.

"Did you hire a caterer?" Tati asked as she took off her coat, boots, mitts and hat.

"Nope. Even better." He led her to the living room and settled them on the soft couch in front of the fireplace. "Wait right here."

First, he took their bags to the bedroom. Then, he went to the kitchen and pulled the casserole dish from the warm oven. He would have to give Frédérique a special thank-you gift for arranging the food and setting up the chalet for them. She was determined to keep Tati and Céline happy, and that meant a lot to him.

He filled the plates and put them with the platter of hors d'oeuvres on a large serving tray. Humming, he lifted the tray and brought it out to the small table beside the couch.

"I contacted the club and when I said I was looking for a special meal to share with you, Jacques offered to send the cassoulet. Then, Chef Marc-François prepared some other delicacies to accompany it."

"People really do love you, Thomas." Tati's smile warmed his heart.

"This is all you. After you sent Jacques a thank-you card last week, he phoned me up to say again how much he liked you. And if we broke up, then I was going to have to give him your number." Tati laughed, while Thomas wrapped her in a bear hug. "I'm never letting you go, though."

She kissed him. It was fierce and sweet and all Tati.

They talked about family and friends as they fed each other from the tray. Although Thomas always looked forward to sexy times with Tati, he also enjoyed the intimate conversations and peaceful moments they spent with their clothes on. She was enchanting in every way.

He sat back when they were finished eating. Tati leaned against him, her back flush with his chest. He breathed in the fruity scent of her hair and snaked a hand around her waist.

"I will always be here for you, Tati," Thomas began. "I might make mistakes, but I will love you unconditionally."

Tati looked up at him. The adoration in her eyes compelled him to keep talking.

"I will always have the urge to protect you from harm, even though I know you can take care of yourself."

"I thought you liked my independence," she said.

"I do. I wouldn't want you any other way." His heart skipped a beat.

"I'm not going to change."

"I want you to keep pushing me. Relationships aren't easy, but I'm a better man when I'm with you."

"You accept me as I am—most of the time," she said.

"And I'll try to do that all of the time. I'm sorry I got so upset about you using your powers to help us locate the Frères Gris." He'd overreacted, he could see it now.

"I understand why you felt that way. But I'm glad you realised you can't control me."

"I was being selfish. I know I can't be a strong leader unless I empower you to be the same." He swallowed. "Will you forgive me?"

"Of course," she said. She turned around to face him. "I'm sorry I didn't come to you first. I was afraid you would say no, but I have to trust you."

"We have to trust each other. We will work things out, no matter what," he said.

"We are partners. Nothing else will work."

"I understand that now." Thomas fumbled beside the table and placed a black velvet box in her hands. "I bought you a necklace to apologise."

"You didn't have to do this, you know." She shook her head, snuggling against him while she opened the present. "I can't believe I'm getting used to your luxurious lifestyle."

"You've seen how we use our wealth to help our communities," Thomas said.

"I see how effective this mindset is for your family and clan. You're using your money and privilege for good."

"If you join our family, you will also have opportunities to do this, if you like."

"Join your family?" She looked up at him, her eyes shining.

"I know it's early, so I'm not pushing. But I want to spend the rest of my life with you." He held his breath as she pulled the necklace from the box — a delicate gold chain with a small pendant showcasing a crescent moon and six stars.

"You are my moon and my stars," he said, trying to keep his voice from wobbling. He helped her fasten it around her neck.

Her eyes shone as she felt the pendant at her breastbone. "I love it," she whispered, wiping at her cheeks. "Now let me show you the lingerie I picked out for tonight."

He undressed her in record time. After running his fingers along the light pink silk and lace, he carried her to the bedroom at the back of the bungalow. He stepped out of his clothes and reached in his bag for the packet of condoms.

"Wait," she said.

He paused, wondering what she had on her mind. He tried to keep his eyes on hers, even though his gaze kept straying to her beautiful form in the sexy black lace romper.

"When I had my check-up this week, I asked them to do a sexual wellness check." She cleared her throat. "I'm clean. I'm also on birth control. Are you...?" She looked so adorable — her big eyes betraying her uncertainty — he was tempted to rip off her lingerie before answering her. But he knew she needed an answer right away.

"Yes. My last monthly check-up was clean, and I've only been with you." He was proud to say that. His wolf rumbled happily inside him.

Mate.

Yes, Thomas replied. *Mate.*

"No condom, then," she said hoarsely. "I want to feel all of you inside me."

Growling low, he dropped the bag and pounced on the bed. She clambered up beside him, a saucy grin on her face.

Then, using just his mouth, he ripped off her bra and panties as fast as he could. He sat cross-legged on the bed and reached for her. Cupping her ass cheeks in his hands, he lifted her up and lined her centre up with his throbbing cock. Moaning, he impaled her pussy on his member, revelling in the sensations of her flesh and juices. He felt like he had died and gone to heaven.

He groaned as she rubbed her breasts on his chest. He pulled her up so he could thrust into her again, her pussy walls sliding exquisitely along his hard cock.

She bounced against his thighs and moaned. Nestling his face in her chest, he thrust faster as he lost himself in the rhythm, the delicious dance that was theirs alone.

Soon they were both climaxing. She clenched around him, milking his cock as he spurted deep in her pussy. He emptied himself inside her, thinking — wishing — the pulses would never end. Soft and boneless, she leaned on him and caught her breath.

He could hold her like this forever. And maybe, some day, she would say yes and he could.

Chapter Twenty-Five

Thomas sat in the boardroom and looked around the table at his pack. His brothers, Charles and Henri, sat with him at one end. His cousins Michel, Clem and Bertrand were on the right side of the table. Charles' mate, Chantelle, was seated on the left side with his mate, Tatienne. Beside them were Head Mage Gwen and Clan Defender Juana. The top minds and hearts of their clan, strategists and negotiators who were dedicated to the community's safety and wellbeing. He couldn't ask for a better group.

He cleared his throat. "Now that Tati and Chantelle have identified the area to search for the lair, we should coordinate our attacks on the Frères Gris' lair and the Trois-Rivières Clan headquarters."

"Where is it?" Henri asked.

"It's been hidden away," Chantelle said. "The Grey Brothers have one foot in our world so they can use it for their power. But they can fold their lair away in a pocket of the other realm so that we can't find it. Now that Tati's helped us locate it, we should be able to enter."

"But it has to be done soon," Gwen said. "The door between the realms is easiest to access during an equinox, and the spring equinox will be here in two days."

Thomas tried to quiet the murmurs around the table.

"Will the sorcerers be stronger during that time? If they follow the ancient festival of *Alban Eilir*, then their powers might be stronger, too," Clem asked, clenching her fists together.

"It's a chance we'll have to take." Thomas replied.

"We'll be at our full powers, too," Gwen answered. "And we're putting together a team of our best Mages to lead the site identification. There's myself and Chantelle, Gavin and Gareth. Tati will be joining us, too."

"Who will protect your team?" Juana leaned forward.

"Charles, of course. Dominick and Derrick will coordinate the Mage defence," said Chantelle. "My guys are putting together a small group from the security force."

Thomas was glad they had the experience of Chantelle's and Charles' personal security. The two men had been there when their Fae Queen had first used her powers in battle. They had also assisted in Chantelle's rescue when René Reynard had kidnapped her.

Tati spoke up. "What about the women and youth who have disappeared?"

"Since you and Chantelle confirmed they're being used in blood rites by the sorcerers, we've prioritised finding them," Juana said. "We anticipate the Trois-

Rivières Clan is supplying the people to the Frères Gris, so we'll be looking at the clan headquarters. One of the border-patrol captains—Anne—will be leading that team. She was on site for the massacre last month and wants to help find the survivors."

"I've tasked one of my teams at the Frères Gris lair to search for captives at that site," Thomas said. "Clem and I have set up two other groups for the general invasion force. Henri, have you and Juana set up your teams for the Trois-Rivières Clan attack?"

His brother nodded. "Gabriel volunteered—he saw the attack on Tatienne's home in Montréal. He's helping us cut down our long list to a manageable number. Lots of our security force want to take down Roland's clan."

"Once we defeat the Reynards, we'll need a lot of help from our people to restore the Trois-Rivières' community," Charles spoke up. "Henri, I expect you to oversee the clan rebuilding."

Henri's face glowed. "Yes, *Marc-heg*."

"Run us through the sequence of attacks once more, Thomas," Charles said.

Thomas took a deep breath. Charles had revealed to him that he wanted to step back and let Thomas be the public face of the clan. Charles had different priorities right now and he wanted to use this opportunity to mentor Thomas through a big venture.

"Tati is with Gwen, Chantelle, Gavin and Gareth. Derrick and Dominick's team will be with you, too, Charles," Thomas said. "Your groups will begin the invasion, since the Mages will have to identify the precise location of the lair. Once that has been accomplished, Clem and I will lead our teams into the structure to start the physical attack. We are tasked with closing down the sorcerers' power source and capturing them. The remaining team will search for the missing women and children. Once the site has been secured, the Mage teams will join us — unless we need them beforehand. They'll wait on standby."

Charles nodded and Thomas continued, pleased Charles was happy with his work.

"At the Trois-Rivières Clan, Juana and Henri will coordinate the attack. They'll gain entry under the guise of returning the prisoners we took at the ski lodge attack. Céline and Tati's guards, Vicky and Émile, wanted to join us, but we asked them to stay with Céline so that Tati and I can concentrate on our roles." He looked at Tati and she gave him a small smile. "The Trois-Rivières Clan strategy is similar to ours at the Frères Gris' site — secure the location, take down the leaders and find the captives."

Charles looked around the room. "Is everyone comfortable with the plan?"

There were nods across the table.

"Good, let's get to work," he said.

Thomas asked Henri to stay after for a few minutes. His brother came and sat beside him after the other pack members left the boardroom.

"How are you feeling about the attack?" he asked.

Henri bit his lip. "Good, I think."

"Are you ready for the leadership role?"

"Yes, I think so. A lot has happened in the last year. I need to make sure our clan survives this feud with the Trois-Rivières Clan."

Thomas' chest expanded. "I'm so proud of you for stepping up. It's not going to be easy, but you're the best choice to challenge Roland and try to take down the Trois-Rivières Clan."

Henri looked at him. "Do you think I'll have to fight the old man?"

"Possibly. His Lieutenant has been our prisoner since the ski lodge attack. He won't be ready to be his second if Roland calls you out."

"You did a number on his hand, bro, but it's healing well," Henri said. "I'm glad you took care of it, otherwise the rest of us would have kicked his ass for dissing your mate. And I don't know if he would have survived that."

Thomas nodded, his mouth set in a grim line. "What about Juana? Is she ready?"

"You know her, she's always spoiling for a fight."

"She's seemed a little off lately. Quieter than usual."

"Has she said anything to you?" Henri looked at him sharply.

"Is there something I should know?"

Henri shifted in his seat. "I don't think so. She's been avoiding me, ever since that day when you brought Tati to the gym."

"What did you do?" Thomas sighed. His brother's big mouth always got him into trouble.

"I don't know. She says nothing's wrong."

"Tati said something about Juana acting strangely at the ski lodge after the attack. She asked if Juana has magic."

"She doesn't, does she? Maybe it was just a weird glitch. Or else she's upset about the captives because it brings up her own trauma?"

"That's probably all it is, you're right. I'm sure she'll be ready for the invasion," Thomas said.

"I can count on her. She's never let me down."

"Except romantically?"

"That was a long time ago," Henri said. "I've given up my crush on her."

"Wow, you really are growing up." Thomas chuckled. He stood and clapped his brother on the back. "Good luck. You two make a great team."

Chapter Twenty-Six

The mid-afternoon sun shone brightly on the day of the spring equinox. Tatienne and the Mages drove towards the Seven Sister Rapids, following the Rouge River towards its source. It was cold, and would be colder still when night fell, but they hoped the coming darkness would give them an advantage.

Tatienne tapped her foot on the floor of the van as she watched the fir trees go by.

Chantelle gently put her hand on her thigh and leaned over. "You'll be all right."

"I wish Thomas hadn't gone in the other van. It would be easier having him with me."

"It's not easy being partnered with a clan leader," the woman replied.

"I'm so nervous," Tati confessed.

"He brings you peace, doesn't he?"

Tati nodded. "I've never felt this way with anyone before. It's like we belong together."

Chantelle patted her leg again. "I think you do, too."

The van came to a stop. In the front seat, Gwen consulted the map. "We've reached Devil Lake. Time for our search."

The Mages zipped up their coats and put on their hats, scarves and mittens. They'd have to make their circle out in the snow. Gavin grabbed the flares while Chantelle picked up the duffel of supplies.

After piling out of the van, they looked around and selected a spot beside the water. Tati wished she could see the red sand of the banks. It would make her dreams of blood seem less real.

Gavin and his partner Gareth prepared to use water energy in the working. Gwen could use all the elements, as far as Tati could tell. And Chantelle — she'd heard stories. She possessed a complex form of magic. It was probably more like Gwen's, but earth and air seemed to be the foundational elements. Chantelle's links to emotions reminded her of her own psychic manipulations. Tati was comforted by the points of connection between her and Chantelle. They were kindred spirits.

Chantelle turned to make sure Tati had followed her down to the water's edge. The little lake was frozen solid. As the sun sank lower on the horizon, pinks and oranges reflected off the fishing huts dotting its surface.

After they drew the pentacle and moon structure in the snow, the Mages arranged themselves at the points — five Mages, five points. This time, Thomas wasn't here. Tati's stomach pitched until she was enveloped by the support of the whole pack, buoyed up by the clan. She drew in her power as the moon crested over the horizon.

They began the working. As the chanting floated over her, Tati let herself fall into the dreamscape. Chantelle's presence held firm beside her.

Darkness surrounded her. She stood still, listening for whispers or humming, anything to lead her forward. She extended her reach, the tendrils smoothly working their way beyond the points of the pentacle, still visible in the vision realm. She drew Chantelle's presence along with her as she followed the whispers.

The sounds grew louder. Along the banks of the lake, the purple lines glowed, leading to a row of nearby hills. A dim purple light emanated from the closest hill, showing an outline of a small building. Could it be the chapel from her vision?

She pulled Chantelle closer to the small structure. As soon as she touched it, she knew it was the entranceway into the Frères Gris' lair.

"This is it," she whispered to Chantelle.

"Now we go back and tell them," Chantelle said.

Tati hesitated. Now they were here, she wanted to investigate. "Shouldn't we take a quick peek before we go back?"

"You know what happened last time you entered their lair," Chantelle said, her presence dark.

"Maybe we could find out where the captives are."

Chantelle's fear twirled around them.

"Let me contact Gwen." Chantelle's presence floated away. When she returned, she said, "Gwen agrees. We come back, no heroics."

"Is she letting Thomas and the others know what we found?" Tati asked.

"Yes."

Tati considered going on alone, then relented. "We'll go back. But if they need us, I want to be ready to come back."

"We'll get our van closer to the site and prepare," Chantelle said.

Tati pulled them back to the lakeside working. It took a few minutes for her to regain her bearings while the rest of the team tidied up their site. Tati was on edge, nerves jangling as she found her seat. When they arrived at their designated spot, Gwen, Gavin and Gareth climbed out to coordinate with Thomas and Clem. Tati couldn't see the other vans since they had split them up.

Turning to Chantelle, she asked, "Now what do we do?"

"We wait." Her friend held her hand. "Our team will monitor comms and magical energies at the lair. They'll call us in if necessary."

"I'm having déjà vu about being left behind," Tati grumbled. "And look how well that turned out last time."

Chantelle smiled grimly. "Just meditate and stay sharp."

Tati took several deep breaths to settle her mind. She reached out to her connection with Thomas, drawing some comfort while trying not to distract him from his mission.

Something brushed against her consciousness.

A whisper by her head made her shiver. She turned in the dreamscape.

Deacon Brébeuf was behind her, a wide grin on his face. He looked slightly different in her subconscious — more hawklike, his image hard to pin down. But she would have known him anywhere. He put a greasy hand over her mouth and started chanting, pulling her out of the dreamscape.

She was back in the van with Chantelle, four large men holding their arms. She struggled as their attackers put magic-dampening cuffs on their wrists. When the cuffs took effect, she sagged against the man and they dragged the women out of the vehicle.

Under the moonlight, the entrance to the Frères Gris lair looked almost benign, a simple rock cave mouth surrounded by brush and stones. But when they passed through the entryway, the walls widened and were covered with purple slime. Orange moss hung off the sides in clumps.

The men marched Tati and Chantelle to a small room where Father Genette and Deacon Brébeuf waited.

"I knew it was you." The deacon smirked. "And this must be the other Ducharme bitch."

Chantelle kept silent, narrowing her eyes and jutting out her chin.

Father Genette spoke to the guards who had brought them in. "Take the women to the sorcerers and watch them. They're cunning."

The guards looked at the ground.

"Now!" yelled the priest.

The men jumped into action, pushing the women out of the room then down a dark corridor. Father Genette and his assistant Deacon Brébeuf came up behind them when they reached a spiral staircase. When Tati stumbled on the stairs, the deacon grabbed her arm and hauled her back up. His oily grip made her shudder.

At the bottom of the steps, they crossed a doorway and entered a large space lit by torches. It looked like the cavern in her visions, but chaotic and dirty. There was a dank smell that mixed with smoke from the fire and turned her stomach.

The guards led the women to the large, dark cauldron set on a fire pit on the far side of the cavern.

"Are you okay?" Chantelle whispered.

"Yes. Can you reach Charles or Thomas?" Tati hoped the dampening cuffs didn't limit Chantelle's powers.

Chantelle shook her head. "They must have felt their connections to us fade. They'll be looking for us."

Tati heart raced to think of Thomas being captured because of her. The clan's teams had to fulfil their mission. Stopping the Frères Gris — and saving the women and children — was more important than rescuing her.

There was a commotion as three figures in grey robes entered the cavern. The sorcerers radiated foul energies, their auras twisting and turning as though they had a mind of their own.

The sorcerers began arguing with the guards who were gathering iron tools by the cauldron. Fury rolled off them in oily waves, causing the people around them to shrink away.

Father Genette turned back to the women. He ordered his assistant to tie up Tati and Chantelle. The deacon led them to the wall behind the cauldron, where three sets of iron shackles had been attached. Tati could make out some runes written on the wall and on the bands. She struggled and Chantelle kicked when the men carried them to the chains, but it was no use. The guards secured them in the shackles.

Tatienne said, "I won't cooperate. You'll have to kill me."

"Oh, you'll cooperate." Deacon Brébeuf smiled menacingly. "We've got the right motivation."

Tati's heart sank as they dragged a familiar figure through the door and into the cavern.

Thomas' head pounded. The last thing he remembered was an explosion going off in the tunnel as he fought a shifter from the Trois-Rivières Clan. Now someone pulled him through a doorway and left him in a heap on the floor. He opened his eyes. Well, one eye. The other was too swollen. He touched it gingerly before a burly man grabbed his arm and pulled him to a stand.

The room was large and dark, but he could sense his mate was there. Apprehension churned in his stomach as he peered around the cavern.

Father Genette stepped towards him. Tati cried out from the other side of the room and his heart stuttered.

The priest looked back at Tati. "If you don't cooperate, woman, then we'll kill your boy-toy."

"Thomas!" she sobbed. "Are you okay?"

He smiled at her. "Just a slight headache."

Tears ran down her face. He wished he was by her side so he could make her feel better.

"I trust you will help us now," Father Genette said to her.

She nodded, sniffling. Thomas tried to reach out across their bond — it was weak. Her shackles must be spelled. How was he going to help her and Chantelle?

"What do you want her to do?" Thomas ground out.

One of the sorcerers glided towards him, his ragged grey robes twisting around his unearthly form. "We're going to harness this one's powers for our rites. We can draw on her magics to help us drain the others."

"No!" Tati cried.

Over my dead body. His wolf growled and came to the surface. They both wanted to tear the priests and sorcerers to pieces. Two large men held him tight and the number of magic users in the cavern were too many. What could he do?

"I will not allow you to use my mate in that way," Thomas snarled.

"That's what women are for. For centuries, we have taken what we need to survive and thrive."

"You're no better than anyone else," he said, clenching his fists.

"Of course we are superior," the creature purred. "We are ancient. The humans and shifters we take are unimportant. But your woman is different—and the one with her. With them, we can take your territory and drain all your people."

Thomas pushed against the guards, but they only gripped him tighter.

"I won't help you." Tati rattled in her chains. "Don't you know the strength of humans and shifters comes from love and community? You just know hate and anger."

"Hate and anger win every time." Father Genette chuckled. "Your Church knew that. That's why they exploited the Indigenous peoples when they came to this supposed 'new world.' And your government, too. It's still going on."

"We're trying to learn how to do things differently," Thomas said, his gut churning.

"Women and children go missing every day in this country. Nobody cares about most of them—unless they're rich and white."

"That's not true. In our clan, every person matters."

"Still, you can't stop us from taking your people." The sorcerer's laugh made the hairs on the back of his neck stand up.

Thomas thought he would burst out of his skin. He threw himself at the brothers and slipped out of his guards' hold. The Grey Brother raised his hand and sent Thomas flying into the wall, near Tati.

His mate sobbed as he landed on the ground near her feet. When he looked up at her, his heart sank.

"Now we start," said the sorcerers. They approached the cauldron and began chanting. One of them picked up a knife while another grabbed an iron bowl. It was just like Tatienne's vision. He couldn't let this happen to her.

Tati fought the guards when they undid her irons.

"Just give in. It will make it easier." Father Genette sneered.

She started screaming when they set her beside the cauldron and filled the bowl with her blood. Chanting, they added her blood to the large vessel. Thomas tried to shift into his wolf form, but Deacon Brébeuf came forward and stopped him with a quick spell.

"Stay down," the deacon warned.

Thomas fought to hold himself together while Tati screamed and his bond with her grew weaker. He could hardly sense her anymore and his chest ached.

When she stopped screaming, Thomas thought that was even worse. He was empty, numb inside.

The sorcerers shouted for the priest. "Genette, is she dead?"

No, no, no, she can't be.

Thomas reached for their bond. There was still a small pulsing, but could it just be an after-effect? He had to see for himself.

Thomas crawled to Tatienne, mourning for his mate. He found the bloodied knife on the floor beside her and cut through his ties. Then he gathered her in his arms, weeping.

Chantelle was sobbing, still chained to the wall.

Tati's skin was warm against his. Did her fire still burn? A glimmer of hope awakened in him.

By the cauldron, the sorcerers were arguing with Father Genette and his assistant. Tati had short-circuited the focuser. She had sacrificed herself to stop them.

Deacon Brébeuf ordered the guards to bring more prisoners. They would try to restart the cauldron with new infusions of blood.

The argument was interrupted by a shifter from the Trois-Rivières Clan. "The Alpha's headquarters are under attack!"

The sorcerers rounded on Thomas as he held his mate. "You'll never win. We will crush all of your little people and take all the power from your land."

Thomas fought through the fog of his sorrow and despair. There was still a piece of Tati inside him, feeding his strength, intertwining his ice-cold rage with the fire of her devotion.

He growled at the brothers. "Over my dead body."

Father Genette laughed. "I can live with that."

The sorcerers turned their backs on him as the three prisoners arrived from their dungeon. The group busied themselves with their preparations for the next round of bloodletting.

Chapter Twenty-Seven

Thomas heard a small whisper in the back of his mind. A light caress rippled across his soul.

He took Tati's hand. A faint pulse throbbed at her wrist. It was thready, but it was there. She was alive.

He tried to keep the relief from showing on his face. He flicked a glance to Chantelle and mouthed, "She's alive."

"You have to claim her," Chantelle whispered, a spark in her eye. "It's the only way to save her."

"Doesn't it happen during sex?"

"Times of crisis will work, too." Chantelle looked over at the sorcerers. "Do it while they're busy."

Still holding Tatienne in his arms, Thomas summoned up all his love and passion. She was his mind's peace — the one who gave his life meaning and made him whole. He had to bring her back. His skin prickled as he focused on his Tati. Her face, her body, her soul. She was his and he was hers.

Magics swirled around them. The tendrils of her abilities circled him, combining with his to make something of their own—something more powerful, more beautiful and timeless.

Her eyelids fluttered. She reached a hand up to his face. "I claim you," she whispered.

He kissed her and sank his canines into the skin at the base of her neck. Pressing his lips against the join with her shoulder, he shuddered. Ecstasy, possession, pleasure, delight and claiming—all these feelings and more rushed through him. It was how it was always meant to be.

He saw them paddling a canoe on a moonlit night, the stars sparkling in the water. They were together and happy. Friends and family laughed and sang.

Back in the cavern, she reached her hands up to tug at his hair. She wound her legs around his torso. Her powers surged through him as she gathered strength from their bond. Then she opened her eyes and looked into his soul. "Yes," she sighed.

Through their bond, Thomas felt joy ripple through her. The sorcerers couldn't control her anymore. She was the warrior princess she was destined to become. The leader who protected her clan and its people. The mate who loved and supported him.

She stood up and faced the cauldron. She flicked a hand, and the deacon went flying in the air to land near the doorway. Father Genette gasped and looked up. She raised her hand again and he landed beside his assistant. Thomas could feel her balance her fire with his ice to maintain control. She could do anything now.

Tati turned back and faced Chantelle. One flick of her wrist and Charles' mate was free from the chains.

"Can you connect with Charles?" Tati asked her, while Thomas tried to process the transformation.

Chantelle closed her eyes as Tati swept an arm and pushed the guards and sorcerers to the other side of the cauldron. Tati pointed and the flames from the firepit grew to make a barrier between them and their enemies.

Chantelle opened her eyes. "Charles is coming. He's connected to me again."

Thomas waited anxiously until Charles burst through the door. His security team, including Dominick and Derrick, were close behind. His group quickly secured the guards, who looked dazed.

When Gwen, Gavin and Gareth arrived, Charles took Chantelle's hand and they all advanced on the sorcerers, who were pinned in a ring of fire. Chantelle and Gwen had revealed the purple lines of power used by the sorcerers and the women were wrapping the lines like ropes around the evildoers.

Chantelle and Gwen grunted under the strain. Thomas connected with Tati. As the sorcerers' power coursed through her, she grew tired and afraid, but Thomas reached out with their bond and steadied her.

Still, it wasn't enough. They couldn't contain the sorcerers for much longer. Their foes had too much ancient power.

Tati's powers were at their limits. They were still new and she didn't know how far she could push them.

Charles was muttering to Chantelle, something about a "magical whammy." Chantelle's attention wavered and the sorcerers tried to breach their bonds.

Chantelle's magical EMP. That was what Charles meant. But if Chantelle broke from the current containment working to create the spell, then the sorcerers might break free before she could disable them.

"You have to try, Chantelle," she yelled.

"But how?" Chantelle said.

"Let me try and use the fire as ropes. I can add them to the restraints while you slip out of that working."

Tati thought about the purple lines of power while she examined her fire energies. Were the two that different? The sorcerers used blood magic—a potent force—but fire was also powerful. She twisted the flames from the firepit, twirling them into ropes before lassoing the Grey Brothers. She held her breath as the flames clamped around the figures. It was working.

"Now, Chantelle," she cried.

She sensed it when Chantelle left the working a moment later, but the sorcerers couldn't budge. Tati stood tall as their opponents crumpled to the ground, knocked out by Chantelle's enchantment.

They had at least ten minutes before the ones who were affected would gain consciousness. Maybe more, since this time Chantelle's working seemed stronger than the last one Tati had witnessed. As Chantelle started to wobble on her feet, Charles grabbed her and sat down with his mate in his lap. He rubbed her stomach and nuzzled the top of her head.

Tati looked for Thomas. He was overseeing the removal of the Grey Brothers, but she felt the bond pulsing between them. She sent a little burst of love along their connection and he sent back a calm caress to reassure her everything was all right. She took a big breath and let it out.

Gwen approached her. "We've removed the contents of the cauldron and broken it into pieces.

Could you melt it down? Or do we have other options?"

"Are there markings on it? Like the knife?" Tati asked.

"Yes." Gwen thought for a moment. "Let's take it back to the compound and evaluate it before we decide on a course of action."

Tati agreed. "Tell them to be careful with it. We don't know its full power."

Thomas started shouting. There was a struggle as the guards tried to remove the sorcerers' robes. Two looked small and pitiful without their cloaks to power them. The third one, however, was not who she expected. Instead of a Grey Brother, Deacon Brébeuf was hiding under the robes.

"One of them got away," Tati breathed.

Chantelle was by her side immediately. She reached for Tati's hand and they searched her dreamscape for any sign of the missing sorcerer.

It was silent. No whispers, no humming. No glowing purple lines. It was like he had disappeared into thin air.

"What do we do?" Tati asked, as dread pressed down on her chest.

Chantelle squeezed her hand. "We'll find him."

* * * *

Thomas' cousin Clem came by with an update. "We've just heard from the Trois-Rivières Clan teams. They're all right."

Tati breathed a sigh of relief. "Did their gambit work?" she asked.

"Yes. They made it into the clan compound and confronted the leaders."

"Is everyone okay?" Chantelle asked.

"No casualties, just some injuries."

The exhaustion hit Tati. She was glad the conflict was over.

"Did Henri challenge Roland?" Charles asked.

Clem nodded.

"All his training with Juana paid off," Charles said. "I knew it would."

"He's growing into his role," Chantelle said. "You were right to believe in him."

"Juana said something strange happened during the combat. Roland had an attack or something," Clem said.

"What happened?" Tati asked.

"He was wearing a talisman of some sort. It was glowing at the beginning of the match, but when it lost its light, Roland started fading, too," Clem said.

Tati gasped. "I wonder if it was connected to the sorcerers and their magical workings?"

"It could have been powered by them," Charles said. "And when the cauldron was destroyed and the sorcerers defeated, he lost his power, too."

Chantelle took Charles' hand in hers. "Is it really over? Have we stopped the Reynards once and for all?"

Charles smiled and nodded.

"Did they find the missing people?" Tati asked.

"Yes," Clem said. "They got them out."

Tati breathed a sigh of relief.

"It will be a long road to healing for the prisoners," said Chantelle, her eyes glistening.

Tati tried to imagine what that path might look like. She thought she might like to help with the healing. Contribute what she could to the clan's growth.

A thought struck her. Tati asked, "So, if he fought the Alpha and won, then Henri is clan leader, right?"

Charles nodded. "That was the outcome we hoped for. Henri will have a chance to grow into his potential and we will have a pack member leading the neighbouring clan."

"That's a big change," Tati said, pursing her lips. A Ducharme leading another clan, bringing their people under the family's protection.

"It won't be an easy transition, but we'll support him. Send him staff and schedule visits to help him secure his place. Don't worry, he won't be alone."

A warm glow settled in Tati's chest.

Soon after, Thomas came over and escorted her outside. Chantelle and Charles walked with them.

"Do we have to do anything else here?" Tati asked, stifling a yawn.

"Not right now," Thomas said. "Let's get you home."

Home. That sounded right. To the compound, with Thomas and Céline, and the rest of the clan. Tati sighed happily and took his hand.

Chapter Twenty-Eight

Tati glanced out through the window of her parish church in Montréal. The summer heat shimmered on the sidewalks. The strains of jazz from the festival lightened the steps of the pedestrians.

Tati stepped into the blush-coloured, floor-length silk gown.

Céline arranged the headpiece and veil. She stepped back. "*Voilà*! You look gorgeous."

"I do, don't I?" The sweetheart neckline showed off her cleavage in an elegant way, while the elegant skirt swished down her full hips. Looking at herself through Thomas' eyes over the months had helped her see her beauty — both inside and out.

She took her sister's hands. "Am I doing the right thing?"

Céline held her hands and shook them up and down, nodding vigorously. Then she pouted. "I wanted Thomas to walk me down the aisle."

"Thomas has to wait by Father Andre. And you've been paired up with Diego – his cummerbund matches the pink of your dress."

Céline looked down at the sugar confection of her gown. "Okay. When do we start?"

"When Lynne comes to take us in. She's waiting for all the guests to be seated."

"I thought you wanted a small wedding. There are so many people in the church."

"I did. But by the time we included our friends and his family, and then all the people from his community who wanted to come –"

"And my friends, too," Céline piped up.

"The church is full. But we can all still fit inside the St Patrice Club for our reception, so it's okay."

"Are you happy?" her sister asked, tucking a strand of Tati's hair under the veil.

She nodded, her heart full to bursting. "Very. I hope you are, too."

"Very." Céline clapped her hands.

Lynne knocked then opened the door. "It's time."

The women walked down the hallway towards the back of the church. The strains of music from Bertrand's string ensemble started up as they stepped into the aisle. Céline stood with Chantelle, Clem and Juana while Lynne orchestrated their entrances. When the women had done their wedding marches down to the front of the church, Lynne turned to Tati and offered her arm.

"Are you ready?" she asked.

"Yes," replied Tati. She looked ahead and saw Thomas. His charcoal-grey morning suit matched his grey eyes, with the little flecks of gold she loved so much shining in his irises. And his smile – she could bask her whole life in that expression.

Father Andre waited beside her groom. She was so pleased he was well enough to officiate the ceremony – she couldn't imagine the celebration without him. It had been difficult to meet him at the church to discuss the wedding plans, since all she could think about was Father Genette and Deacon Brébeuf. But by the time they performed the traditional marriage counselling sessions with him, she had covered the bad memories with better ones. In fact, Father Andre had taken a shining to her fiancé and Thomas had even gone to a couple of hockey games with the priest. Everyone fit so well together.

Tati walked down the aisle beside Lynne, Bertrand's cello singing out and soothing her the way only the Ducharmes could.

She looked at the wedding party – Charles, Chantelle, Henri, Juana, Céline, Diego, Clem and Michel. Their families united and sharing this public declaration of their love. This was a chance to celebrate their bond and share their joy with their loved ones.

There had been a few surprises with her bridal party. Chantelle had confessed she was pregnant when they had a dress fitting and her gown needed to be let out. The gown shop had broken out the champagne when they had heard all the shrieking. Everyone jumped for joy at the news. Their Alpha pair was moving into the next phase of their lives. She and Thomas would have to step up more during this time, but it was a blessing to support her pack and share in their happiness.

She had agreed right away when Thomas had suggested Juana as a bridesmaid. She had been like family to Thomas and his brothers, and Tati felt a strange but familiar connection with Juana. It was like the one she had with Chantelle. Probably because they were family now. Clem was shyer than Chantelle, but she was loyal and kind. Tati had been glad to get to know her a little better since they had defeated the Trois-Rivières Clan.

They reached the end of the aisle, and she smiled up at Thomas. Lynne made her declaration to Father Andre. Then Tati took Thomas' outstretched hands in hers. It was time to move forward into her future, with her family and friends by her side.

* * * *

The Sunday wedding brunch for Tati and Thomas took place at Grandmaman Marie's country house. They held it outside in the garden, amid the blooming bushes and cottage flowers. Family and friends laughed and shared memories of the happy couple.

After everyone had eaten, Thomas brought them to attention. "A toast to my wife, who starts her library science programme in the fall. May all our new beginnings bring you as much happiness as they have to me."

The group cheered and drank an assortment of fizzy beverages.

Thomas then made a toast to his brothers. "Charles, you have always been our rock. We've gone through so much, and still you have the strength to support me and Henri while taking care of the entire clan. I'm glad to be here with you as we both embark on the next stages of our personal and family journeys. I couldn't do this without you."

Charles, eyes shining, raised his glass in one hand and squeezed Chantelle's shoulder with the other.

"And, Henri," Thomas said, "you are becoming everything I knew you would. I loved getting into trouble with you when we were kids. You and Juana were always my partners in crime. I am grateful for your loyalty and camaraderie. And I'm so thrilled you are taking over the Trois-Rivières Clan and bringing your compassion, strength and sense of humour to the community. They need you."

Henri's face grew hot as he raised his glass and smiled. This was going to be a challenge in so many ways. But he was glad to be stepping up and taking a leadership role for the family. He'd had his time to play, and now it was time to get to work.

Juana was seated beside Henri. She was part of the challenge. She was still angry he had falsely said she was his mate a week ago. He wasn't sure he'd done the right thing, putting her in the line of fire like that, but when the Trois-Rivières Clan elders approached him to say they expected him to marry a seventeen-year-old girl, he had panicked. Apparently, the girl had been promised to Roland and therefore she belonged to the new Alpha. The elders had waited for Henri to settle in, then they had presented it to him as a done deal.

He had gotten flustered and told them Juana was his mate.

She had been furious when he had told her, but she'd agreed to go along with it "to save your *culo.*" She'd rather have a fake relationship than make that poor young girl get stuck with him. And it *had* saved his ass. Nobody was offended that he was mated to the strong and striking Clan Defender. In fact, his new clan seemed happy — maybe even relieved — by the news.

Charles and Thomas had laughed when he told them.

"I knew you'd try and get her in your bed somehow," Thomas had said.

"I couldn't marry the underage girl, even if they said that was their custom. It was too icky."

Charles had asked, "How long will Juana have to go along with this?"

"Just a few months. Then, we'll stage an amicable break-up and go our separate ways."

Then Thomas had looked at him. "Will you be willing to give her up? Just like that?"

"I'll have to." Henri had blinked his eyes. "Lately, there's been something between us, but she's ignoring it. And I don't want to push it."

"That's smart. She'll beat your *culo* if you did."

Henri had laughed along with his brothers. There was too much to worry about right now. He just had to manage the transition for the Trois-Rivières Clan. Then he could worry about Juana touching his ass.

Want to see more like this?
Here's a taster for you to enjoy!

Sin City Kilts: Heart of Stone
January Bain

Excerpt

I jumped naked from my bed, the stone floor bracing against my bare feet and the early morning chill raising quick goosebumps on my flesh. The clash of swords and shouts of men I led into battle nightly in my dreams still rang in my ears before I stretched and let the images fade away.

Last night's full moon still lingered and false dawn approached, that liminal moment when the sun has yet to appear. My ancestors believed it heralded glimpses of the future and great secrets to be shared. Me? I thought it time to be up and about.

Throwing on my shirt, kilt and boots and strapping my claymore to my back, I descended the steep steps from the north tower. Despite myself, I sensed something of import with the night's Hawthorn moon—a time of masculine power, potency and fertility, even more so than the other eleven months of the year.

Fingers of heavy mist crept across the vast estate toward me, intensifying the fresh woodsy scents of heather and moss. The low-lying fog obscured my long view of forest and hedgerows, but I knew they were there.

Untold numbers of Creigs had carved this land and battlements out of solid rock eons ago on *Eilean maddah-allaidh*, or Wolf Island as it was known to those from away, creating a legacy that would stand for generations to come. A sanctuary that was mine to oversee and care for...which included being alive to any messages sent my way.

"Okay, fine," I sighed to whomever or whatever might be listening, and, giving in, stood in the shadow of Castle Creigbourne, awaiting a glimpse of what lay beyond the ken.

An intense flickering in my peripheral vision hit my senses hard before the world disappeared entirely, sending me back to that timeless realm with no name and no season. Then a glimmering of light appeared as my third eye opened, sending flashes of blue and gold to strike my retinas. The blue of eyes and the gold of hair?

I grasped for more but the partial image vanished in an instant. "That all?" I snarked, shaking off the disquiet that the vision left in its wake. No answer came. Shrugging, I strode across the ground toward the stables. The first rays of light glinted on the dewy grass now as the sun returned, creating a field of ephemeral sparkling diamonds that never failed to put all human efforts to shame.

A series of soft chuffs broke the quiet stillness as Loki came trotting over to greet me. The legendary deerhound voted most likely to be mistaken for a large pony swiped his tail to a steady beat.

"Ah, this is the time we like best, isn't it, my Loki boy?" I bent to give his thick, wiry fur a quick rub.

He followed me into the stable, sneezing as the sharp scent of manure tickled his nose. I opened the door to Roam's stall, then led the magnificent stallion out into the alleyway and swiftly saddled him. The scent of oiled leather and clean horse flesh permeated the air, grounding me.

I swung a leg up and over the coal-black beast, both of us impatient to be off. Roam stomped the hard ground with loud thumps of his massive hooves. A destrier, he was of sturdy stock with bloodlines that harked back to tournament fields and knights in armor. He needed to be to carry the likes of this Highlander — six-foot-three of solid muscle, thanks to the daily regime of the claymore.

"Let's go."

A loud whinny of agreement followed, the stallion's breath whitening the brisk air in pillowy clouds as we surged away from Castle Creigbourne. I gave Roam his head and we raced across the glen, Loki running by our side, the three of us as ancient as any legend.

"Creigbourne Loch?" I suggested.

Roam knew the way and barely needed my touch on the reins before his strong haunches were eating up the miles across a greenscape as brilliant as any that existed on this Earth. For one brief moment I caught a glimpse of the spot where my cousin's fated mate had died. Averting my eyes, I forced the image away. It was far too beautiful a day to spend grieving for what could not be changed…although it haunted me.

The clean air and the colors of nature worked their usual wonder on me and helped to place the morning's vision in perspective. "Second sight is sometimes a gift, sometimes a curse," I told my animals. Which was the hazy impression sent to me this morning? The blue and gold could be either, depending on opinion.

Blue eyes, gold hair… Personally, I was not looking for the female prophesized by the elderly woman at last year's Spirit of Creigbourne festival. I had no need of distraction. My life in the Highlands of Scotland was filled with dealing with the needs of my clan, and I'd have it no other way. Family honor and loyalty was everything.

The edge of the loch loomed and I dismounted. My shirt tugged over my head, I threw it on the ground and took up my broadsword.

Swiping and lunging at demons and enemies, I cut a swathe across the clearing. Under the canopy of forest, I swung the claymore with precision and speed, savoring the perfectly balanced weapon in my hand. It was born of the finest steel and crafted with such remarkable precision that I'd been offered a king's ransom for its possession. *Never. Not enough money on this earth to entice me to part with the pride of clan Creig.*

An hour later, my bare chest dripping with perspiration that pooled in the ridges and valleys of my fairly earned six-pack, I removed my sturdy boots and kilt and dove into the frigid waters of Creigbourne Loch.

Sluicing back my long hair from my face, I swam out a fair distance from the rocky shore, enjoying the pull on muscles that were well-used from my workout. A bark from Loki and a whinny from Roam alerted me a second before a long-winged shadow skimmed across the water. I stilled, treading in place for a moment to observe the interloper. *Damn.*

The fierce falcon, named Tyr after a special god of bravery — a nod to my ancient Norse ancestors and to The Creig — settled on a rock nearby, his golden eyes beady and ever watchful. Then with a series of proud screeches to announce his departure, the giant bird of prey flapped his shoulders, rising into the air on powerful wings designed to catch the wind currents home or to hunt.

I swam swiftly to shore and pulled on my boots. Wrapping my kilt around my waist, uncaring of my wet skin, I whistled for Roam and Loki. "Time to head in. We have a visitor waiting," I told them.

The ride back to the castle was all too short. I curried Roam and fed him fresh carrots on top of his full share of oats and nutrients, making sure the stallion had all his needs met before heading into the conservatory where the visitor whose herald had summoned me held court.

I rolled my shoulders, the unease of dealing with whatever had prompted the visit bringing back the tension that my early morning exercise had almost eliminated. I had no choice on the matter though — when *this* visitor called, any Creig with a whit of sense answered.

I girded my loins and strode through the doorway. "Morning, Grandmother."

"Morning, Grandson," The Creig, the elder of the clan, replied, turning her stately head with its elegant upswept hairdo to present her cheek for my buss. Dressed in the customary Creigbourne tartan of black and green plaid with gold threads running through it, she perched on her throne, slight enough to be blown away in a stiff breeze. However, no one in their right mind would dare share that intel.

"Ye're soaking wet, Lachlan. Dinna ye think to bring a towel?"

I laughed. "No need. I have the constitution of an ox, the strength of a bull and the fortitude of a conqueror. Why waste time?"

"And the lasses in these parts would add...and a heart of stone," she said, then added, "Aye, but yer right, it's precious it is, time. Never enough of it."

She nodded sagely, her piercing green eyes still not requiring correction though she was ninety if she were a day. No woman admits her age, according to The Creig. She'd been thirty-nine forever before she finally quit discussing the matter entirely. Her birthday cake was only allowed one candle to this day.

"What brings you here on this fine morning?" I asked though a pall had been laid over the morning. I sat down across from her. *Might as well get it over with.* The Creig never showed up unless something difficult was afoot. Unease reared itself in my mind, making my nerves rankle. I knew the next words out of her mouth would have a cost.

"Ye're needed in America, Grandson. Cristaldo of the House of Luceres has asked for our help in a personal matter and has a business opportunity he wishes to discuss. Which means it's time to pay our debt to him."

She looked at me more keenly when I remained stubbornly silent. I detested owing a duty. So often the wishes of another burdened beyond compare.

"But I see ye already knew something of this." She pursed her lips. "If the second sight is talking to ye, then it's settled."

I ignored her last words, instead pushing myself out of the chair and beginning to pace. I preferred to think on my feet. "I have a great deal on my plate at the moment, taking care of our vast holdings. I can't just rush off to America at the whim of another."

I was venting, knowing I would have to answer the call. As head of the clan, paying the ancient debt the Creigs owed to the house of Luceres fell to me, and I would honor that, not even think about sending my brothers, Calan or Logan, or even one of our cousins.

"I knew it would come to this one day, but not now," I muttered. A warrior chooses his own path, his own battles. Of course, once I wanted something, I would not be deterred from obtaining it by any means necessary. How else could I have doubled our billions in the past decade alone? "But, of course, honor above all."

"Aye." The Creig picked up her dram of spirits she'd poured earlier. She swallowed it a single gulp. "Spectacular year."

"It is." I waited for her to come to the point.

"Was your vision any clearer this morn?" Her question hung in the air between us, those few words filled with more portent than the most dramatic soliloquy and, knowing what she was asking, I shook my head, a bit more riled than I let on.

She leaned forward to add weight to her words. "Well, ye must think of the future, Grandson. Ye are heir to all we possess, as is the right of the first born. And ye are not getting any younger." She pointed her glass at me. "And neither am I. Would you deny me grandchildren?"

I snorted. "You're going to live forever. And it's blatantly unfair, the structure of inheritance. Archaic laws that need changing."

"Be that as it may, if ye canna find your mate on this side of the water, she may exist in the new world."

Her words clanged like warning bells, especially when allied to the reason for her visit. "Grandmother, I'm not looking to upend my life. A lass from another country with a different culture causes too many complications. I have too many responsibilities right here. Obligations that cannot be set aside on the whim of another."

"We must learn from the past, but embrace the present, Grandson. You won't be the first to cross the water for your mate. Your *one*. Besides, it might lighten ye up!"

I grimaced and let The Creig's words sink in as she poured us both a drink of Scotland's finest. My life was so regimented, the needs of others firmly set before my own, as it should be for the alpha of a clan, especially one who needed to lighten Grandmother's load as she aged.

And yes, over the quickly passing years, I had become less light-hearted and more solemn, though the love of wit and laughter called strongly at times. Things an adult must set aside. *Isn't that the proper way of it? Not kicking over the traces?*

I glanced at my favorite painting of all time, hanging in its place on the conservatory wall. Backlit spectacularly by the artist, it depicted my great-grandfather doing a sleight-of-hand magic trick, a gaggle of his grandchildren huddled at his feet, their tiny faces alight with amazement.

I'd always been fascinated by stories of him, and his personality, leading to my lifelong enjoyment and practice of the art of magic, everything from close-up to illusionist tricks. My brothers had called me cracked for spending long hours at this, but I enjoyed it and had got pretty skilled.

Then, as if Great-Grandfather were calling to me, a thought struck me. If I had to visit Las Vegas, or Sin City as it was more rightly called, maybe I could recapture something of my lighter side, and do something I'd always wanted to do? Take some recompense for the interruption to my life? Could I? I looked at Great-Grandfather. *Yes.*

"Fine. But I get to do it my way," I said, crossing my arms over my chest.

The Creig's eyes gleamed with interest and she stared at me, but I remained stubbornly silent. *Where do you think I got my need to turn the world my way?* She tilted her head, as if listening to something I couldn't hear, then nodded. "Good. It's settled then. Now, how about some breakfast?"

Taken aback, I muttered, "Of course," and mulled over the situation while we ate the tempting dishes the servants brought at her request. I quickly consumed vast quantities of steak and bacon, sausage and eggs with sides of toast and oatcakes in short order. I had a great deal of preparing to do and little time to accomplish it.

"If you'll excuse me, I have somewhere I need to be."

The Creig nodded as I took my leave, her expression expressing pleasure at the outcome of our meeting. As if it were ever in doubt. I always uphold the honor of our family.

"Off with ye, grandson. I look forward to my invite."

The Creig had passed the second sight on to me, the first born, though her advancing years had added immeasurably to her ability. She knew far more than she would ever admit about what awaited me in Vegas, but it would be no use asking her to divulge it, and I was too proud to beg.

Exiting the castle, I tore off my kilt and boots, ready for my real exercise — my wolf run. Creigs were weres, our secret ancestral heritage, and this would be my last chance before heading off to Sin City. I wanted it to count. I wanted to feel the wind in my fur, the scent of life in my lungs and the world dropping away as I raced across the moors.

I pushed my way from our realm through the glimmering portal into the next dimension so tantalizingly close to ours, the process necessary to shift my energy from man to wolf, the actual transformation occurring in an instant. All those painful experiences expressed in novels? Patently untrue for any werewolf I knew—a small mercy.

The world had now mutated to an array of colors unknown to the human eye, blacks and browns and grays with subtle shadings that my brain converted to what my human side saw—blues and greens, yellow and reds. I breathed in deeply, my olfactory nerves sharpened by the cool, moist morning Highland air, each scent more rousing than the last.

A chorus of howls erupted in the distance, begging me to join them. I took off at a quick lope, overcome with a sense of urgency. This might be my last chance for a while.

I slipped off the bonds of duty, my worries over the Creig estate and concerns about the journey to America. Instead, I embraced my animal nature, letting it take over. The grasses compressed beneath my massive paws, acting like a springboard to my prowling.

I stood taller and larger than the thought-to-be-extinct dire wolf and, blessed with sharper tracking ability, soon picked up the scent trail of Calan and Logan.

Around a thick stand of birch and oak trees, I caught sight of them with my superior vision, my younger brothers lying in ambush, hoping to catch me unaware. My wolf mouth stretched in a grin.

I'd teach them a thing or two.

About the Author

Mimi B. Rose writes fantastic tales filled with steamy enchantment and tender-hearted fulfilment to thrill strong women. As a teen she read V.C. Andews's *Flowers in the Attic* and Anne Rice's *The Vampire Lestat* and she was hooked on fantasy romance and paranormal romance. Some of her favourite tv shows are *Sleepy Hollow, Grimm,* and *Once*--and the reboot of *Beauty and the Beast* starring Kirstin Kreuk (does anyone remember that series?).

She loves all kinds of shifters and vampires. Her all-time favourite authors are Faith Hunter, Ilona Andrews, Nalini Singh, and more recently Richelle Mead.

Mimi likes a sassy heroine who is independent but finds a strong hero who can keep up with her and treasure her for their uniqueness--including her flaws!

Mimi loves to hear from readers. You can find her contact information, website details and author profile page at https://www.totallybound.com

Home of Erotic Romance

Sign up for our newsletter and find out about all our romance book releases, eBook sales and promotions, sneak peeks and FREE romance books!

www.ingramcontent.com/pod-product-compliance
Lightning Source LLC
Chambersburg PA
CBHW031111030726
47496CB00002BA/495